BY JAMES M. TABOR

FICTION

Frozen Solid
The Deep Zone

NONFICTION

Forever on the Mountain
Blind Descent

FROZEN SOLID

FROZEN SOLID

A NOVEL

James M. Tabor

BALLANTINE BOOKS
NEW YORK

Published in the United States by Ballantine Books, an imprint of The Random House Publishing Group, a division of Random House, Inc., New York.

BALLANTINE and colophon are registered trademarks of Random House, Inc.

LIBRARY OF CONGRESS CATALOGING-IN-PUBLICATION DATA
Tabor, James M.
Frozen solid : a novel / James M. Tabor.
pages cm
ISBN 978-0-345-53063-9
eBook ISBN 978-0-345-53885-7
1. Women scientists—Fiction. 2. Bioterrorism—Fiction.
3. Overpopulation—Fiction. I. Title.
PS3620.A258F76 2013
813'.6—dc23   2012051358

Printed in the United States of America on acid-free paper

www.ballantinebooks.com

9 8 7 6 5 4 3 2 1

FIRST EDITION

Book design by Dana Leigh Blanchette
Title-page and part-title photograph: © iStockphoto

THIS BOOK IS DEDICATED TO
T. ALAN BROUGHTON,
WHO SHOWED ME THE WAY

Growth for the sake of growth is the ideology of the cancer cell.

—EDWARD ABBEY

We must shift our efforts from treatment of the symptoms to the cutting out of the cancer. The operation will demand many apparent brutal and heartless decisions. The pain may be intense.

—DR. PAUL EHRLICH,
Bing Professor of Population Studies,
Stanford University

PART ONE

Continent of Pain

Great God! This is an awful place.

—SIR ROBERT FALCON SCOTT,
AT THE SOUTH POLE

1

SETTING UP ITS FINAL APPROACH, THE C-130 PITCHED NOSE DOWN
and snapped into a thirty-degree bank, giving Hallie Leland a sudden
view of what lay below. It was the second Monday in February at the
South Pole, just past noon and dark. Two streaks of light, thin and
red as fresh incisions, defined the runway. Half a mile distant, the
Amundsen-Scott South Pole Station appeared to float in a glowing
pool. The air here was clear as polished glass, red and white and gold
lights sparkling jewel-sharp a full mile below.

"Pilot having a bad day?" Hallie yelled at the loadmaster, the only
other passenger. Glum and silent, he had spent the flight reading an
old issue of *People* magazine. The peace had been unexpected and
much appreciated. She'd been traveling for four straight days and
nights, and her need for sleep was like a desperate thirst. But the aircraft was designed for cargo, not comfort. Her seat was nylon web-
bing that hung, hammock-like, along the entire length of the fuselage,
and four roaring engines made seeking sleep like trying to doze behind a waterfall. So for most of the flight's three hours she'd alter-
nately revisited the bad parting from Wil Bowman at Dulles and tried

to visualize diving a subglacial lake with twenty-two-degree water— her primary reason for coming here.

"Just a little fun." A bit more cheer in the loadmaster's voice. "It gets boring, flying McMurdo to Pole and back. Plus, if he goes in, there's just them up front and us two back here. Know what I mean?"

She wasn't sure she did. But she was watching, down on the ice, a clump of white light break into jittering pinpoints. "What's that?"

"There's a Polie saying: 'Two best days of your life are the one you fly in and the one you fly out.' Lot of happy flyouts down there." He peered at her. "We don't usually get incomers this late. You a win- terover?"

"Looks like you'll be full heading back to McMurdo."

"Tell me about it."

"You don't sound happy."

"Most'll be drunk before they get on. Always a lot of throwing up and fistfights and such."

"Drunk? It's noon."

He looked at her. "First time down here?"

The cowboy up front could fly, Hallie gave him that. She barely felt the Herc's steel skis kiss the ice, no easy trick with sixty tons in the scant air of thirteen thousand feet. The plane taxied, stopped, low- ered its cargo ramp. She paused at the top to don a face mask and pull up her fur-trimmed hood.

"I wouldn't linger, ma'am. They'll run you right over." Beside her, the loadmaster gestured toward the mob down on the ice.

"Sorry. You don't see that every day, though," she said, looking up at the southern lights, unfurling like green and purple pennants across the black sky.

He frowned, hunched his shoulders. "Not supposed to look that way at noon."

On the ice, a wall of bodies in black parkas blocked her way, faces hidden behind fur ruffs, headlamps on top, fog of liquor breath. The pack shuffled and stamped like horses at her family's farm in Char-lottesville.

"Coming through, please," Hallie called.

" . . . come through *you*," somebody slurred, and a few people laughed, but nobody moved. She walked around them. The loadmas-ter yelled, "Board!" and jumped aside like a man dodging traffic. Eventually, he dragged her two orange duffel bags down onto the ice.

"Welcome to hell froze over, ma'am. Enjoy your stay!" the load-master exclaimed. It was the first time she had heard anything resem-bling good cheer in his voice.

"How come you're happy now?" she yelled.

"Ma'am, 'cause I'm flying outta here."

She watched the plane claw its way back into the thin air, turn toward McMurdo, and then she was alone on the ice. She had never been in a place that looked and felt so hard. The sky shone like a dome of polished onyx etched with the white flecks of stars. The ice could have been purple marble, scalloped into sastrugi. The wind was blowing twenty miles an hour, mild for the Pole, where a thousand-mile fetch delivered hurricane winds all too often.

A digital thermometer hanging from one zipper pull read sixty-eight degrees below zero. The windchill dropped that to about one hundred below. She had heard firefighters describe fire as a living, hungry thing. This cold was like that, seeping through her seven lay-ers of clothing, attacking seams and zipper tracks and spots of thin insulation. The exposed skin on her face felt as if it had been touched with lit cigarettes.

It occurred to her that she could die right here where she had de-planed, with the station in plain sight. She decided that all the sages were wrong about hell. It would not be fire. It would be like this. Cold, dark, dead. She rotated 360 degrees, saw nothing but the sta-tion. In this pristine air it looked closer than a half mile, but she knew the distance from maps at McMurdo. She kicked the ice, scarred and dusted with chips like a hockey rink after a game. Her head felt light and airy; silver sparks danced in her vision. Her ears were ringing, she was nauseated and short of breath, and her heart was pounding. Altitude, Antarctic cold, exhaustion—and she had just arrived.

She had brought her own dive gear, and each duffel weighed forty pounds. At this temperature, the ice was like frozen sand. Dragging the bags was going to hurt. She had made this trip on short notice—no notice, really, for such was the life of a BARDA/CDC field investigator. But it was still bad form, she thought, letting a guest freeze to death out here.

"Let's go, then," she said. Inside four layers of gloves and mittens, her hands were numbing already. She managed to grab the bags' end straps and headed for the station, hauling one with each arm. It was like trudging through deep mud—at altitude. After thirty steps she stopped, lungs heaving, muscles burning, body cursing brain for making it do this mule work. The station seemed to have receded, as if she were drifting away from it on an ice floe in black water, like Victor Frankenstein's pathetic monster.

She looked up and saw a light detach from the distant glow and dance toward her. Several minutes later, the snowmobile slewed to an ice-spraying stop. Its operator was about the diameter of a barrel and not much taller. He was all in black, right down to his boots. She kept her headlamp trained on his chest to avoid blinding him.

"It was getting cold out here. I didn't expect a marching band, but—"

"Honey, you ain't seen cold." Hoarse, but definitely not a him. Woman with an Australian accent. "Graeter said you were supposed to come tomorrow. Lucky for you, the pilot radioed about an incoming."

"Graeter?"

"Station manager. Think you can grab maybe one bag?" Hallie heard condescension, irritation, or a combination. She dumped both duffels onto the orange cargo sled.

"So why are you here? Nobody ever comes early for winterover," the woman said. She sounded angry, though Hallie was hard-pressed to understand why. Chronic ire of the short? But then, going from cozy station to one hundred below for some clueless stranger could do it, too. A coughing fit left the woman gasping. She straightened, breathed in gingerly.

"That sounded bad," Hallie said. "Bronchitis?"

"Pole cold. Don't worry, you'll get it. So *are* you a winterover?"

The woman got on the snowmobile and motioned for Hallie to sit behind her. The wind had picked up. "Does it always blow like this?" Hallie asked.

"No."

"That's good."

"What I meant, it's usually stronger."

Before she gunned the engine, the woman peered over her shoulder at Hallie. "I *got* it. You're replacing that Beaker who died, right? What's-her-name."

"Her name was Emily Durant," Hallie said.

2

"WELCOME TO ARSE," THE BARREL-SHAPED WOMAN ANNOUNCED. "Stands for—"

"I got it. ASRS. Amundsen-Scott Research Station." Hallie had regained her breath. "It looks like a Motel 6 on stilts."

They were standing beside the parked snowmo at the bottom of the yellow stairs that rose to the station's main entrance.

"Wind blows underneath, stops snow buildup. Otherwise, five years, we're buried. Just like Old Pole."

"Everything happens here? Living, research, all of it?"

"Now it does. Summer people are gone. Beakers are finishing up projects. And there's a skeleton crew of Draggers."

"Beakers? Draggers?"

"Pole slang. Scientists are Beakers. Support workers are Draggers like me. As in 'knuckle draggers.' "

Inside, they shoved Hallie's bags against a wall, peeled off outer layers. The other woman was five inches shorter and a good bit heavier than Hallie, who stood five-ten and weighed 135. She wore her brown hair in a crew cut. Her cheeks were pitted with old acne scars, and she had a kicked dog's wary look. She peered at Hallie, took in the short, almost white-blond hair, high cheekbones, large, turquoise-blue eyes, and whistled softly. "Gonna have your hands full with boy Polies. And some of the girls. So you know."

"What's your name?" Hallie asked.

"Rockie Bacon."

"Rockie?"

"As in Rochelle. What's yours?"

"Hallie Leland." She was peering, nose wrinkled, down a long, dim corridor. "Clean, well-lighted place you have here."

"Energy conservation. Just enough light for safety. Motion sensors turn them on and off as you move along."

"I was being ironic," Hallie said.

"Gathered that. I've read the story. Faulkner, right?"

Hallie's nose kept her from setting Bacon straight about contemporary American fiction. "What *is* that reek?"

"Eau de Pole," Bacon chuckled. "Diesel fumes, disinfectant, burned grease, and unwashed bodies. You're here just for five days?"

"Why is the floor vibrating?"

"So you're one of those."

"What kind of those?"

"Who answer questions with questions. It's irritating."

"Is it?" Hallie could keep the grin off her face, but not out of her eyes.

"Fungees." Bacon scowled.

"What's a fungee?"

"Fucking new guy. Or girl."

Bacon's cough had sounded bad outside. It was worse inside, without the face mask and the covering noise of wind. She was flushed, her eyes were bloodshot, and her nose ran.

"Picornavirus heaven," Hallie said. "Everybody sealed in like lab mice, passing germs back and forth."

"You a doctor?"

"Microbiologist. Where's the cafeteria? I need water and coffee."

———

The U.S. Navy dug the first South Pole station out of solid virgin ice in 1957. Buried thirty feet deep now, that original facility, called "Old Pole," still survived. So did some vestiges of naval tradition. Thus the current station's cafeteria was a galley. By any name, it was like the dining hall in a big high school or penitentiary, one open rectangle redolent of fresh floor wax and old grease, crammed with scarred green tables and chairs, and buzzing at lunchtime. The kitchen and serving line were in back. In a fit of festivity, somebody had once strung multicolored Christmas lights from the ceiling. Most were burned out now, and their wires hung like thick green cobwebs.

"How's South Pole food?" Hallie was in line with Bacon.

"Ever been in prison?"

Before Hallie could say, "Not yet," a red-haired woman in a lab coat stood up too quickly, knocking her chair over backward. She was clamping a wad of paper napkins to her face, trying to stanch a bad nosebleed. Blood quickly soaked the makeshift compress, ran down the skin of her hands and pale wrists, and dropped in radish-sized spots onto her white lab coat.

For a few moments, nothing more happened. Then the woman's eyes bulged and her chest convulsed. She coughed out a thick, red stream. Took a step, stumbled, mouth thrown open, blood spewing. She staggered, knocking over chairs. Grabbed for a table. Blood kept pouring out, splashing the front of her lab coat, splattering tabletops, the floor. People scrambled away.

She fell over backward. Her head hit the floor with a sharp crack. A PA system boomed:

"Code blue in the galley. Code blue in the galley. EMTs to the galley. Repeat, code blue in the galley."

"Somebody called comms," Bacon said.

A heavy man in black coveralls knelt beside the woman. He put his face close to feel for breath, shook his head, and began performing chest compressions. Another man knelt by her head with a mask-style ventilator, but there was too much blood flowing to use it.

Two EMTs in blue jumpsuits burst into the galley. They suctioned the woman's airway, then went to work with a ventilator bag and defibrillator. After ten minutes and four sets of shocks, the instrument's computerized voice droned, "Victim not responding."

The EMTs rocked back on their heels. "She's gone," one said.

Hallie had seen victims on mountains and in caves badly hurt, drowned, and, several times, killed and disarticulated by long falls, but she had never seen so much blood. The woman lay completely surrounded by an oval, dark red pool. The two men and the EMTs looked like battle casualties.

The big room had been absolutely silent while the EMTs worked. Now it became even louder than before. When she'd entered, Hallie had seen dozens of faces, each one distinct. Now they all looked very much alike, reshaped by horror. Someone—she couldn't tell whether man or woman—was sobbing softly off to one side.

"What the *hell* happened here?" Hallie turned to see a tall man dressed in pressed khakis. She was struck by the pallor of his skin and how his clothes hung off his knobby frame. His voice was raspy. Heavy smoker or bad sore throat, she thought. Maybe both.

"I was sitting close." A woman in the onlooking circle, red-faced, close to tears. One hand was clasping a table edge, the other at the base of her throat. "Harriet stood up all of a sudden. I thought it was Polarrhea. But then she started vomiting blood. I never saw so much blood. Look at it."

"She wasn't vomiting," one of the EMTs said. "No foreign matter there. Just blood."

"Some kind of hemorrhage," the other EMT said. He, like everyone else in the room, was still staring at the woman on the floor. Her skin was now almost as white as her lab coat. The smell of her fresh blood overwhelmed the wax and grease and everything else. Hallie's stomach heaved. With the initial shock wearing off, she felt stunned, sorry for the woman, and, she was honest enough to admit, afraid.

The man in khakis keyed a radio and spoke: "Comms, Graeter. Get Doc and the biohazard team to the galley." He had a bud in his right ear, so only he could hear the other side. He spoke again: "There's blood. A lot. One female down. Harriet Lanahan." To the EMTs he said, "You help them with the body when they get here. Doc will need to see it and take photographs. After, secure it in the morgue. I'll get a flyout as soon as possible."

He turned on the crowd of onlookers. Hallie saw anger in the abrupt move and heard it in his voice. Maybe it's the default condition here, she thought. "I want witness statements in my email by thirteen hundred hours."

"What if we didn't see anything?" someone called.

"Then say that in your email, for Christ's sake. I may talk to some of you later. Listen up: paging response has been shit-sloppy. If you hear your name, I'd better see you in my office pronto or learn a good reason why not. Now let's clear this area. The bio team will be here soon."

Hallie started to follow Bacon and the others out, but a hand landed on her shoulder. She turned to see the man in khakis.

"You're Leland?" he asked.

"I just got here. I was going to see you after—"

He looked as if she had said something offensive. "Zack Graeter. Follow me."

3

"WAIT ONE," SAID GRAETER.

His desk was a massive steel relic from the 1950s that occupied practically half of the office. He turned away and began jabbing his computer's keyboard with two long, stiff index fingers.

She decided to give nice a try. "My grandfather had a Buick about the size of that desk."

He didn't look up. There was no other chair and not much to see. The smudged, lima bean–green walls were bare except for a gray metal cabinet hanging behind him and an eight-by-ten color photograph of a woman thumbtacked to the wall opposite him. Throwing darts were stuck in and around the photo, which looked like it had been blasted with No. 8 birdshot. He stopped typing and turned back to her.

"Your ETA was tomorrow." He made no effort to stand and shake hands, causing Hallie to wonder if he was protecting her from germs or just rude.

He *looked* rude, if such a thing were possible. There was not much more to him than muscle strung over bone and wrapped in white skin. Steel-wool hair, high forehead, cheekbones like golf balls. A thin, hard mouth cast in a downward curve. His khaki pants and shirt were crisp, his black shoes and brass belt buckle polished to a sheen.

I'll eat that skinny little tie, thought Hallie, *if he's not ex-Navy.*

"McMurdo had a flight with space. I figured an extra day would be valuable, with winterover so close. But—"

He waved off the explanation. "I don't like unscheduled arrivals. I can't give you the safety tour today."

A woman just bled out and we're talking about schedules? "What happened back there?"

"In the galley?" he asked.

"Unless somebody died in another place that I'm not aware of."

That got more of his attention. "It looked to me like Dr. Harriet Lanahan suffered a fatal hemorrhage. She was a glaciologist. From the U.K. But Merritt does the Beakers."

She waited.

He waited longer.

"That's it?" she asked.

"If you know more than that, please enlighten me."

"It's what I don't know that's bothering me. First, how could it have happened? And second, I'm struck by your *sang* . . . by your lack of concern."

"I know what *sangfroid* means, Ms. Leland. Annapolis isn't Harvard, but it's not a goddamned community college. First, we won't know how it could have happened until the medical examiner in Christchurch performs an autopsy and issues his report. Second, that wasn't my first fatality." He fixed her with what was obviously meant to be a commanding glare. "In case you hadn't noticed, this is the South Pole. It is very easy to die here."

She folded her arms, looked around for some clue to this strange man, but saw only the dirty green walls, punctured photograph, and that cabinet.

He sighed, raised beat-up hands. "Would you prefer it if I cried and beat my breast? Tore out some hair?"

Talking with him was like striking flint to steel. But this was terra incognita, after all, the manager and the station and the South Pole. The whole *continent,* for that matter. Until she understood everything better, she would do her best to be civil. "Had the woman been sick? Was there any warning that this might have happened? A precondition, maybe? There's a doctor here, right?"

"Why all the questions? You didn't even know her."

"First, she's a human being. Second, I'm a field investigator for CDC. Pathogens are what I do. Third, once the word gets out, reporters will be asking questions. It would be nice if my boss had some answers. Yours might be wanting some, too, I'd bet."

In his eyes she saw a new flicker—amusement or irritation, maybe both. "If she had been sick, Agnes Merritt would know. She's the chief scientist. Lanahan was a Beaker and worked for her. If there had been some precondition, Doc might have known." He hoisted his eyebrows, pointed one bony finger. "For the record, I don't give a fiddlefuck about bosses, and my job description does not include grief counselor. I won't bore you with the details of my workload, but with winterover four point five days away I am well and truly—excuse my French—*fucked,* and you are keeping me from getting unfucked."

"I'm sorry to hear that. But if you recall, it was you who asked me to come in here."

"And if *you* recall, it was not to talk about Dr. Lanahan."

"What happened to your hands?" They were painful to look at, red and cracked, oozing.

"Pole hands. Basically zero humidity here. Skin takes a beating."

Pole throat, Pole cold, Pole hands, she thought. What's next? Pole brain, probably.

"It looks painful."

"At first. Then the nerves die."

"Good thing you don't play piano."

"Actually, I do. Just not allegro anymore."

She tried to imagine him banging out show tunes at cocktail parties. The image wouldn't gel. "That happens to everybody?"

"Pretty much. You don't look so good yourself, Ms. Leland. Maybe you should think about catching the next flight out."

4

IT WAS EARLY MONDAY MORNING. DON BARNARD, WHO HAD NEVER been a late sleeper, was sitting with coffee in the study of his Silver Spring home. He was a big man, twenty pounds heavier than in his days playing tight end for the University of Virginia thiry-five years earlier. His hair and mustache were both white and the skin of his face was heavily creased from squinting in the bright sun while sailing on the Chesapeake Bay. His wife, Lucianne, was still in bed.

Barnard glanced at the clock on his desk: 5:12 A.M. It was 5:12 A.M. on Monday at the South Pole, as well. All lines of longitude converged there, so it existed, in a way, out of time. Since the National Science Foundation, just outside Washington, ran operations there, NSF time was Pole time. Not only habit had gotten Barnard out of bed early that morning. He had been awake for at least an hour before rising, thinking about Hallie. And he had suffered the same thoughts, off and on, for two days running.

Donald Barnard, MD, PhD, was the director of BARDA—the Biomedical Advanced Research and Development Authority—created by President George W. Bush in 2006 to counter biowarfare threats.

BARDA also conducted a clandestine initiative called Project BioShield. Thus Barnard's work required that he keep secrets—a good many, really. He was not the kind of man to keep secrets from himself, however. An only child whose father had died when he was seven, Barnard had always envied friends from big families. He had wanted a sprawling family of his own, had entertained visions of himself old and doting, rocking in a large chair in front of a fire, his lap overflowing with grandchildren while his sons and daughters stood around drinking wine and laughing over old sibling dustups.

But then, during his postdoc in Strasbourg, he met Lucianne, and later they got married in the States. It was 1979, and everyone understood that the earth was a lifeboat sunk to the gunwales by proliferating billions. He and Lucianne agreed that having just one child was the right thing to do, and that had been Nicholas. Barnard had never felt bad for their son. There were some drawbacks to being an only child but more advantages, emotional and material both, as he himself knew.

Still, another of the secrets he had not kept from himself was how much he would have appreciated a daughter, and especially one like Hallie Leland. There were many things to admire about her, but perhaps more than anything else he loved that she was a challenger. He sometimes joked that, given the power of speech at birth, she might have questioned the obstetrician about his credentials. She accepted no wisdom as conventional, no practice as standard, and reflexively distrusted authority in all its forms. Barnard hadn't seen many people like her in his time, and he knew that the few who had the intellect to match their skepticism were those rare and precious creatures called natural-born scientists.

It took one to know others. It also took one to understand how they, especially when young, simmered along in an almost continual state of impatience, waiting for sluggards to deduce what they had discovered long ago. Barnard had been like that earlier in his career. Hallie was like that now. He had not been the easiest person to be around then, and she was not now.

But all of that was old knowledge. This was Monday, and Barnard was dealing with something new. Hallie had flown out on Thursday afternoon. She had called from LAX very early on Friday morning and sent an email from Christchurch on Saturday. Having heard nothing since, he didn't even know if she had arrived at the South Pole.

But communication wasn't the thing bothering him most. It was, rather, the South Pole assignment itself, which he had given her. Had been directed to give her, more precisely, by his own boss, DCDC—Director, Centers for Disease Control. He could have pushed back, of course; he'd been around long enough and earned enough respect to do that. CDC directors were political appointees, came and went, and he had seen more arrive and depart than he cared to remember. At the time, though, there had seemed no reason to object. And Hallie herself had been thrilled, as he'd known she would be, with the opportunity. Most microbiologists would spend their entire careers without getting to the South Pole, one of the most extreme—and coveted—research postings on earth.

But by Friday afternoon, something had started bothering him, a mental splinter that at first he could not tease out. He looked at the possible reasons, one after another. The South Pole was a dangerous place, true, but no worse than other realms Hallie's work had taken her into. The previous year, for instance, she'd almost died in a Mexican supercave called Cueva de Luz, Cave of Light, which had been full of traps. A swamp of bat shit teeming with pathogens. Acid lakes. Five-hundred-foot sheer drops. Flooded tunnels. At least the South Pole was aboveground, settled, and civilized. So the problem wasn't where he had sent her.

The work itself—technical ice diving—was also hazardous but, again, not worse than other diving her work had required, in caves like that vast Mexican labyrinth or on deep wrecks involving possible biohazards, to name just two. So it wasn't what he had sent her to do, either.

He had known where he was sending her and what she would be

doing, and he had been, if not happy with those challenges, at least comfortable that she was equal to both. It was only after some time that he'd realized that his unease derived not from the destination or the work.

He had called the director back. Laraine Harris had taken her PhD from Tulane and retained a rich and musical Louisiana accent. Barnard could have listened to her talk all day long, about pretty much anything, just for the sound of her voice.

"I had a question about Emily Durant," he said.

"The scientist who died," Harris said.

"Right. When you told me about Emily, I didn't think to ask how she died. Do you know, by any chance?"

If Harris thought his question odd, her tone didn't suggest that. "I asked them—NSF—the same question."

"What did they say?"

"I'm sorry, that information isn't available. Quote, unquote."

"Does that seem"—what was the right word here?—"unusual?"

"Maybe a little. But it was an official personnel request, not a next-of-kin notification. They might not know themselves."

That rang true. Communication in Washington was as complex and nuanced as a Japanese tea ceremony. Laraine had just described one of the invisible rules. If someone said information wasn't available, back off. Frontal attacks rarely worked here. Much better to find and exploit the vulnerable chink or flank.

They said goodbye, and he sat staring out a window. The view from his office wasn't much: a big parking lot, mostly empty this late on a Friday, followed by vacant buildings and warehouses. Beyond those, the green woods were usually pleasant to look at. Today, though, was standard winter weather in Washington, and the distance held only gray fog.

He became aware of a big paper clip that he had twisted and bent, without realizing it, while they'd talked. He set it aside, picked up the white meerschaum pipe he hadn't smoked for sixteen years, then set that down, too. Stared at the blank legal pad he kept on the right side of his desk, toyed with the fountain pen stationed on top of the pad. He picked up the pen and wrote one word:

Bowman

He added a question mark: *Bowman?*

Not yet, he thought. Wait to see if Hallie calls. But not much longer.

5

"THANKS FOR YOUR CONCERN. TRUTHFULLY, I DON'T FEEL SO good," Hallie told Graeter. "Which isn't surprising because it took four days and nights to get here, and I can't recall when I really slept last. But don't worry on my account. I've been to twenty-four thousand feet on mountains and almost two miles deep in caves."

He snorted.

"You find that funny?"

"We get lots of climbers down here, all full of themselves. 'I got this high on Mount Rumdoodle' or whatever." Shook his head. "You stay on one of your mountains, what, a week or two? Hit maybe forty below? Deal with fifty-, sixty-knot winds? People stay at Pole for a year. It *averages* one hundred and five degrees below zero in winter. Hurricanes with hundred-knot winds can last a week. Crevasses big enough to swallow locomotives. So yes, I do chuckle at the ignorance of fungees."

She waited, understanding that he was enjoying himself, impressing a newcomer.

"You'll feel worse, believe me," he went on. "There's something called T3 syndrome. Your thyroid shrivels up. Memory goes. Wild mood swings. Some people start seeing things, hearing them."

"There's a thing in deep caves called the Rapture. It—"

"That movie, *The Shining*? Where Nicholson starts chasing his family with an ax?"

"Yes?"

"T3 syndrome. You probably won't be around long enough to get a bad case. But a lot of people here have been. So you know."

She needed to tell him something else. Or maybe ask. What? Altitude addlement leading to brain cramp. Buy some time. She nodded at three framed photographs of young men in Navy whites on his desk.

"Your sons?"

"No."

She waited again.

So did he, again. The hell with small talk, then.

"You probably know this already," she said, "but, for the record, I'm here on temporary assignment from the Biomedical Advanced Research and Development Authority, BARDA, part of CDC, in Washington. On loan to the National Science Foundation to help Dr. . . . um . . ." What the hell was his name? *Lots* of syllables.

"Fido Muktapadhay," Graeter said. *Mook-ta-POD-hay.* "Who everybody calls Fido, for obvious reasons."

"Right. To help complete his research project. CDC rushed me down here. I was told that he and Emily Durant were working on deep ice-core samples and found something unusual. Finishing before winterover was urgent."

"Was there a question in there somewhere?"

"Do you know any more about their research?"

"No. More importantly, you haven't been briefed about this place."

"I did talk with—"

"Not by me. My point."

"Could this wait until I get some sleep?"

"Here's the quick and dirty. I'm in command here. Just like the captain of a ship. I can marry you and bury you. The only law at Pole is SORs, and I enforce them."

"SORs?"

"Didn't you read your prep material?"

"Nobody gave me prep material."

"Jesus Christ. SORs are the Station Operating Regulations. They must be obeyed to the letter. Failure to do so gets people hurt. Or dead. Clear?"

She gave a curt nod. Poked in the chest like this, Hallie was more inclined than most to poke back harder. She had inherited that tendency not just from her soldier father but also from her horse-trainer mother. Growing up with two older brothers had sharpened it nicely. Now, standing half-asleep and fully irritated in the stinky closet of an office, she was finding it harder not to poke, terra incognita be damned.

Then he woke her up a little. He opened a desk drawer, removed a black leather ID folder and what she recognized as a SIG Sauer semiautomatic pistol. He flipped the folder to show a brass, star-shaped badge, then set it and the pistol on his desk, the gun's muzzle pointing to one side, watching her all the while.

Maybe we're going to play spin the pistol, she thought, immediately recognizing the weirdness of that idea. Be serious. He wants to see how I do with guns.

"Something else you need to know," he said. "The station manager is a deputy U.S. marshal. Sworn and trained. So I am the law here. Literally."

At its deepest, exhaustion was like being drunk; it dissolved restraint, invited mischief. Her next action had a life of its own.

"May I?" Before he could speak, she picked up the SIG, released the magazine, caught it in her left hand, worked the slide to eject the chambered round, caught that spinning in the air in her palm beside the magazine. It pleased her no end to see how much effort it took for him to look unimpressed. "You like the forty-cal better than the three fifty-seven?" she asked.

"So you know guns," he said. "Fine. Now put my pistol down."

"Grew up on a farm in Virginia. I like the magnum's muzzle velocity, myself." She popped the magazine back into place, thumbed the slide release and then the trigger release, set the pistol back on the desk, and stood the fat ejected round beside it. "I don't like one chambered. No safety on a SIG," she said.

"The forty-cal is what they issue. Safeties are great for target punchers. Slow in a fight, though." He put the badge folder and gun away. "To finish up, just so we're clear. Merritt keeps the research going. I keep people alive. You, just long enough to ship out in a few days." It was the first time anything resembling pleasure had crept into his voice. That did it.

"Mr. Graeter, what could I possibly have done to piss you off so much in the very brief time we've been acquainted?"

His expression did not change. Did the man have any muscles in that face? "Bringing you down here pissed me off."

"Why would it do that? I'm here to help. And we've never met."

"Nothing personal. This is the easiest place on earth for the inexperienced and unwitting to die." He fixed her with a hard stare, but not before his eyes flicked to the photographs on his desk.

"I'm experienced. And, most of the time, relatively witting."

If he appreciated the irony, it didn't show. "Nice to know. Keep this in mind at all times: we are like an outpost on Mars, except colder and darker."

"I get it. I really do." She just wanted some sleep.

"One last thing: do not go near the Underground or Old Pole."

"What are they?"

"Read your station manual."

"I didn't get a station manual."

"Jesus keelhauling Christ." He closed his eyes, shook his head. "Did the CDC at least take care of you?"

"Centers for Disease Control? In Washington, you mean?"

"Clothing Distribution Center. At McMurdo. For your extreme-cold-weather gear."

"Yes."

"Wait one." He unlocked the gray cabinet on the wall behind his desk. Scores of door keys hung from small numbered hooks. He removed one. The keys on all the other hooks were duplicates. There was no key left behind on the hook from which Graeter had taken this one.

"Where's the backup?" She pointed to the empty hook.

For the first time, he looked more uncomfortable than angry. "Missing." He locked the cabinet and pushed the key across his desk. "Dorm wing A, second level, number two-three-seven." He told her how to find it. "Believe in ghosts, Ms. Leland?"

"Yes." It pleased her immensely to see that he wasn't expecting that.

"Good. You may have company. It was Emily Durant's room. That bother you?"

"Not one bit. We were good friends. I hope she visits." Ha, she thought. Got him again.

"You *knew* Durant?"

"She worked at BARDA before NSF. We did a lot of things together. She saved my life one time, after we got avalanched climbing Denali. It's been a few years, though. Do *you* believe in ghosts, Mr. Graeter?"

His eyes flicked again to the black-framed photographs. "No," he said, and even though she had just met the man, she knew he was lying. Maybe she would find out why. At this point, she was too tired to care. But she was curious about one thing.

"Why that room?"

"With winterover so close, the field units are closed and all personnel, Beakers and Draggers alike, have moved into the station. Every room is occupied. Durant's opened up when she passed. Come see me tomorrow at noon. We're finished here now."

"Actually, we're not. No one in D.C. knew much about Em's death. How did it happen?"

His face changed, and it was like watching water suddenly freeze. "See Merritt. I told you. Durant worked for her. She found the body."

"Maybe, but you're the station manager. I'd appreciate hearing—"

"I just said to see Merritt. In the Navy, once was enough, Ms. Leland."

"*Doctor* Leland. And this isn't the Navy."

She waited for him to snap or shout. The more someone did that, the calmer she became—you couldn't see to fight if you were blind with rage. But his voice was flat.

"No. But this *is* my office, and I have work to do. Go see Merritt." A beat. "If you please."

He turned around and began typing on his computer keyboard. She stopped with her hand on the doorknob, looking at the photograph on the wall. The woman had shoulder-length brown hair. Her red blouse's two top buttons were undone to show swelling breasts. Good skin, upturned nose. Cheerleader-cute rather than model-beautiful. But eye shadow too thick, lips too red, and dark-circled eyes too old for the face spoiled the cheerleader image.

Hallie knew the type. Every branch had them. Picture-pretty, nail-hard, girls who had fun when the men were gone. She didn't know what the Navy called them. In the Army, they were known as layaways.

"Ex-wife, am I right?" It just slipped out. Like the thing with the gun.

Graeter's head snapped up.

"Wonder what she's doing with *your* picture."

He turned away, the creased back of his neck reddening. He started typing again, and it sounded like little machine guns firing.

6

IT WOULD TAKE TWO TRIPS TO GET THE DUFFEL BAGS TO HER ROOM. She bent down, reached for one. Silver sparks filled her eyes and she had to stand quickly, one hand on the wall.

"Please allow me to help with those."

She turned toward a light touch on her shoulder. A smiling, very muscular man put out his hand. He wore jeans, work boots, and a black turtleneck stretched by bulging pectorals and undulating abs. His legs, in tight jeans, were skinny and short. Wil Bowman, the man in her life, had once talked about "prison muscles" on men with massive upper bodies and bird legs. But this fellow did not look like one who had done time. No knuckle tattoos, a firm but not painful handshake, eyes direct but showing hello rather than some odd hunger. A Cousteauean nose and black watch cap worn askew gave him a jaunty, faintly nautical air.

"Rémy Guillotte," he said. *Ghee-YOTT.* "You are just arrived, I think."

"I didn't hear you come up. And yes, you are looking at a total fungee."

He laughed. "So you are learning to speak Pole already. Excellent. Dr. Leland, am I right?" He pronounced it *Lee-LAND*. "I heard you were meeting with Mr. Graeter. I am the station's dive operations manager, so we will be working together while you are here."

It just popped out: "Did you work Emily's dives?"

His expression changed. "Poor Dr. Durant. No. That man flew out several days ago. I am a winterover."

She would want to see all his certifications and credentials, but not now. "We can talk about the diving later. I really need to get some sleep."

He flipped both bags up onto his shoulders. Forty pounds each, she thought. "So let us go find your room."

She gathered up her ECW gear and followed. Sensors turned overhead lights on as they approached and off again when they had passed. It was like flowing in a luminous bubble through dark tunnels. Similar to cave diving, in fact. They saw only three people. One had his head down and appeared to be talking to himself. The other two went right on by, slack-jawed, eyes fixed in thousand-yard stares.

After they passed, Guillotte said, "I heard what happened in the galley."

"I saw it," Hallie said.

"Is it true that Dr. Lanahan was vomiting blood?"

"Probably not vomiting. A hemorrhage, more likely."

"This is so tragic," he said. "In just a few days she would have been flying back to home."

"What's it like? Living here, I mean?"

He looked thoughtful, considered before answering. "A good question to ask. It is strange at first. A place where everything you know is not true."

"How so?"

"Here the sun comes up once and goes down once in a year, for starters. It all flows from there."

"Oh." She hadn't thought of that.

"After some time, you adjust. Or, some people, not."

Room A-237 was in the middle of one of the second-level dorm wings. Guillotte opened the door with one hand. The bags stayed balanced on his shoulders.

"Unlocked?" she asked.

"Apparently so. The cleaners probably forgot after they are finished." He followed her in, set the bags down gently, switched on the room light.

"Thank you very much," she said. "I could have gotten them myself, but—"

"Of course you could have. Clearly you are in very fit shape. But this was better, I think. Until you are acclimatized."

"You're right. I'm grateful."

"And I am happy to help. Maybe I can show you around later. There are many unusual things here in this Pole place."

Alone, she leaned back against the door, too tired to wonder how he had known her name and which room was hers. It was tight even by Motel 6 standards—no bigger than a supermax cell, really—and furnished like a college dorm: white acoustic-tile drop ceiling; single, high bunk bed with drawers underneath; a tall, narrow window that could have been a sheet of black marble. Under it sat a tiny desktop with a computer monitor and keyboard. The computer's boxy CPU was on the floor beneath the desk.

She knew what she *should* do: email Don Barnard, her boss, and Wil Bowman. Her last contact with Barnard had been by email at Christchurch, so he wouldn't know she'd arrived. Her last with Bowman had been the previous Thursday and less than pleasant. As such scenes are wont to do, this one kept replaying in her mind despite her best efforts to make it stop. It was like trying not to think of a camel after someone says, "Don't think of a camel."

Bowman drove her to Dulles. Minutes from the departures area, she said, without preamble, "I have always been regular as a clock. Every four weeks on the dot. This time, I was eight days late. Until night before last. I really was starting to think . . ." She let the rest of it trail off.

"Why didn't you say anything before?" It took a great deal to discomfit Wil Bowman, but her statement clearly had.

"I wanted to be sure."

Something in her tone must have caught his ear. "That wasn't the only reason, though."

"No, it wasn't the only one," she said. She knew he was waiting for her to say more, and she knew, as well, that she should. Why couldn't she? And why hadn't she told him sooner? She wasn't really afraid that he would be angry. In their year together, she'd seen him genuinely angry only three times, and two of those had been with himself. He was not, by any stretch, meek or mild. He was perhaps the most balanced, synchronous man she had ever met, and he was certainly the most dangerous—though not to her. She understood that his work for some unnamed entity buried deep in the intelligence labyrinth occasionally involved killing—"but only those who really need it," as he'd once said. The thought that he might up and leave had never entered her mind.

As he sensed and she admitted, there was something else. The trouble was that she hadn't then understood what, and that was why she hadn't said anything until they were almost to the airport. Didn't want to fly off holding a secret, but didn't want to talk in detail until she'd had more time to sort things out.

He was already double-parking in front of the soaring terminal. Fifty-five minutes until her flight boarded and her with two huge bags, one full of dive gear that would certainly catch the TSA agents' attention. Cars were stacking up. A taxi honked. Wind whipped grit against their faces, into their eyes, as they stood by the curb. He tossed her bags onto a redcap's wagon, then drew her aside.

"We need to talk more, Hallie."

"We do. But I have to go."

He held her with his eyes. "There are things you don't know. About me."

That surprised her. He never spoke like that, hated the international-man-of-mystery air some people in his profession affected. She retained enough composure to say, "And about myself, apparently," which seemed to startle him as well.

She glanced at the terminal, saw automatic doors clamping shut on a suitcase towed by a limping woman. Those doors weren't supposed to do that. Electric eyes or infrared sensors. She looked back at Bowman.

"I have to leave now, Wil." She kissed him. He held her shoulders lightly, kissed her back, then again, and touched her face. That a man his size could touch so softly never failed to amaze her. "I'll call from LAX." She motioned to the redcap, who followed her into the terminal.

She had needed time to understand her own behavior. Four days and nights of travel with the scene replaying in her head like an endless film loop had been enough. She composed an email on the room's station computer:

Hi Wil

Sixty-eight below and pitch-dark when I stepped onto the ice—at *noon.* Beats my previous record low by about 25 degrees. I'm exhausted already, four days and nights in planes and terminals, and work hasn't even started. The South Pole is a very strange place. The people, too—so far, anyway. Mostly, what you notice right off is the dark. Dark outside for thousands of square miles. It's even dark *inside.*

At Dulles, you asked why I didn't tell you sooner. I didn't know myself right then. Now I do. I was afraid you'd say that I had no business even thinking about being a mother. And that you might have been right.

So it was all me. Nothing about you.

Love,

Hallie

She sent that email, then wrote one to Don Barnard, shorter, saying that she had arrived safely, describing the place. She turned off the light, jumped up onto the chest-high bunk, and fell asleep still dressed.

Guillotte reached the end of Hallie's corridor, turned into another. After looking up and down that one, he used his cellphone.

"You may make the call now."

7

SHE AND EMILY WERE SWIMMING IN FRIGID WATER, THICK AS SYRUP, green and purple swirls coiling around them. In a black sky, iridescent birds circled, screaming. Hallie sank away from Emily, floating slowly down, flapping her arms, trying to breathe water now as viscous and silver as molten mercury.

She awoke and lay still, pulling herself up out of the dream, watching false light images glowing and sparking in her eyes. The room smelled of Lysol and, thanks to four days of traveling without a shower, her. And something else, so faint she had not noticed it until then. Licorice, of all things. She turned on one side, sniffed. The scent, barely discernible, was coming from the bunk mattress. Emily had had a sweet tooth, though more for dark chocolate than licorice, as Hallie remembered. Doubtless a year in this place could change a person in many ways, and who knew—licorice might have been the only candy she could get.

It had been a long time since Hallie had slept in a top bunk. She sat up, swung her legs over the side, stretched tall, and accidentally punched two of the ceiling's acoustic tiles, which lifted out of their frames and then fell back into place. For a few moments she didn't move. Then she got down and turned on the light.

She climbed back up and knelt on the bunk. Using both hands, she raised one of the tiles she had accidentally hit and laid it aside. She reached up through the vacant space and carefully explored the back of the second tile. Her fingers touched something metallic, shaped like a deck of cards, but with sharp edges and corners. She lifted the tile carefully out of its metal frame and set it on the mattress.

There was product information on the object:

BrickHouse XtremeLife DVR Camera
SXp1w3r
PIR Motion Detection

Two wires ran from sockets in the surveillance unit's case. One connected to a microcamera that looked like a metal toothpick half an inch long with a tiny bulb at one end. That had been pushed down into a hole in the tile. The other was connected to a shorter, thicker metal tube—the motion sensor, she guessed. It, too, had been inserted into a hole. Hallie worked both loose, freeing the device, and saw a USB port on one side of its case.

She connected it to her laptop computer and set it on the bunk so that it was almost at eye level. On the screen appeared a black camera shape with the same information she had seen on the case. PIR, she knew, stood for "passive infrared," the same motion-detection system that worked intrusion alarms and automatic lights like those in the halls. And—strange to think of it now—that should have prevented the airport door from clamping down on the crippled woman's suitcase as Hallie had said goodbye to Bowman.

She double-clicked on the icon and a new screen appeared, showing nine MPEG-4 files. Hallie watched the first, created on January 23. It showed what the microcam had seen: a fish-eye view that included half of the room. There was no audio, and just enough ambient light for the camera to record grainy images. That light, Hallie reasoned, might have been coming from luminous numbers on a digital clock somewhere in the room, or perhaps from a night-light, or both. She saw a shape moving onto the bunk, vague but discernible as a woman. Emily, caught by her own camera. Or—someone else's? Emily's eyes closed; her breathing slowed. She fell asleep almost immediately.

Hallie kept watching. The camera recorded for three more minutes, then stopped. She thought it was probably set to turn off automatically after detecting no motion for a predetermined period. Hallie fast-forwarded through a number of false alarms triggered by Emily's movements while asleep. Then she opened the most recent file, from January 31. Sixteen days ago. The same scene, so dark she could see only shadows moving. Then a flare and, after that died, soft and wavering light.

Someone had lit a candle.

Still too dark for sharp resolution, but better than the other recording. Hallie watched as one person and then another climbed up onto the bunk. Both sat with their backs against the wall. She could see the tops of their heads, shoulders, and their thighs. She could not see their faces.

One was a woman—Hallie could make out the swell of breasts under a skin-tight black suit of some kind. A wet suit? Indoors? No, a leotard. White stripes on the tops of the thighs suggested a skeleton costume. Emily. The figure next to her was larger, with bigger shoulders and hands. He had coarse black hair and what looked like bolts sticking out of his neck at the base. A baggy shirt with ragged sleeves.

A skeleton and the Frankenstein monster. So they must have come from a costume party. Or were going to one.

The man produced a metal flask, unscrewed the top, and drank. He passed it to Emily, who almost dropped it. He caught the flask and handed it to her more carefully. She drank, appeared to cough, waved a hand in front of her mouth.

She and the man talked. There was no sound, but it was easy to recognize what they were doing by their nods and touches and body movements. Occasionally they drank from the flask. After several minutes, the man peeled off fake scars and removed the plastic bolts that had been held in place by a semicircular wire running behind his neck. He pulled off the wig, which was attached to a bulging rubber forehead. He tossed all of the costumery down onto her desk chair. He was undisguised, but the overhead camera angle still kept Hallie from viewing enough to allow her to recognize him if she saw him later.

Emily half-turned and kissed the man, put her arms around him, pulled him closer. They kissed more seriously.

She had a lover. Well, good for her. A year is a long, long time. But, Hallie thought, should I keep watching this? It doesn't feel right, spying on her like this.

Think. This is a surveillance camera. If she had wanted to make a sex tape, they would have used something else.

Emily lay down on her back, giving Hallie the first direct look at her face. Painted skull-white, it was brighter than anything else in the frame. The man lay down beside her, his face buried in her neck, nuzzling, kissing, hidden from the camera. His thigh slid over hers. One hand scurried over her body, nibbling, rubbing, pausing longer here and there. Emily's back arched as though in spasm, and Hallie saw her mouth open, a silent moan.

She whispered something in his ear.

And fell asleep.

That seemed very strange. Emily never used drugs, rarely drank more than a beer or two, and here she was passing out?

The man sat back against the wall and watched her. It was maddening—Hallie could see the top of his head and shoulders and thighs, but nothing else. After several minutes, he climbed down from the bunk and out of the picture. When he reappeared, he had on tight-fitting latex gloves. Working carefully and without haste, he unzipped Emily's leotard and pulled it off, leaving her in bra and panties.

The son of a bitch. He'd drugged her. With that flask? He'd been drinking from it, too. Or maybe just pretending. Something else, before they got to the room?

Hallie's breath came faster. She felt angry and afraid for Emily. Said, out loud, "You better not touch her."

He disappeared from the frame and reappeared with two hypodermic syringes. The barrels were the same size, but the needle on one was much longer. Using the smaller syringe, the man injected something into the vein, in Emily's right arm, from which blood was typically drawn. Hallie watched with growing horror.

"Leave her alone!" She said that aloud, too.

Oddly, he was dressed. A date rapist would have been naked by now. He stood beside the bunk, watching. Emily was still asleep, her chest rising and falling slowly. After several minutes, her eyes floated open. She didn't move or try to speak. Hallie strained, but she still could not see the man's face.

He climbed up onto the bed and knelt between Emily's parted legs, holding the syringe with the long needle up for her to see. Her blink rate and respiration increased. He took a deep breath, shoulders rising and falling, leaned closer, and began using the needle. Emily's eyes stretched wide and her whole body tensed, but she didn't move.

He had given her some kind of short-acting paralytic. Oh God.

Hallie thought she might vomit. Shaking with rage, she had to pause the video. It was some time before she could turn it on again. Now there was no question about watching. It was a thing she had to do.

The man went back to work.

God. Please make him stop.

He did not stop. Horror washed Hallie's mind clear of words. Her jaw was clenched so tightly it ached. Her stomach churned, and she pulled the wastebasket close.

There was no blood. Only agony. He kept at it until Emily's body went limp.

Tears of grief and rage were running down Hallie's cheeks, blurring her vision. She brushed them away, blinked her eyes clear.

I will find you, she vowed. If it takes the rest of my life, I will find you. Wil Bowman will help me. And you will pay.

The man climbed down off the bunk. She still could not see his face, but the bulge of an erection was unmistakable.

Emily was unconscious but still breathing. He tapped his gloved fingers against the inside of her right elbow to bring up the vein and, with the smaller syringe, pierced it in several places without injecting anything. Then he took her right hand and pressed her fingertips to the syringe, her thumb to the top of the plunger, and moved to the vein inside her left elbow. He performed a smooth venipuncture and pushed the plunger all the way in, emptying the syringe. He left it attached to her arm.

He put the spent vial on her bunk and laid several more, still full, beside her body. He moved out of frame for a few moments, and when he came back into view he had the flask. He moistened a paper towel and used it to swab Emily's lips, neck, other places where his mouth had touched her.

DNA wipe. He wants people to think she overdosed. Why in God's name would anybody do this?

The man disappeared from the frame one last time. Seconds passed, and the wavering light went out.

He'd snuffed the candle.

The video played for three more minutes, then stopped.

She could not remember anything more horrible than what she had just watched. She grabbed the wastebasket and vomited. She tried to look out the window, but it was solid black. She could almost touch both walls with her arms outstretched. It felt as though the room were shrinking.

Something was trying to claw out of her. She felt sick, disgusted, enraged. If the man had been there, she might have attempted to kill him with anything in the room that would tear flesh and break bone. Including her bare hands.

A sound, part sob and part howl, erupted from her throat. She buried her face in the pillow, sat on the floor, and wept until her belly hurt. Exhausted, she stood, one hand on the bunk's edge for support, trying to think rationally. The images of the man and the things he had done to Emily stayed where they were. Might as well try to push black clouds out of the sky, she told herself.

Keening wind suddenly hit the station, which jumped and shook like a plane flying through turbulence. The ceiling light blinked several times, and somewhere in the room a fly began to buzz. A final gust, strongest of all, and the room went dark. Dizzy, she lost her balance, flailed at empty air for some firm hold, finally grabbed the bunk.

The light came back on, flickered, then died and stayed out.

She thought: *What if that man is still here?*

8

"DHAKA MAY BE THE ONLY PLACE I KNOW WHERE FEBRUARY IS LIKE July in Washington," David Gerrin observed cheerily. He was in his late fifties. Dark-haired and with a thin, efficient body, he had been a marathoner until knee injuries had ended the running, a decade earlier. An epidemiologist, not truly famous but with a university laboratory named after him and several books to his credit.

"Could do with a bit less jollity," said Ian Kendall. "I mean, it's a bloody steam bath, isn't it?"

Jean-Claude Belleveau said nothing. Out of respect for the conference, he had worn a suit. White linen, but still sweltering. He wiped his face with an already soaked handkerchief.

It was late afternoon. The three men, walking back to their hotel after the last day of a U.N. global conference on sustainability, were trapped in a mass of bodies on a sidewalk that radiated heat like a giant griddle. Leaving the Bangabandhu International Conference Center, Kendall had suggested a taxi, but Gerrin had pointed out that in the capital of Bangladesh, traffic in the streets moved even more slowly than people afoot. Day and night, masses of bodies clogged sidewalks and alleys and roads and overflowed into main highways, so that solid lanes of exhaust-spewing buses and trucks and cars measured their progress in mere yards per hour.

And it was also true, Gerrin had said, that a walk would keep their Triage focus sharp.

With only the backs of necks and heads to look at in front of him, Gerrin glanced over at a woman sitting by the curb under a sign prohibiting public defecation. The woman was not terribly old, but her mouth showed more gums than teeth and her skin was the color of ashes. She tilted over and slowly fell onto her side, her left arm flung across her body, her right arm trapped under it. Her fingers curled around a few coins in her right hand. Her head hung at an awkward angle, just touching the filthy sidewalk beside her shoulder. Flies lit on her eyes. Others crawled into her nostrils, and her tongue tried to push them out of her mouth.

Arrayed in front of her on a square of green cloth were things she was selling: yellow pencils, a blue pack of Player's Navy Cut cigarettes, cards with images of Jesus Christ, Buddha, Muhammad, packs of chewing gum. She wore a torn yellow dress, and her swollen feet looked like black melons. One eye was opaque with a cataract. She was still alive, Gerrin figured, because the other blinked when flies tried to crawl into it.

Gerrin pulled out his cellphone, dialed the emergency services number. It was not easy, in the jam, keeping the phone close to his ear. He elbowed people who elbowed him. Dhaka was many things, but polite it wasn't. Gerrin kept listening to the ringing. Then he noticed Belleveau, who had been behind him, plowing through bodies, on a course for the woman.

"Jean-Claude," he yelled. "Wait!"

Belleveau was already there. Gerrin and Kendall held doctorates, but Belleveau was the physician, the oath taker. He knelt beside the woman and took from his briefcase a CPR face-shield mask with a one-way valve. Gerrin knew that Belleveau never ventured into places like this without one, though truly it was intended for use on his own companions, or even himself. From years spent living and working in New Delhi, he knew that things unimaginable to Westerners were the stuff of everyday life in places like this. Gerrin watched him turn the woman over, feel for pulse and breath, tilt her head back to open the airway. He put the shield mask in place and turned to Kendall. "Ian—compressions, please."

"Yes, of course." Kendall, no longer young, clambered down onto his knees.

Gerrin stood, listening to the ringing, keeping some space clear around them. Belleveau and Kendall were busy, but Gerrin had time to look at the faces. The people could have been mannequins for all the feeling they showed. He understood. Death was far from an oddity here; it happened so frequently and so visibly, in fact, that it was only banal, if that.

After a while, Belleveau sat back. "Finished," he said.

Belleveau and Kendall stood, both sweating so heavily that their dress shirts were soaked through and clinging. One knee of Belleveau's white trousers was torn. Red, scraped flesh showed through. He cleaned his mouth and hands with sanitizing gel, handed the bottle to Kendall. No one was watching them or the woman now, most people focused on weightier concerns, cool drinks, the approaching dinner hour. Again, Gerrin understood. Not their fault. The way things were. He heard ringing still coming from his phone, forgotten and dangling in one hand. He broke the connection and put it away.

"Someone should do something," Kendall said, sluicing sweat from his forehead with the palm of one hand. "I mean, someone will come for her, won't they?"

Their guide had grown up in Dhaka and had told them how, as a child, he'd survived by eating cats and dogs and rats. Now even those had grown scarce.

"Someone will come for her after dark. There are fifteen million people in this city. Half of them are starving."

Two hours later, they stood on a twelfth-floor hotel room balcony.

The light was failing, and through the haze Dhaka shimmered like a city under foul water. A putrefying reek rose even this high. Clots of red taillights blocked every street and highway as far as they could see.

"Behold the future," Gerrin said.

"London in fifty years, give or take," Kendall said. He was a blocky man with a boxer's face and an earl's accent. His appearance, which included an ear like a handful of hamburger, came not from prizefighting but from four years of Oxford rugby. A geneticist, he was old and brilliant enough to have worked under Francis Crick and was, as well, the kind of Englishman who never made mention of that.

"Paris, as well. *France,* for that matter," Belleveau said. He had remained slim despite a childhood overly rich in every way. His skin was pale and, after kind, curious eyes, his best feature was lustrous curly black hair. Born to wealth, he had earned a medical degree from the Sorbonne and could have practiced obstetrics and gynecology in a gilt-edged *seizième arrondissement* office suite. He worked in New Delhi instead, caring for any and all, payment accepted but never requested. Mostly he delivered babies and, as frequently these days, aborted them. He had come, as had Kendall, to meet with Gerrin one last time before Triage launched. After that, there would be no stopping it, and thus no reason to meet again.

"But for Triage." Gerrin raised his tumbler of Laphroaig, and they touched glasses.

They drank, watched the darkness congeal, and no one spoke. Sometimes there was only waiting. Then Gerrin's phone chimed. He answered, listened, hung up. From the room's wall safe he retrieved a Globalstar satellite phone. He walked out onto the balcony, adjusted the long antenna, input a string of numbers, waited. Again he listened, very briefly this time, hung up without saying a word.

"The replacement has arrived," he told the other two.

"Thank God." Kendall sounded like a man breathing air after surfacing from great depth. He drank, shook his head, looked straight out, away from Gerrin and Belleveau. "We've always been honest with each other, haven't we? So I must tell you that I am afraid, a little anyway, now that we are almost there."

"No shame in that, Ian, given what we are about," Gerrin said. "Galileo was lucky not to be burned at the stake."

"One wonders how many others *were* burned, doesn't one?" Kendall asked.

"Your countryman Edward Jenner," Belleveau said. "Accused of serving Satan. Cutting children and scraping animal pus into their wounds. His own *son*. He was fortunate to escape the gallows."

"Given druthers, some might've drawn and quartered poor old Darwin," Kendall said.

"Still," Gerrin said, and the others smiled.

"I, for one, am glad that capital punishment is no longer used," Belleveau said.

"Tell that to Saddam Hussein. And bin Laden," Kendall said.

"We are *not* like them." Gerrin was their firebrand, Belleveau their heart, Kendall their diplomat.

"Of course not. Such a comparison is odious," Belleveau agreed. "But the point is that their actions would be viewed as mischief compared to Triage."

"Without Triage, this planet is *doomed*." Gerrin turned to look directly at them.

"We all agree on that, David," Kendall said, his hand on Gerrin's shoulder. "Else we would not be here, would we?"

"No. We would not." Gerrin drank his whiskey, his expression softening. "I'm sorry. I think we are all a bit on edge."

"I wonder if this is how the men who flew to Hiroshima felt? Just before it dropped?" Belleveau asked.

No one spoke for a moment. Then Gerrin said, "Not even close, my friend. Not even close."

"We are certain that the threat to Triage no longer exists?" Kendall asked.

"Absolutely certain." Gerrin did not smile often, but now he did to support his reassuring words. Triage had been long in the planning, and they had known one another for some years. From anyone else he would have found the question annoying, might have snapped off a retort, but he understood how this man's spirit was tuned.

"Might there be others, though?"

"It's not impossible. Our security asset is looking into that."

"And if he finds others?"

"Then he will do more to earn the considerable sum we're paying him."

No one spoke for a time. Belleveau looked up from his drink. Gerrin knew that, as a physician, he was concerned perhaps more than the others about such things. Necessary, unavoidable—these concepts he understood. But still . . . that oath. "Would it be accident or suicide?" Belleveau asked.

"Too many accidents might draw undue attention, though, mightn't they?" Kendall asked.

"It would take more than a few," Gerrin said. "Death is no stranger there. You know that was one reason we chose it."

"Yes, and because it is the world's best containment laboratory," Belleveau said.

"You're right," Gerrin agreed. "The South Pole certainly is that."

PART TWO

Ice on Fire

Death drifting from the doors and blood like rain!

—AESCHYLUS, *AGAMEMNON*

9

THE IDEA OF SLEEPING IN THE BUNK WHERE EMILY HAD BEEN TOR-
tured and killed revolted Hallie. She sat on the floor, in the dark, sick
and seething, full of feelings she had never experienced before. Feelings without names, animal and raging. Far beyond those even her
father's death had aroused. But that one had been natural.

She had just witnessed a murder.

A murder by torture.

Of a friend.

By someone who might be living in the next room, for all she
knew.

On Denali, climbing with Emily, she had been buried by an avalanche. One second she was leading a pitch on the Cassin Ridge route;
the next, the avalanche had swept her away, consolidated around her,
and encased her like cement. Only her tongue and one eyelid could
move. She could not even struggle.

That was how she felt now, on the floor in the dark.

So many questions. Why was there a surveillance camera in the
room? Emily must have placed it herself. If someone else had put it
there, they surely would have removed it before Hallie arrived. What

reason could Emily have had for doing something like that? She must have been afraid, but why, and of what? Of *whom*? Hallie knew that Emily had been an inveterate video blogger. Maybe she just wanted to record time spent in the room without having to activate a camera every time she returned.

What should *she* do now? Tell somebody? Who? Not tell anyone? But then what? Was the killer still here in the station? Killers, plural? Who else was in danger? Was concealing evidence of murder a crime in its own right?

She was suddenly, intensely claustrophobic. A very experienced cave explorer, she had not felt that way for years. She did now, squeezed into the tiny room, gripped by the dark station, trapped by the wasteland that stretched a thousand miles in every direction. Ironic in a way, feeling like that in a place with more empty space around it than any habitation on earth. Like an outpost on Mars, Graeter had said. Just words at the time. Not any longer.

She awoke where she had fallen asleep, sitting on the floor, back against the wall, feeling no less confused and exhausted. She stood, breathed deeply, and the licorice smell, faint before, now was stronger, heavy and cloying. Almost as unpleasant as the smell of her own body after five days without bathing. In gray sweat clothes, towel in hand, she stepped into the hall and nearly ran into a bulky man. He had long, greasy hair and needed a shave. He wore black bunny boots and Carhartt coveralls that had been tan when new but were now dark with oil and hydraulic fluid.

He looked her up and down, with bloodshot eyes, as though she were stark naked.

"Lookee here. A new girl Beaker. Whooeeee." His voice was rough, his breath heavy with liquor. It was not yet eight A.M. She was very aware of being alone in the hall with him. As far as she could tell, there were no surveillance cameras in the station. She took a step back.

"Excuse me?"

"Escuse me. *Escuse* me." He laughed as if those were the funniest words he had heard in months. "They ain't no 'scuses here, fungee." She could see the hunger in his eyes. The tip of his tongue peeked from between his teeth, flattened, a third lip. Her stomach twitched. She started to walk around him. He sidestepped, blocking her path.

His tongue slid out like a thick, pink-skinned eel and kept coming until its tip hung even with his chin. He gave a slow, leering lick to something Hallie could not see but had no trouble imagining. The man reeled his tongue back in, winked, and lurched off.

She watched him go, her heart racing and hands shaking from the adrenaline surge.

Was it him?

If only there had been sound, or better image quality, or just one good look at the killer's face. From now on she would wonder the same thing about every man she met here.

In the women's shower room, she lifted her face to steaming spray, washed her hair, stepped out of the stream to work up a soapy lather all over her body. Before she could rinse, the water stopped.

"What the hell?"

"Two minutes is all you get," said Rockie Bacon, just entering.

"How could you stay clean showering two minutes a day?"

"Two minutes a *week*."

"You're screwing with a fungee, right?"

"Takes a lot of energy to melt ice. That shower will reactivate after five minutes, but there's an honor system." She gave Hallie a long look. "You got soap all over. Take some of my time to rinse." Hallie wasn't sure she had heard right. But Bacon said, "C'mon, c'mon," and Hallie went.

Afterward, while they were toweling dry, Hallie thought, *Tell her?* but decided, *Not yet.* Instead, she related what had happened outside her room.

"That was Brank. Total, dead-end, asshole loser. And a mean drunk. He put two Draggers in the hospital a month ago. One was a woman. Stay clear of him."

"Why is he still here?"

"Ever try finding normal people willing to spend a year in Alcatraz on ice?"

"The money's supposed to be great."

"Yeah. But a year here is . . ." She shook her head, as if unable to find the right words.

"What does he do?"

"As little as possible."

"He has the longest tongue I ever saw on a human."

Bacon chuckled. "His most prized possession." She considered that for a moment. "Well, probably the second most."

Hallie was thinking: *Put a woman in the hospital.* And: *Why did he just happen to be walking past my room?*

"You want eggs with them waffles?" The galley server was about five-five, with a ferret face and a voice like squeaking hinges.

"Sure," Hallie said.

He deposited a soft yellow pile.

"Are those fresh?" she asked.

He grinned around spotted teeth. "Honey, the only fresh thing around here is the tube steak."

"The what?"

He pointed his spoon at a discernible bulge and waited for her reaction, which was to say, "Mouse in your pocket?"

Hallie sat by herself. The eggs and waffles and coffee all tasted of chlorine. It felt utterly bizarre sitting there eating breakfast, or trying to, overhearing snatches of conversation, taking in the new surroundings, all the mundane trappings, while carrying around the secret of a horrible, violent death. It occurred to her that a spy would have it this way, hoarding secrets and telling lies, fear a constant shadow. It would have to corrode your soul. She'd been carrying her secret around for only a few hours and it was already starting to feel like some live thing wanting to claw out of her.

She understood, suddenly, that this must be exactly what the killer himself was experiencing—unless he was one of those monster psychopaths who felt nothing, including remorse. Regardless, he and she were connected by Emily's death, although only she knew that.

An odd sensation came over her, and she glanced around. It felt like people in the galley were looking at her. It had to be her imagination, of course, another side effect of the secret. Or some weird form of Pole-induced paranoia. But then, working her way through the awful food, glancing up now and then, she realized it was not her imagination. People really were looking at her strangely, some staring, others peering out of the corners of their eyes. A couple even pointed. Four men in particular, at a table halfway across the room, were making no attempt to hide their interest. Then one of them rose and walked over.

"Hey." He was smiling—smirking, actually—and standing with his head cocked to one side. He wasn't bad-looking, but his eyes kept flicking around, scanning for something or someone more important. She was surprised to see eyes like that down here. In Washington they were as common as flies.

"Hi," she said.

"Maynard Blaine." She took his extended hand and, eventually, had to pull her own free.

"I might need that someday."

"Need that someday. Ha, ha." His laugh was like two little coughs. "So you are Dr. Holly Leland, replacement for Emily Durant and the newest addition to our distinguished team of Beakers."

"How did you know that?"

"Are you kidding? Fresh face, you stick out like a sore thumb."

That was why people had been looking at her. "It's Hallie, not Holly. You knew Emily?"

He hesitated, then shook his head. "No. Well, just to say hello."

"I knew her." Hallie was surprised at how surprised he looked.

"You did?"

"Very well."

His features became disarranged, like a turned kaleidoscope. Putting them back in order took a few moments. "Tough break," he said.

"For me or her?"

"Both. But I meant her dying like that."

"Like what?"

He shook both hands beside his head, like a man warding off bees. "Enough about her. I came over here to make you an offer you can't refuse."

"Like *what*?" Hallie wanted to learn what he knew about Emily's death, but he misunderstood. He thought she was very eager to hear his offer.

"How would you like to be my ice wife?"

10

UNDER OTHER CIRCUMSTANCES, SHE MIGHT HAVE BANTERED— *Where's the ring?* and *Why aren't you on your knees?* Not now.

"I'm in a relationship."

He winked. "What happens at Pole stays at Pole."

"How about ice friends." She hoped the words, and her tone, would ease his exit.

"Like, friends with *benefits*?"

"Not that kind."

Blaine's smirk faded, his shoulders sagged.

"Friends?"

He sighed. "A friend indeed leaves a man in need." But he shook her outstretched hand, and once again she had to pull free. "Holly," he said. "A thorn by any other name is just as sharp."

"*Hallie.*"

"What's your field?"

"Microbiology. What's yours?"

"Genetic virology."

She decided that a serious insult to speed his departure might not be wise on the morning of her first full day here. It was entirely possible that he had killed Emily. Or knew who did. Be smart, be civil, try to learn something.

"What science are you doing down here, Maynard?"

"Do we have to talk shop?"

"I'm sure your friends would enjoy having you back."

"Picornaviruses."

"Mostly common cold pathogens."

"Right."

"Using human subjects?" she asked.

"Do I look like Josef Mengele? Mice."

"What strain?"

He seemed surprised by the question. "Um, BALB/c. Why do you ask?"

"I work with mice, too, back in the world. I like to keep abreast of the matches between strains and applications." In fact, she was very current on the optimal mice strains for picornavirus research because work conjoining those viruses and bacteria was hot right now. BALB/c was not one of them. Why in God's name would anybody lie about such a thing? Maybe he wasn't lying—just wrong. Or maybe those were the only mice he could get down here. Before she could ask, he said, "So you'll be doing time with Fido."

Curiosity overcame her dislike of talking about absent people. "Why do you say it like that?"

"Fido is one crispy critter."

"As in burned out?"

"He hasn't been playing with a full deck for some time. And Emily's death knocked him for a loop."

Whoa, she thought. I'm wasting a golden opportunity. "Since we're friends now, can I ask you something?" she asked.

"I guess."

"Do you know how Emily died?"

His face did that thing again. He lowered his voice. "Through the grapevine—overdose." His voice became more distant, and he glanced back at his table.

So the killer's ruse was working. Assuming this man wasn't the killer, she thought.

"Wasn't there an investigation?"

"You're barking up the wrong Beaker."

She had noted by then that his speech consisted largely of trite idioms. "What do you mean?"

"Merritt found the body."

Before she could speak, he looked over her shoulder and said, "Uh-oh."

She turned. A woman, eating alone several tables away, had jumped to her feet. Her eyes were wide, mouth open, face contorted. She screamed once, grabbed her belly, dropped to the floor.

A tall, thin man with the paper-white skin of an albino was sitting not far away. He wore dark glasses even in the dim galley. He moved quickly and knelt beside the woman, whose paroxysms reminded Hallie of childbirths she had witnessed.

"Who's that?" Hallie asked Blaine.

"Doc. The station medical officer. Orson Morbell."

The woman's pain appeared to ease. Panting, she said, "I don't know what happened. I was just sitting and all of a sudden . . ." She stared not at his face but overhead. Hallie looked up. Nothing but the burned-out Christmas lights.

"You lie still, Diana. I'm going to have people bring you down to the infirmary. It's probably appendicitis." Over his shoulder Doc said, to no one and everyone, "Call comms. Get the EMTs in here. Tell them we need a gurney."

Hallie thought the woman was about forty. She had olive skin, black hair pulled back into a ponytail, and a Spanish accent. Her hands looked like Graeter's, and a gold wedding band and engagement ring shone brightly against the reddened skin.

"It's Diana Montalban," Blaine said quietly. "She's a biochemist. University of Madrid."

"Look." Loud whisper from somewhere to one side of Hallie.

Montalban wore a black sweatshirt, gray sweatpants, and running shoes. Something was happening to her belly. It swelled as though inflating, rising above the waistband of her sweatpants, pushing them down. Hallie saw the ragged pink line of a C-section scar.

"What the hell is going on?" Someone else, not whispering now.

"Diana?" the doctor said. "What's happening? Talk to me."

She screamed, cutting him off. People started edging back, pointing.

"Somebody get a goddamned gurney!" the doctor shouted. "We need to bring her to the clinic."

The woman's hands were clamped over her belly, covering the scar. She began to writhe. As Hallie watched, blood started seeping through her fingers, then flowed freely. The doctor put his hands over Montalban's, applying hard direct pressure. Someone offered a folded-up lab coat, which Morbell grabbed. He pushed Montalban's hands away, and in the split second before he applied the makeshift compress, Hallie could see blood pulsing from where the healed incision had reopened into a gaping red slash. The sweet stink of blood filled the cafeteria.

Three EMTs arrived this time, one carrying medical kits, the other two pushing a wheeled stretcher. Blood had pooled all around the woman's torso, soaking the doctor's legs and hands.

"Everyone clear this area *NOW*!" Graeter yelled, behind Hallie. She hadn't heard him arrive. The doctor was telling the responders to prep an IV coagulant while he kept the sopping lab coat pressed in place. Hallie and Blaine joined the flow of people heading for the galley exits. She heard Graeter key his radio and say, "Get the biohazard team to the galley. Yes. That's right. *Again,* goddamnit."

11

HALLIE ARRIVED LATE FOR HER MEETING WITH THE STATION'S CHIEF scientist, but Agnes Merritt seemed not to mind. Before Hallie even sat, the older woman blurted, "Did you hear what happened in the galley?"

"I was there. Yesterday and today both."

Merritt shook her head. "What an awful introduction to Pole, Dr. Leland. I can't imagine how I'd feel in your shoes."

"Thank you. Please call me Hallie."

"Good deal. I'm Agnes. Aggie to my friends, which is just about everybody."

Merritt's office was slightly bigger than Graeter's, and she had two folding chairs for visitors. A coffeemaker sat on a small table in one corner. Merritt filled mugs and handed one to Hallie. Then she passed a plate of chocolate chip cookies.

Hallie had left most of her breakfast back in the galley. She nibbled one cookie, then gobbled another. "These are great."

"Grandma's recipe. I love to bake. Sneak into the galley during off-hours."

Unlike Graeter's office, Merritt's was adorned with framed pictures. One wall was all Antarctic shots: Merritt boarding a C-130 at McMurdo, standing in her Big Red parka beside the station's "barber pole" ceremonial marker, hoisting a champagne glass in honor of some holiday or memorable occasion. The other wall's pictures were from back in the world. Most of them were grip-and-grins, Merritt receiving or holding awards and certificates. A typical bureaucrat's wall, Hallie noted, except that there were no family pictures.

Merritt looked to be in her late forties. She wore comfort-cut jeans that stretched tight across her wide rump and a black turtleneck with a red fleece pullover on top of that. She had a round face red from high blood pressure or windburn or both, a red-veined snub nose, and a small, moist mouth that formed circles around words, as though she were blowing bubbles when she spoke. "So tell me what happened."

Hallie did, and then everything slipped out of focus. She realized that Merritt was speaking. "I'm sorry. What?"

"Dear, you just zoned right out."

"God. I'm sorry."

"Don't worry. Pole's tough." She patted Hallie's knee.

"Agnes . . . Aggie, two deaths like this, so close together. That has to be unusual, even for the Pole."

"I thought so, too. But have you ever heard of dehiscence?"

"No."

"Me, neither, until Doc called. Part of Harriet's esophagus was removed last year. Some kind of precancerous condition. They severed and reconnected some major veins and arteries."

"You're saying they ruptured?"

"Doc thinks so. When surgical scars reopen, it's called dehiscence."

"Why now, though?"

"Goodness, why not? Altitude. Extreme temperature fluctuations. Radiation. Stress. Bad food. Hard work. On and on."

"I never heard of something like that."

"How many folks do you know who've had esophagectomies?"

"What about Diana Montalban?"

"You mentioned a C-section scar. Could have been the same thing, Doc said."

That seemed like too much coincidence to Hallie. At the same time, it wasn't hard to understand why Merritt would want to rationalize the deaths. Minimize threats beyond your control. Unknown is always more frightening than known. And as chief scientist, Merritt would have a vested interest in showing that on her watch, deaths were caused by problems the victims brought with them, rather than any they'd encountered here.

Or maybe the deaths were connected in some way to Emily's, and Merritt knew about all of it. Since Hallie had arrived in the chief scientist's office, the question had been blinking in her mind. *Should I tell her?*

There was something else. With each new encounter, it was getting harder *not* to tell. The secret wanted out. More properly, something in her wanted it released. It felt like a tumor, ugly, foreign, and dangerous. A friend with cancer had told her, "Once you know that thing is in there, you just want it *out*." Hallie understood that much better now.

"I'm so glad you're here." Merritt brought her back. "Fido will be overjoyed. He's just been, oh, what's the word . . . distraught since Emily's death."

"I hope I can help," she said. "I was sent in a huge rush. Emily and he were researching an extremophile found in a subglacial lake, or so I was told. I didn't know there were any lakes at the Pole."

"There weren't supposed to be. It was a huge surprise. Russians found the closest one hundreds of miles away, called Vostok. Bigger than Lake Ontario. Ours is tiny by comparison—about a thousand feet in diameter."

"How deep?"

"Two miles, give or take."

Hallie thought she might not have heard right. "Two *miles*?"

"Yes."

"And Emily was diving this lake, right?"

"It's called a cryopeg. Yes, she was. Poor Emily." Merritt looked away for a few moments, appeared to compose herself. "She found the extremophile colony only a hundred feet down and retrieved a biosample. They had it in the lab, but it went moribund in three days."

"So that's the reason you needed another ice diver."

"Not *just* a diver. One who knew extremophiles and could function in the Pole environment. *And* who could get here fast, because of winterover. If we can't take more biomatter out of the cryopeg in the next few days, it'll be nine months before we can put anyone down there again. Who knows what will be left, now that we've breached the ice capsule?"

"What makes this thing so special?"

"I'm just a garden-variety epidemiologist, Hallie. Fido can explain it better. When were you thinking of diving?"

"That depends. Is there a recompression chamber here?"

"Oh dear, no. There was never any need for one until now."

"Not good. The water is twenty-two degrees, right?"

Merritt nodded.

"That's brutal. Did Emily mark a route?"

"Yes."

"How much ice do you have to pass through to reach the water?"

"It's a thirty-foot shaft, flooded to surface level."

"This is going to be very dangerous. Without a recompression chamber, there's no margin for error. I'm tired, dehydrated, feeling the altitude. It's all a recipe for decompression sickness."

"The bends."

"Yes. Let's shoot for later this afternoon. Might even need to wait until tomorrow."

"Oh, either will be fine. Need you healthy, after all." Merritt seemed not at all disappointed by the possible delay, which surprised Hallie, given the urgency to get her down here. Then Merritt asked, "Have you seen Doc yet?"

"No."

Merritt sat back, her smile fading for the first time. "Please do that as soon as possible." Also for the first time, she sounded more like a boss than a kindly aunt.

"I'm not sick. A cold, maybe, but nothing serious," Hallie said.

"It's not about being sick. It's to start your Pole medical file."

"My medical file should have been sent down."

"Might have been."

"Then why—?"

"Studying people at Pole is critical. In a way, the biggest experiment here is us. So everybody gets an incoming physical. Creates a research baseline."

"I'm leaving in four days, though. Why bother?"

Merritt shrugged. "The rules come down from on high, and we follow them. Would appreciate your doing the same."

"All right."

Merritt looked ready to finish, but Hallie was not. "Can we talk about Emily? Graeter said you knew the details of her death."

"What did he tell you?"

"Nothing. He told me to see you. Not very nicely, either."

She nodded. "Graeter went through some bad times. He wasn't in such good shape when he came down here. And he's been at Pole way too long, poor man." Merritt sipped her coffee.

"What happened?"

"He was the executive officer on a nuclear sub. The *Jimmy Carter.* An accident in the reactor area killed three sailors. May not have been his fault, but the captain had better connections up the chain. Graeter got the blame, and his career was over. Then his wife left him for another man—the same captain who had tossed him under the bus. Can you believe it?"

"Did he tell you all that?"

"God, no. You met him. The man talks like every word costs ten dollars. No, that information came from other sources." She looked at her hands, then back at Hallie. "I'm going to share something gal to gal: be careful with Graeter."

"Careful how?"

"The man is a sad case, but he has problems."

"Other than disliking women, you mean?"

"Oh, yes. He's obsessed."

"In the clinical sense?"

"He's not certifiable. I don't think he's a bad man, deep down. But he can be like a little Hitler with his rules. Just don't get sideways with him."

"Forewarned," she said. "But about Emily."

Merritt scratched a fingernail over her desktop, as if trying to scrape away something crusty and foreign. "It's tricky, with all these confidentiality regulations now. You're not family, so I don't—"

"What I hear stays here. I *promise*."

"Why are you so interested?"

"Emily and I worked together at BARDA, part of CDC, and got to be good friends a few years back."

"I didn't know that." Merritt seemed surprised and, for some reason Hallie couldn't fathom, unhappy to hear that. "Not sure any of us did. No matter. It was very sad. That young woman was so sweet, and had such potential. What an awful waste."

"What do you mean?"

"Maybe this will help you understand why I wasn't eager to talk. The sad fact is, Emily killed herself."

Hallie knew that this was not true. She also knew that it was important not to let anyone else know that yet. She did her best to look and sound horrified. "*Really?* My God."

"Isn't that just the most tragic thing you ever heard?"

"Suicide? Emily Durant? It's hard to believe."

"I didn't say suicide."

"You said she killed herself."

"Accidental drug overdose. There is a difference."

"Who determined that?"

"The station manager, Doc, and me. I found her and wrote up the report, since technically she worked for me. But the others had to sign off."

"How did you come to find her?"

"Her partner—Fido—started to worry after she didn't show up in the lab. He went to her room and knocked. No answer. Called and asked me to look in on her." Merritt shook her head. "Oh dear. It was very bad. She was dead on her bunk with a syringe stuck in one arm. There were injection marks in other places, syringes, more drugs. Just . . . just *awful*. I'm not used to that kind of thing."

"How do you know about the injection marks?"

"She was almost naked. You couldn't miss them. I'm no expert on druggies, but Doc said they find all kinds of strange places to shoot up."

"I seriously doubt Emily Durant was a druggie," Hallie said.

"Pole changes people. Emily had been here almost a year. You've just arrived."

"Emily never used drugs when I knew her. She rarely even drank. She was a nationally ranked ski racer in college. Stayed in top shape."

"To tell you the truth, her health had been deteriorating for some weeks before she died. I saw it. Others did, too."

"How so?"

"The poor girl was exhausted. Depressed. Not eating. Forgetful."

Must have been watching her pretty closely to know all that, Hallie thought. But then, a good chief scientist would.

"It's called getting Polarized," Merritt said. "Happens at the end of a long stay."

"Why didn't she just leave?"

"Don't you know, I suggested that very thing? But she'd been given a sizable grant. And signed a contract. If she had to withdraw for mental health reasons . . . Well, I don't have to tell *you*. Poor thing. It would have ended her career."

"It might have kept her alive."

Merritt gave Hallie an odd look. "Did you have any more questions about this?" Her tone indicated that she hoped Hallie's answer would be no.

"What was the drug?"

"We don't know just yet. But—and it pains me to say this—it's like Alice's Restaurant here. You can get anything you want."

"What did the medical examiner's report say?"

"We haven't seen one yet."

"Isn't that unusual?"

"Not really. The ME at Christchurch does the autopsy and sends his report to the New Zealand Police. They give it to State, and *they* send it through diplomatic channels to Washington. After all that, it might be routed back to NSF and, if the powers there see fit, shared with us worker bees."

"Did the doctor do a tox screen?"

"No, we're not equipped for that."

"You said you found injection marks, as in plural?"

"On her thighs and both arms."

"Were photographs taken of the body? The death scene?"

"No."

That struck Hallie as odd, too. "Does everybody know you were the one who found Emily's body?"

"No, just Graeter, Doc, and Fido. Details like that are all confidential." She hesitated, then continued: "And honestly, Hallie, you wouldn't either, if I hadn't learned you were friends. If details start leaking before the muckety-mucks get their paperwork, I could wind up in very hot water."

"I give you my word, nothing I heard leaves this room."

Merritt smiled. "I knew the minute we met that I could trust you. Just a feeling you get about some people."

That sounded like a closing statement to Hallie. She got up to go. "Thanks for taking time, Aggie. I appreciate—"

Merritt waved her down. "Whoa, hang on. All we've done is talk work. What about *you*? Married, have a family?"

"No husband, no kids."

"There must be a Mr. Right, though. Beautiful girl like you."

"As a matter of fact. We've been together about a year."

"Making family plans yet?"

"Excuse me?"

"You know, family plans. Marriage, babies, all that."

Merritt's questions were mild in tone and accompanied by a

sincere-looking smile, but they felt strange to Hallie. They had known each other for only twenty minutes. And why would she care about Hallie's family plans, of all things?

"We haven't gotten there," she said. Which was true, if you discounted her recent close call and the impasse with Bowman it had caused on the way to Dulles. Merritt didn't need to hear any of that, but Hallie felt it would be discourteous to just walk out now without showing some personal interest in return.

"How about you, Aggie?"

"Married, you mean?" Long sigh. "Once. Not anymore."

So, death or divorce, Hallie thought, either of which could bite if you reached too far. She nodded, waited to see if Merritt wanted to continue. She did.

"He came from a big family. And wanted a big family. We—I— couldn't have children at all. He didn't want to adopt. So he found a better breeder."

"I'm sorry."

"Oh, I'm over it long since. Seems like a dream now. Nightmare, actually."

Are you over it? Hallie wondered. Something in Merritt's tone and expression suggested otherwise.

"You two tying the knot anytime soon?" Merritt asked.

Hallie had not heard that expression for a long time, but something in Merritt's tone made it sound more like a hanging than marriage. She shrugged. "We both travel a lot and do dangerous work."

"Can get addictive, though, right? That kind of work?"

Hallie had been thinking about that a good bit recently. Still, the question surprised her, coming from a relative stranger.

"Honestly, yes. I'm always glad to be home. But then I can't wait to get out again."

"Interesting choice of words."

"How so?"

"Most people would have said 'leave home' or maybe 'go away.' You said 'get out.' Like from prison."

12

WIL BOWMAN LIVED ON A HUNDRED REMOTE ACRES IN NORTH-
western Maryland, in a stone house built in the 1850s by a farm family named Mongeon and refurbished at odd intervals since. Bowman's
place was accessible by a dirt service road that curved and twisted
more than a mile from State Route 550. The land was mostly mixed
hardwood forest on the southern flank of Piney Mountain. Remnants
of an orchard intermingled with native trees off to one side of the
house. Bowman was slowly bringing the apple trees back, heirloom
varieties like Northern Spy, Orange Pippin, Winesap, Roxbury Rus-
set.

A quarter mile behind the house, a sheer granite face rose vertically for 150 feet and ran a half mile in either direction. In spring,
freshets poured down the mountain above the cliff and joined into
foaming cascades at several places. In winter, those waterfalls froze
solid. In front of the house, Bowman had cleared several sloping acres
to reclaim what, once upon a time, had been sheep pasture bounded
by ruler-straight, knee-high stone walls. When time between operations allowed, he kept working to open things up beyond the fields.

He liked making space for the big maple, beech, and oak trees to have light and flourish. He also liked clean, open sight lines.

He sat at an oak table in front of a cavernous fieldstone fireplace. It was fitted now with a Vermont Castings Defiant woodstove, which heated the house all winter on four cords of seasoned wood, which he cut, split, and stacked himself.

He had been trying to write an email to Hallie for some time now, starting and stopping, uncharacteristically twisted up in his own thinking. He had not liked the way they had parted on Thursday. On the way to Dulles, she'd told him that she had thought she was pregnant. It had come as a surprise, but no more so than the fact that she'd waited until they were almost at the terminal.

"Why didn't you say anything before?" he asked, wanting her answer and fearing it in about equal measure.

"I wanted to be sure," she said.

He looked over. Something in her tone. "That wasn't the only reason, though."

"No, it wasn't the only one."

Perhaps that was why she had waited until they were so close to the airport. Before more could be said, he double-parked in front of the terminal. He knew that she had to board in less than an hour and had two huge bags to check, not to mention passing security. He could feel her impatience. Cars were lining up behind them. A cabbie honked, then another. A dirty wind came up, making them both blink to clear the grit. He tossed her luggage onto a redcap's wagon, then drew her aside.

"We need to talk more, Hallie."

"We do. But I have to go."

He held her with his eyes. "There are things you don't know. About me."

"And about myself, apparently."

That surprised him. Shocked, almost. Hallie never spoke about herself that way, was virtually allergic to the argot of self-help books and guru mantras.

He held her, and they kissed. She promised to call from Los Angeles, or maybe it had been New Zealand. She waved to the redcap, who followed her into the terminal.

A green minivan pulled to the curb directly in front of him and disgorged people: business-suited man, woman in white parka and jeans, young girl with shining blond hair in red jacket and white cap. The man hauled a suitcase out of the van's back, faced the woman, and they embraced. The girl fluttered around them.

Bowman turned away. More honking, a woman leaning out her car window, gesturing, yelling something. He heard none of it.

He started another email:

> Hallie,
>   I didn't like the way we left things at the airport. I was caught off guard by what you told me and did not respond appropriately. Since we hadn't talked at all about anything relating to

No, he thought. Sounds like a fuddled college kid. He deleted that attempt, got up, walked around. Looked out the front windows. It was midafternoon, the sun dipping behind the mountain's western shoulder, white woods turning blue, wind spinning through the forest, twirling up snow devils in the old sheep pasture. Bowman looked out, watched shadows stretch, thought about climbing one of the frozen waterfalls. Tossed that idea away. Quit stalling, mister.

He went to the bathroom, used the toilet, saw his reflection in the mirror while he washed his hands. Bowman liked living among old things. Some young Marylander might have gazed at himself in that mirror before heading off to Antietam. Bowman had bought it for the oval frame of hand-carved butternut and had never replaced the glass, though it was cracked and dulled with age. It was like looking at himself through fog—not such a bad thing, actually. Thirty-nine, not old, but not much youth left in that face. Had he ever looked young? Must have, once. The job ages you. Other people told you, so you knew that when you took it on. Like being a soldier. Or a cop in a big city. People thought the fighting ended when the bad actors swung, but it never really did end. Just smoldered underground, out of plain sight, waiting to flare again like roots that reignite forest fires.

There were certain rules he never broke. Some had to do with killing. Always finishing what he started was another. One of his favorite books was *Personal Memoirs of U.S. Grant,* and one of his favorite passages described young Grant's attempt to ride home, on a short leave, before deployment separated him from family and friends. At one point he had to take a green horse across a rain-swollen river. Mixing fast water and young mounts was a good way to produce dead riders, as Grant, possibly the finest horseman ever to pass through West Point, well knew. But he wrote, "One of my superstitions had always been when I started to go anywhere, or to do anything, not to turn back or stop until the thing intended was accomplished."

Bowman had never forgotten that sentence, thought it worth adding to his collection of personal commandments, and allowed it to guide actions large and small. An email was one of those small things that could have very large consequences, and he would not let this one go unfinished. Now, though, he felt the way he imagined Grant's horse must have, knowing it had to go, wanting like hell not to.

Walking back to the table, he felt, rather than heard, some disturbance. *Might* have been a very faint sound like a slap. He stood where he was for several seconds, then went to the kitchen and moved a switch that killed every light in the house. He stepped out onto the small back porch—the noise, or whatever it was, had come from that direction—leaving the door open. He stood there for a long time, listening, feeling the dark, and finally went back in.

At the table again, he sat and stared at the screen and reeled in his mind when it started to wander. Finally, to break something loose, he sipped coffee that had grown cold sitting next to the computer, took a deep breath, and tried a jump-starting trick a writer friend had once showed him:

Dear Hallie,
        What I really want to say here is

Stopped. Waited for more. Waited longer. Rubbed his forehead. Leaned back, closed his eyes, grunted. Stood, cursed, and went to make dinner.

He rose the next morning before sunrise, had coffee, and set out on snowshoes. Twenty minutes of easy cross-hill climbing brought him to the base of the biggest frozen waterfall. As far as he knew, he was the first to climb it, so he'd had the privilege of naming the fall: Revelation.

It rose vertically for almost 150 feet. The exit on top was barred by a rounded, bulging cornice that required very careful climbing. Unusual to have the crux of a route so near its end, but the velocity of flow in this stream caused water to shoot out beyond the cliff face, forming the cornice as layer after layer froze. At some point the cornice would break off of its own weight.

It was about ten degrees and still, perfect weather for climbing here. Everything—rock, ice, snow—was blue in the predawn, though the sun would appear soon, in an hour at most. Above him, the ice looked like giant drips of melted white and blue wax. His passage had silenced the woodpeckers and chickadees, ermine and hares, the wraith deer. The only sounds were his breathing and small, sharp cracks as the ice shifted, compressed, expanded. Every part of it that he could see was frozen solid, but deep inside there was always something happening.

He stamped a firm circle and stepped out of his snowshoes, clipped into his Grivel crampons, took two leashless Black Diamond Cobra ice tools from their holsters on either side of his climbing harness. Accustomed to solo climbing, he carried just a few carabiners and ice screws. The only other tool was a Desert Eagle Mark XIX pistol in .44 magnum caliber, black stainless steel with internal laser sight, carried under his left arm in a custom Bianchi shoulder holster, which also held two extra eight-round magazines. Bowman never went anywhere unarmed.

He stepped to the ice, found secure placements for both tools above his head, set one pair of front points, then the other at the same level. He hung straight-armed from the ice tools for a few seconds, knees bent and legs relaxed. He stood up straight, removed and replaced his left tool higher, stepped up with his right foot, moving diagonally to center his body on the tool, set the left front points, set the right tool, and stood again.

The ice was perfect, solid enough to be secure, with features and porosity for good penetration of the tools' picks. Then he really began the climb, not stop-go, stop-go, but in a continuous flow, arms and legs always moving, body constantly, smoothly rising, as if he were being hoisted by an invisible cable.

When he had climbed sixty feet, the sun rose over the treetops and he saw it strike the ice twenty feet below him. He was tempted to hang and let it catch him, because it would feel good to be there like that, sandwiched between the heat of the sun and the cold of the ice.

He started up again, moving in that easy rhythm, and stopped at 130 feet. The cornice overhang loomed above him. Beneath that, a massive fracture had left a band of clean rock ten feet high and cutting completely through the ice column. He was surprised not to have seen the debris down at the bottom, but then he reasoned that it must have shattered upon impact with the ice column's solid base. There had been less than full light, too, when he began. He understood that the ice section's cracking and fall was what he had heard the night before.

He could try to climb past the smooth swath of granite. It wasn't the rock he was worried about, though it looked dauntingly clean.

Worse, all the ice above that section was now unstable, held in place only by adhesion to the face. It might carry ten climbers his weight or come off with one strike of an ice tool. The sun was moving. Warmth touched his calves like slowly rising water. In ten minutes, maybe less, it would reach that ice hanging above him.

He leaned back, surveyed the rock band, looking for a line. Saw two ledges the width of a guitar pick that could hold his front points and, above them, a crack that would take the pick of one tool. He could get that far, but the ice above would still be a foot beyond his longest reach. It would require a dynamic move, launching himself off those ledges and swinging the free tool all at once, to reach that ice above, with no guarantee that it would take his weight long enough for him to place the other pick.

Two hours later, climbing gear stowed and coffee poured, Bowman added maple logs to the Defiant and sat at the oak table. Like Hallie, he came to decisions quickly and did not look back. He put the mug down and started typing.

Dear Hallie,

I have been at this for some time without producing anything worth sending to you. So I'm going to let words come as they will. I said there were things you don't know about me. I wasn't referring to the work. Not directly.

I was married before, and we had a child. My wife's name was Arden. Our daughter was named Sarah. One time some people came to where we lived then and killed them both. I was not there to save them.

It was never my intention to deceive you. Only guilt and shame kept this locked down. It cuts every day.

You doubtless would have thought me a paltry excuse for fatherhood before. I cannot imagine that this will improve your estimation much.

Wil

He sent the email, wondering which would disturb Hallie more: that he had had a family, or that they had been killed, or that he had taken a year to tell her about it.

His cellphone chimed while he was in the kitchen breakfasting on raw lemons and blood-red *otoro*.

"How's BARDA today, Don?"

"All good. Are you planning to be in D.C. anytime soon?"

"Why?"

"Something I'd like to discuss with you."

"About our mutual friend?" Bowman put his chopsticks down. He could not think of another reason Hallie's boss would be calling him. And if Barnard had been on the phone with good news, he would not have hesitated to speak about it immediately.

"That's right."

"I'll see you in two hours."

13

SITTING AT THE TINY DESK, HALLIE WATCHED A FLY HANGING UP-
side down from one of the white ceiling tiles. She wondered briefly how
a fly might come to the South Pole, much less survive there. Then she
wondered if she was seeing things. And then—she was learning the
Pole's way of deranging thought—she recalled Charles Lindbergh.
He had become legend for flying solo across the Atlantic, but it wasn't
true. Not strictly, anyway. Hallie's father had known one of Lindbergh's
children, who told him something about the flight few people knew.

After twenty-two hours without sleep, still flying in the dark over
the ocean, Lindbergh began to hallucinate. He saw, or thought he
did, a fly in the cockpit. He had opened the *Spirit*'s windows several
times during the flight, hoping the cold air would keep him awake,
but apparently the fly—or at least his vision of it—hadn't been blown
out. To keep himself awake and help ward off thoughts of death,
Lindbergh began talking to the fly. He realized that it was an aviator
of sorts itself, and he considered that the hazards his tiny companion
had to deal with outnumbered his own many times over. He began to
feel something like affection for the fly and conversed with it as he
might have with a copilot.

Now Hallie tried to work up some feeling for the fly on her ceiling, just to see what would happen. Lindbergh had his copilot. She could do with a little confidant. Try as she might, the thing remained an insect that vomited *before* it ate and thought shit was earth's greatest treasure.

But if Lindbergh had his fly, she had the farm in Virginia. At times like this, she found it helpful to close her eyes and visit. It was called Marley, for her ancestor Constant Marley, who had acquired the land virgin in the 1720s and made it into a farm. Fifty acres were in pasture and hay. The remaining hundred were woodland, home to white-tailed deer, black bears, coons, and coyotes.

And copperheads. In summer, they glittered on gray basking rocks and, for Hallie, inhabited the same mystic realm as mares foaling and springs bubbling from stone. Just beyond striking range, she would sit watching sun glint off their hammered-metal heads. The yellow, black-pupiled eyes and golden, pentagonal scales made her think of jewels and treasure. Still, she understood the danger and always kept a respectful distance.

Except once. Thirteen, drawn by something in the ancient eyes, she'd inched closer, slow and smooth. She could have touched the snake's head, and almost did, just to see how it felt. Coiled and relaxed, it swelled and shrank its bellows flanks, and the pink tongue licked the Virginia summer-thick air. The back of her neck reddened, and sweat bubbled from her forehead. It was like staring into fire, a trance, and the world arranged itself around them.

Then the snake moved.

It could have been a hawk flashing in the sky, or some threat scent caught by the flicking tongue. In a blink the metallic head rose, its snout stopping a foot from her eyes. Even without being struck, she felt like an electric shock had hit. Adrenaline burned the oxygen in her system, leaving her breathless and weak-muscled. Fear very nearly overwhelmed her. She retained just enough mind to back away, slow as a shadow following sun.

Even safely distant, it was as though she had grabbed an arcing wire. The shock did not fade for a long time.

That was how she felt now. And backing away was not an option.

She awoke from restless drowsing, checked the time. Still an hour before she had to meet Graeter for a station tour. She stood, stretched, rubbed her face. Stared at the door, trying to make sense of everything. The meeting with Merritt was still fresh in her mind. There were only two possibilities about the chief scientist. If Merritt believed that Emily had given herself a fatal overdose, the killer's ruse was working. If she was lying, she had to be involved in some way. *Had* Merritt been lying? It was hard for Hallie to imagine the matronly, cookie-baking woman committing or aiding a horrible murder. Merritt's interest in Hallie as a person made it seem even less likely. Women did kill, of course, but really—one like Merritt?

The normal procedure, she assumed, would be to tell Graeter, with his claim to be a marshal. The man was a martinet, and a nasty one at that. Did that make him a murderer? Definitely not. But Graeter was also angry down to his core and obviously hated women. Did all of that make it easier for Hallie to see him killing a woman? Definitely so.

What about Maynard Blaine? He seemed about as likely to commit murder as Merritt. But that was only an assumption. If she knew nothing else, at least she knew one thing, and Guillotte had said it:

A place where everything you know is not true.

For the time being, she would obey an ironclad rule: *Assume nothing.*

The secret would have to stay where it was.

"Talk to me, Em," she said.

Silence.

What did she expect, really? Ghostly voices from the ether? Apparitions floating around the room? She looked at the window, which showed nothing and reflected nothing, and only then realized that the room had not one mirror.

She needed to write to Barnard and Bowman. But how secure

would the servers be? Some people always had access. IT techs and managers like Graeter and Merritt certainly would. God knew who else. And the off-and-on comms. Even if they were up, email would have to wait.

She sat back, looking around, wishing there had been something of Emily's left behind. Then: maybe there was. Think like a cop. What would one of them do? Start with the body. Lacking that, the death scene.

She turned over the mattress, examined its underside, felt it all over for bumps or bulges. The bunk's plywood platform was bare and clean. She checked under the computer's CPU, examined its monitor and stand, picked up the keyboard and the mouse. She searched the inside of every cabinet and, standing on the desk chair, looked at their tops. Then she worked her way around the room, moving the chair, lifting and peering above all the other acoustical tiles.

Nothing.

She sat back in front of the computer desk. What the hell. Worth a try. Get some sleep.

She rose, but the space under the desk was so tight that her foot caught between the computer tower and the desk frame. She called the computer a foul name and started to yank her foot loose.

Then she stopped.

She *hadn't* searched everywhere.

14

SHE BOOTED UP THE COMPUTER.

"Talk to me, Em," she said again, and accessed the hard drive. Found the usual: Word, Excel, Explorer, Outlook. All the libraries—documents, music, pictures, videos—were empty. Someone must have cleaned them out as carefully as they had scrubbed the room. Not surprising, really—standard procedure in any organization after an employee left. So she would find nothing on the hard drive.

Wait.

Not *on* the hard drive.

What about *in* the hard drive?

From her own laptop she transferred to the room computer a program called Golden Retriever, given to her by Bowman. It was like the data-recovery programs you could buy on the Web but *much* more powerful. She searched for documents created by "Durant."

In 0.976 seconds, it displayed a message: *No matches.*

She would try more search terms. First, an adjustment. The computer keyboard lay flat on the desktop, and Hallie preferred typing on a tilted keyboard. She turned this one over and unfolded the plastic legs from their compartments on the underside. When she popped out the right one, something fell, hit the desktop, and bounced to the floor. The light was so dim in the room that she had to crawl around on her hands and knees to find the object. It was a blue microSD card the size of the nail on her little finger.

She was about to insert the card into a port in the station's computer. Then she stopped and disconnected her laptop. She pushed the tiny card into one of that computer's ports. There were thirteen folders, "date created" numbers showing that they started with the previous year's January and ended with January just past. The folders held varying numbers of files—all .wmv format.

It was a video log. Emily had been an avid amateur shooter, loved video calls and YouTube. It was natural that her journal would be in this form. She had arrived in January of the previous year. Hallie opened the first file from that month and suddenly there was Emily looking back at her from the screen. She double-clicked on the image, and Emily spoke.

"So. This is January sixth. My first full day here at Pole and my first entry into the video log."

Hallie hit the Pause symbol and wiped away the tears that were filling her eyes. Emily looked like the young woman Hallie had known at BARDA—auburn hair, freckles, lively green eyes, an infectious smile. And a honey-sweet Georgia accent. So full of energy that Hallie could feel it coming through the monitor. Involuntarily, she found herself smiling back through the tears. She recalled things she and Emily had done together, the great climb on Denali, the avalanche, Emily digging her out, their decision to keep going, making the summit, all the hard-ass climbers cheering and buying them endless rounds when they stumbled back into the Talkeetna Lodge.

"Emily," she said.

She touched one finger to the side of Emily's cheek on the screen. Gave herself a few moments, then hit Play, and Emily started talking again.

"This is such an amazing place. It's dark twenty-four hours a day and cold as hell—seventy-one below outside right now, according to the intranet. Makes Alaska seem almost tropical. Everything is just . . . *extreme.* I can't wait to look around more. It's like being out in space, totally alone. There's even a greenhouse where they grow vegetables. Somebody said they grow pot in there, too." She frowned, shook her head. "The vegetables are a good idea, anyway.

"This is a once-in-a-lifetime experience, and I'm going to keep a record of my time here. I can record footage of other things in the station and here in the room and outside with my video camera and produce something later when I have time."

Emily stopped, yawned again, rubbed her face. "But right now I need to get some sleep. I am just about out on my feet. Nap time. More later!"

The image faded.

Hallie jumped to an entry from July, seven months into Emily's stay. Dark circles had developed under her eyes. The freckles, brighter against pale skin, looked like little scabs. Her lips were cracked, and when Hallie hit Play, Emily came to life, but her smile did not.

"Let's see. It's July twenty-ninth. About halfway through my stay. What's the big news? Not much. Unless you count the partying. I've never seen so many people walking around drunk and high. Pot, of course, but not just. You wouldn't believe the booze they stockpile here. I mean, gallons and gallons, all top-shelf—Chivas, Jack D, Stoli, you name it. And they make moonshine! Some of the Beakers built a still. The stuff is clear like vodka, but it's about 160 proof and tastes like I think jet fuel would if you drank it. They call it Poleshine.

"I'm tired. No, exhausted. Everybody said this is a hard place to be, and it is. The disgusting food, being dirty all the time, annoying people, so much darkness. And getting sick. If you don't have Polarrhea you have a cold, and vice versa. There are scientists from so many different countries, who knows what kinds of bugs are floating around this place? I'm the only one from North America this year. Pure luck of the draw, the way grants shook out. We just keep swapping germs back and forth."

She looked into the camera without talking for several moments. "Need to get some sleep," she said, and the screen went blank.

Hallie jumped ahead again and opened a video from early in the

January just past. Emily's appearance last time had been disturbing. Now it was shocking. Weight loss had sharpened her face to points and edges. Her hair looked dirty and uncombed, and her teeth were yellow, with little wedges of plaque between them. There was a scabbed scratch on one cheek and blue-black circles under her bloodshot eyes. Her lips were chapped and cracked.

Emily stared blankly at the camera for several moments after turning it on. Her eyelids fell and rose slowly. She ran her tongue over her lips, grimaced, and then did something that struck Hallie as odd: she half-turned and looked over her shoulder. Was someone in the room with her who the camera wasn't showing? Had someone knocked on the door? After a moment, Emily turned back.

"The New Year's Eve party. Unbelievable." She rubbed her face, ran fingers through greasy hair. "Ambie got totally fucked up again." Her eyelids drooped and she nodded forward in a microsleep. Then she came back.

"It's getting harder to think straight. At first, when I heard people talking about being crisp I thought they were exaggerating to freak out a fungee. They weren't. I can't wait to get out of this goddamned fucking place.

"But it's important to record what's happened while I'm here and it's still fresh."

15

AGAIN EMILY STOPPED TALKING AND STARED, EYES VAGUE AND DIS-
tant, seeing something Hallie could not imagine, or perhaps seeing
nothing at all. She came back, sipped from a dirty white mug, and her
hand trembled as she brought the mug down from her mouth.

"Okay. Have to focus. I need to talk about Ambie. We started really hanging out after Thanksgiving. In the world, I don't know.
There's a saying here: 'The odds are good, but the goods are odd.'
Ambie's okay-looking and he can be funny. He has a really amazing
mind. He is a little odd, true, but nothing compared to some of what
slouches around this place. So, okay, we hooked up.

"He's great at some things, but holding his liquor isn't one. He got
really totally shit-faced at the New Year's Eve party. Plus, he mixed
Ecstasy with the Stoli and beer. Offered me some, too. I told him, yet
again, that I don't do drugs. I had to almost carry him back to his
room. Usually when he gets that drunk, he rambles for a few minutes
and passes out. This time was different. He was all jazzed. The Ecstasy.

"He kept babbling about triage, which was odd. I thought he was
hallucinating about a disaster or something. I told him nobody was

hurt. He said triage was about *saving* people. He said some other things, just making no sense at all. Then he passed out. We didn't even have time to make love. Better living through chemistry. Right.

"The next day we were here in my room. He had a horrible hangover. I felt fine. I said, 'What was all that stuff about triage last night?' Incredible. He turned white as the ice sheet. For a second I thought he was going to faint. He looked *terrified*! I said, 'What's wrong?' and he snapped at me, like, 'What the *fuck* are you talking about?' So I explained about the night before, the things he kept saying. He just freaked. 'What else did I say? What *else*?' He actually grabbed me by the shoulders and tried to shake me. I told him to get his hands off me and shoved him away, but it scared me. I'd never seen him like that. Then I thought he might cry. Totally bizarre. He went, '*Please* tell me what else I said.' I actually felt sorry for him then, so I really tried to remember and got some of it back. I told him, "You said triage is coming. Then I said nobody was hurt, why would there be triage? And you said, No, no, you don't understand, nobody is going to die, because it won't kill them and they won't even know they have it.'

"It took me a long time to convince him that this was all I remembered. I said that he had been stumbling drunk and high on Ecstasy, and that you can't hold somebody responsible for stuff they say when they're so messed up. I don't think he even heard that. He sat down and squeezed my hands and made me promise not to tell anyone else. I said, 'Okay, I won't tell anybody. It didn't make any sense anyway. You were drunk out of your mind and all drugged up. Why would I?' "

Emily rubbed her face, and when she looked up again, tears filled her hollow eyes. The monitor screen went dark.

She made her next video entry on January 26: "I'm not sure what's happening. After that last talk with Ambie, I didn't say anything to anyone. Didn't mention it to him again, either. He left it alone, too. A week went by. But it was just too weird. I couldn't get his reaction out of my mind. I thought, Okay, I promised not to tell, but it would be okay to *ask*, wouldn't it? So over the next ten days I did—Agnes Merritt, Doc, two or three others. Not all at once. Everybody said basically the same thing: triage is an emergency medical protocol they use in war and disasters.

"Ambie has changed. Before, he couldn't get enough sex, at least when he was sober. Now he could care less. But even without sex, it's been like he doesn't want to let me out of his sight. Even weirder, right? So I told him to back off, leave me alone. He wasn't happy, but it got me my space."

She paused, closed her eyes, and some time passed before she opened them again. "I feel like I'm being watched. That sounds weird and paranoid, I know. But I can't shake the feeling. It's like that old thing where you're walking by yourself on a dark sidewalk and think somebody's following you, but when you look over your shoulder, there's no one. I haven't said anything about that, even to Fida. But I'm thinking maybe I should.

"One thing's for sure. On Friday I am going to Thing Night. Alone. No Ambie. Wore out his welcome. I just want to drink a beer and dance a little. Have fun. If I can remember how."

The video stopped. It was the last one.

Hallie stared at her laptop's screen. What to do next? First thing, secure the card. She put it back where she had found it. If the thing had stayed there undiscovered this long, it was as good a place as any.

She could not get the afterimage of Emily's ravaged face out of her mind. She wasn't sure she ever would. It took her back to a time when they had both looked like that, after the climb on Denali.

The Cassin Ridge stuck out of Denali's south face like the dorsal fin of a shark and was one of the world's great big-mountain ascents. Before dawn they started up the route on the sixty-degree Japanese Couloir, about 1,000 vertical feet of ice, a long, shining blue mirror. Placing the tool picks and crampon points was like trying to drive nails into slabs of glass. Chunks of ice called "dinner plates" kept breaking off and shattering when they hit the ice lower down. It was some of the most delicate climbing Hallie had ever done. They would have moved to the couloir's rock walls, but those were even worse, encased in a half-inch of clear, brittle ice called *verglas*.

With the chute finally climbed, they stopped on the Cassin Ledge, a rock shelf at 13,400 feet just big enough for two tents. They drank tea and slurped energy gel. The air was clear, a light wind blowing up the face. To the south they could see the Kahiltna Glacier curling around like a vast, white snake and, beyond that, the shining peaks of Mounts Hunter and Huntington, giants in their own right but dwarfed by Denali, the highest mountain in North America and the largest massif on earth.

They moved out, and an hour of moderate rock climbing brought them to a nightmarish obstacle called the Cowboy Traverse, a knife-edged ridge, very exposed, with both flanks dropping away at sixty-degree angles.

They were climbing unroped—simul-soloing—for speed. Hallie went first, straddling the ridge like a horse, crunching through crust over loose sugar snow. She knew that there had to be another hard, slick layer somewhere underneath. An avalanche could start when the weight of new snow—or a wrong step by some climber—sent the whole thing sliding like sand down a tilted mirror. But if you wanted the Cassin, this was how you went.

Seventy-five feet out, Hallie took that wrong step. A crack one hundred feet long opened across the slope, and a slab avalanche two feet thick let go. At first, it felt slow and gentle, unreal as a dream. Three seconds later it was like being spun in a giant dryer full of bricks.

The friction-melted snow froze as solid as concrete seconds after stopping. Upside down, she could move her tongue and one eyelid. She had created a small air space by cupping her hands in front of her face as the avalanche slowed. It was the first time in her life she had known absolutely that she was going to die.

She closed the working eye and said the Lord's Prayer several times. Brought up images of her mother and father, brothers, and Barnard. Moved away from tears. Every trip had a verdict. She'd known that going in. No blame for a mountain.

She was hypoxic and semiconscious when something struck her boot sole a hard blow. Three shovel strokes later, she felt Emily shake the boot and yell at her to keep fucking breathing, goddamnit.

Later, off the ridge and looking back, she saw. Emily had traversed diagonally down and across 150 feet of intact but unstable slope to reach her. That whole section could have slid at any second. *Should* have, really.

"We both ought to be dead right now," Hallie said, still shaking from cold and fear. "You know that."

"What would you have done?" Emily handed her another cup of hot, sweet tea.

She thought about living another fifty or sixty years knowing she had done nothing. "The same."

"See? No choice." And then they both cried.

She wasn't sure how long that reverie lasted, but now she had to think carefully about what she had seen. Who was Ambie? A pet name, obviously. But short for what? There weren't a lot of men's names that began with those letters. Ambrose, Ames, Amal, Amadeus . . . What she needed was a roster of station personnel.

Merritt, overseeing only the scientists, wasn't likely to have that.

But Graeter, captain of the ship, was.

If she could find a man with that name, she might find Emily's killer.

16

HALLIE THOUGHT GRAETER MIGHT SAY HELLO. INSTEAD, HE POINTED at his wrist.

"You're late. Doctor. Leland."

"Actually, I'm not." Having taken his measure yesterday, Hallie had made a point of being precisely on time this morning. She held up her wristwatch as proof. "Twelve noon."

Graeter held up both hands. He wore two watches, one on each wrist. "My time is Pole time," he said. "I have you two minutes late. You might want to synchronize your watch with mine."

"Pole time," she said. "Sounds like a beer commercial." She didn't touch her watch. He was a never-good-enough man, but he would get no bowing or scraping from her. Might mean butting heads, but she would rather butt than bow any day.

"Sleep well?" Graeter asked.

"Is that a joke?"

"It'll pass. Or maybe not. Some never adjust."

"I know altitude. But my mouth feels like I gargled with acid. Do people get sick that quickly here?"

"You're probably not sick. Yet. It's frostbite. When you stepped out of the plane, you went from sixty above to about seventy below. Sucked in air. Involuntary, like what happens if you jump into freezing water. It heals in a few days. Usually."

"Comforting."

"Have you—"

"Did you find out anything more about the women who died?" she asked.

"I thought we covered this yesterday."

"We didn't cover the possibility that some pathogen might have killed them. If that's the case, it could happen to others."

"That wasn't it," he said, much too casually for her mood just then.

"How could you know that? Just about everybody I've talked to so far has been sick with one thing or another."

"Doc called. He said Lanahan had some kind of operation on her throat. Montalban had surgery, too—a C-section."

The same things Merritt had said.

Should I tell him?

Merritt could not have been the killer; the one piece of real information Hallie had—thanks to Emily's video—was that the killer was a man. Graeter—more likely than Merritt, obviously. She would tell him nothing.

He glanced at the watch on his left wrist again. "Let's go. I have a station to run here."

He brushed past her and was out the door before she could protest.

A few minutes later, they were walking along the main corridor when Rockie Bacon approached. She wore bunny boots and black insulated Carhartt coveralls over a red plaid shirt. She held a smartphone in one palm and was texting as she walked, oblivious to Hallie and Graeter.

"Good afternoon, Bacon," Graeter said.

"Good afternoon to you, Mr. Graeter," she said, no great pleasure in her voice. To Hallie: "We just can't stop bumping into each other, can we?"

"Are you headed for the early grading?" Graeter asked.

"That's right."

"How's the cold?"

"Can't seem to shake it."

"I could get Landis or Richards to handle it this morning."

"Thanks, but it takes more than that to keep me off my Cat."

After Bacon walked away, Hallie said, "I thought it was too cold for planes to land now."

"It is."

"So why send her out there, sick as she is, to grade the runway?"

"Not runway. Iceway."

"To grade the iceway."

"SORs say it gets graded twice a day. So we grade it twice a day."

They walked on. As Graeter led them to the first level, Hallie asked, "Why are all the stairs yellow?"

"Human factors experts said fewer people would fall down them."

"Did they do the decorating, too?" She was referring to the irregular polygons in clashing colors—deep blue, fire orange, blood-red, sharp purple—that covered the corridors' walls and ceilings.

"Sort of. They also claimed that asymmetrical patterning warded off depression. In a place that goes dark for eight months, it's a serious problem."

"Reminds me of a badly lit elementary school decorated with paintings by disturbed children. Does it work?"

"Not hardly."

They moved in their pool of light down dark corridors, past a grimy gym and weight room, offices, storage chambers. Descended stairs at one end of the station, came to an air-lock door with a sign:

ATTENTION! LABORATORY ZONE
AUTHORIZED PERSONS ONLY
DO NOT ENTER UNLESS YOU WANT TO GET BURNED BLOWN UP
OR INFEKTED

"Beaker humor. Merritt can take you in there," Graeter said.

Minutes later, they stood beneath the station in a rectangular tunnel, eight feet wide and twelve feet high. The floor and walls were smooth, white ice. Icicles and frost formations dangled from the ceiling. Round metal tubes, two feet in diameter, hung from one wall.

"Welcome to the Underground," Graeter said. "A labyrinth carved out over the years. This main tunnel runs under the length of the station. Other tunnels branch off, and still others branch off them. Imagine a Scrabble board late in the game."

"What is that smell?"

"Sewage and diesel fuel."

They walked on. Graeter turned right down one secondary corridor, right again into another, and kept turning into new corridors for several minutes. "Know where you are?"

"Do you mean could I find my way back to the stairs? Maybe."

"Maybe isn't good enough at Pole," Graeter said.

"Why did I know you were going to say that?" Hallie asked.

"That's what you need to know about the Underground. Let's go back."

"What else is down here?" Hallie asked as they walked.

"Bulk food storage. Generators, primary and backups. Fuel reservoirs. NCS holdings more than anything else."

"NCS?"

"Non–cold sensitive. Everything from old furniture to files."

They passed a chamber whose entrance was blocked by a sheet of heavy black canvas. The other "rooms" she'd seen were open.

"What's in there?" she asked.

"That's the morgue. Lanahan and Montalban are in there, until we get them on a flight out."

She stopped. "Is that where Emily stayed?"

"Yes."

He looked at the black sheet, then back at her. Turned and kept going. She lingered for a few moments, feeling tears start to well up, pushed them back down. Rage came, hot and red. Then grief, and then, last of all, horror.

Something touched her shoulder and she started. *"Jesus!"*

Graeter. He had come back without her hearing. "I told you about ghosts," he said.

17

"COFFEE, TEA, OR GLENFIDDICH?" DON BARNARD ASKED AS WIL Bowman settled into a red leather chair. They were in Barnard's office in the BARDA complex, outside Washington, D.C. It was ten A.M. on Tuesday.

"Nothing, thanks."

They sat with a coffee table between them. Barnard brought a mug of coffee with him. "Thanks for making time on short notice."

"When the director of BARDA calls, I answer. Especially when it has to do with Hallie."

"It's good to see you under happier circumstances. The last time was . . ." Barnard shook his head, unable to find the right word.

"Scary as hell," Bowman said.

"Amen."

It was at BARDA, thanks to Don Barnard, that Bowman had first met Hallie Leland, a year earlier. Barnard had assembled a team of scientists to search the world's deepest cave for a natural antibiotic that might stave off a pandemic. He made no secret of the fact that people could die. When an uncomfortable silence extended—these were scientists, not SEALs—Hallie stalked to the front of the room and declared that this was the opportunity of a lifetime: millions of lives might be saved. The rest of them might not go down into the cave, but she sure as hell would. Alone, if she had to. Bowman, in his government's service, would go, of course. The others could choose. In the end, they all went, and Bowman had never forgotten how she'd galvanized that team.

Not many men outsized Don Barnard, but Bowman was one. Six feet four, 230 pounds of hard muscle. A natural mesomorph, big-shouldered and narrow-waisted, clean-shaven, with a straw-colored brush cut. His nose showed the effects of nonverbal conflict resolution, and a thin pink scar divided his right eyebrow into two short dashes. His was a lean face of juts and angles, hardly handsome but surprising enough to attract stray glances and hold them.

Bowman worked for, or was attached to, or emanated from—Barnard had still not found the right word for Bowman's affiliation—some dark entity hidden invisibly deep in the government's intelligence labyrinth. Bowman had never volunteered its name, and Barnard had never pressed him for details. He suspected that Bowman had a military special operations background. Hallie had said he held a PhD in some esoteric engineering subspecialty.

"Have you heard from Hallie?" Barnard asked.

"No," Bowman said. "You?"

Wil smiled rarely and frowned almost never. If Barnard had been pressed to describe the man in a word, it would have been *centered*.

"No."

"Really? I was sure she would have contacted you."

"I thought the same thing about you," Barnard said.

"That's not like Hallie at all. Do you know if she actually reached the Pole?"

"Not even that. I got an email from her at McMurdo on Sunday, but nothing after."

"I emailed her earlier this morning but haven't gotten an answer. Have you tried to call?" Bowman asked.

"A number of times. Apparently the moon is easier to talk to. All communications to the Pole are satellite-dependent. Right now, there are just two two-hour windows in every twenty-four-hour period. And lots of things can screw those up—storms, solar events, power failures."

"She told me she would be replacing a scientist who had died unexpectedly. And that she'd known the woman here at one time."

"That's right."

"Who was that woman working for? Durant was her name, I think."

"National Science Foundation," Barnard said.

"How long ago did she die?"

"Not exactly sure. Sometime early last week, though."

"And you don't know how?"

"Here's where it gets a bit strange." Barnard recounted his conversation with Laraine Harris.

"There should be an autopsy and a medical examiner's report by now," Bowman said.

"I thought so, too. So I called a man at my own level over there. Director of Antarctic Programs. He didn't know how she'd died, either. I explained my interest and asked if he could look into it. Very nice fellow. He agreed. I made an appointment to see him tomorrow."

"He wouldn't just send a copy of whatever he found?"

Barnard chuckled. "He's a bureaucrat. The normal response to such a request would be to forget about it for a week or two, then hand it off to some subordinate. Bureaucrats learn never to do anything too quickly, because it will be expected of them next time."

"So what happens now?"

"It's like fencing. Can be fun if you understand the rules and weapons. I pointed out that since neither of us knew what happened, it would be better to meet in person. Possible discretion required, et cetera. Slow response is one thing; no response is another."

"You put him in a corner."

"I figured if he was blowing smoke about getting the information, he probably wouldn't have wanted to meet. This gives him a little incentive to really find something."

"Keep that kind of thing up and I might have to recruit you."

"I'll take that as a compliment. But my ops days are over."

Bowman's expression hardened. "I don't like this."

"Me, neither. Less and less, in fact."

"Hallie's supposed to fly out of there before the station shuts down for winterover, right?" Bowman asked.

"Yes. After the last flight, it's totally isolated for eight solid months."

"So if anything happened and she missed that flight . . ."

"It would be a long winter. For all of us."

Bowman stood. "Thanks for bringing me in, Don. I'll look for that report."

"I was hoping you'd say that."

"Let me know when you get through to her. I'll keep trying, myself."

Barnard had been worried not to hear from Hallie but shocked to learn that Bowman hadn't, either. He knew that the two had grown close over the past year, and he knew, as well, that neither was the kind who did that easily. He had watched the relationship change Hallie, rounding edges, softening points. He wasn't sure she'd noticed the evolution herself. Barnard loved Hallie, but that did not keep him from seeing her as she was: an excellent scientist and a lovely young woman, but one who had grown up with two older brothers in an Army family. A colleague of Barnard's had once commented on the "porcupine suit" she sometimes wore.

Barnard stared out a window. Now that he and Bowman had talked, Barnard was feeling the edge of an old dread that rarely visited him these days but slept always in some deep place, ready to wake at the right disturbance. It had come back with him from Vietnam, where night after night he had led soldiers even younger than himself out into the black jungle, knowing with absolute certainty that on this patrol, or the next, or the next, some of them would not come back alive.

18

"SIX MORE DEGREES," SAID GRAETER, "AND WE WOULDN'T BE OUT here."

They were standing in front of the station. It was close to one P.M. and pitch-dark.

"Why is that?"

"It's called Condition One. Eighty and colder, no one egresses." From his parka he took a plastic bag. "Watch this." From the bag he took a chicken leg. He poked it with a mitten. "Raw, right? Soft?"

She nodded.

He stood for twenty seconds, then rapped the chicken on a metal stair rail. The leg shattered like a lightbulb. "See?"

"I saw. What is this, fourth-grade science?"

"Showing beats telling. Especially with someone like you."

"Someone like me?"

"I detect a certain disdain for authority."

"'The wisest have the most authority,'" she said, quoting.

"Socrates, right? If he was so wise, why'd he drink the Kool-Aid?"

"Plato said the thing about authority. Didn't they teach philosophy at Annapolis?"

He squinted at her. "How come a microbiologist knows philosophers?"

"Nothing to do with microbiology. I know about authority from my father. He knew about philosophers."

"An ivory tower family," Graeter said. "Should have guessed."

So he didn't really look at my file, she thought. In any case, he was wrong about her family. She started to correct him, then let it go. She liked him better wrong.

They walked to a row of yellow snowmobiles. Before getting on one, he looked into a red box bolted onto its rear deck, behind the passenger seat. Hallie remembered that there had been one on Bacon's snowmo, too.

"What's that?"

"Emergency kit. These snowmos go out to field camps all the time. Some are miles away. Spare lights, first aid, flares, the usual stuff. SORs require operators to check their kits before using the snowmo. Ready?"

Hallie straddled the seat, and the snowmo jumped forward before she could answer.

Hallie understood that she might be going for a ride with Emily's killer. That she might have been in the Underground with him, too. She had zipped a dive knife into a pocket of her parka. As they drove away from the station, she touched that pocket. With so many layers on her hands, it took a few seconds of fumbling, but then she hit it. The long, sharp knife was there.

After they'd gone a half mile, the headlight illuminated rows of what looked like giant black sausages lined up on the snow. She tapped Graeter on the shoulder, pointed, and he stopped.

"What are those?" she asked.

"Fuel bladders. Two thousand gallons each, hauled on sleds all the way from McMurdo. Eight hundred miles, six weeks in tractor caravans at five miles an hour. Now, *there's* some tough people."

"Can't fly it in?"

"Burns up more than they bring. Hauling over ice is slower but lots cheaper."

He turned right, running parallel to the station. From the skin out, Hallie was wearing regular underwear, lightweight long underwear, expedition-weight long underwear, a wool shirt, fleece pants and jacket, insulated coveralls, and the special Antarctic parka they called Big Red. On her feet, three pairs of socks, thermal boot liners, and bulbous white bunny boots. Silk glove liners, fleece gloves, wool mittens, and down-filled overmitts. Fleece neck gaiter, face mask, down-filled, fur-ruffed hood. A Petzl headlamp. And still her toes and fingers were already starting to go numb.

After a few more minutes, Graeter stopped. She glanced back over her shoulder. The station looked very far away.

"Welcome to the Dark Sector," he said. "They use radio telescopes and neutrino catchers and cosmic ray detectors here. This area extends several miles out from the station limits. It has to be free of light and electromagnetic interference."

"What's that?" She was pointing to something that looked like a giant lunar landing module with a tall silver silo on each side. The silos were one hundred feet from the main structure and connected to it by metal tubes extending from near their tops.

"That is Operation IceCube," Graeter said. "Drillers were sinking shafts a mile deep all around that and putting neutrino sensors down into them. To the left there is the dive shed, where you'll be working. They built it over the shaft that struck water."

"Good to know," she said. "Hey. It is *cold*."

"White Death, we call it," Graeter said. "Sucks heat, not blood. Your brain is the first organ affected. You can be half gone before you know what's happening."

A huge Caterpillar D9 bulldozer, sparkling with red and yellow and white lights, came roaring and clanking off to their right, heading for the iceway. In the immaculate air, its headlight beams were like shafts of crystal.

"Bacon," Graeter said. "Best operator here. Cranky, but she can do surgery with that thing."

The bulldozer drew abreast of them, about a hundred yards to their right. Hallie saw the operator, visible in the red light from the instrument panel. She started to wave before realizing that Bacon could see only what the headlights illuminated. She kept looking. It was hard to know for sure, but there seemed to be something odd about Bacon's posture, her torso inclined forward against the seat belt, head down, almost as though she had dozed off.

"Mr. Graeter, I think there's something wrong with—"

"I see it." He pulled out his radio, then shoved it back into a pocket. The D9 veered right, heading straight for a line of red danger flags twenty feet away. Bacon's Cat crushed the wands and kept on going. Graeter sat frozen for an instant, as if he could not believe what he was seeing.

"Hold on!" he shouted to Hallie.

Opening the throttle too quickly, he flooded the motor. He jumped off and yanked the starter, again and again, but it took half a dozen pulls to clear the flooded carburetor and get the engine to fire. By the time they stopped at the line of red wands, Bacon's Cat was one hundred feet beyond and still moving.

"What's in there?" Hallie shouted.

"It's the area over Old Pole. Completely unstable. Do *not* move!" Graeter yelled. He jumped off and ran into the restricted area. He had gone only ten feet when the D9's front end broke through the surface. The fracturing ice sounded like rifle shots.

"Jump!" Hallie screamed, but Bacon, still bathed in red light, sat motionless, pitched forward, held in place by her seat belt. Hallie watched in horror as the machine, haloed by its lights, sank deeper into the hole, tilting forward like a ship going down at the bow. Then came a huge, crumpling sound, and the D9 disappeared completely. The ice shook under Hallie's feet. She heard a rumbling, then more ice fracturing at the bulldozer dropped deeper into the huge crevasse. *Big enough to swallow locomotives,* Graeter had said.

His headlamp beam danced crazily as he stumbled, turned around, fell to his hands and knees. A fracture line opened between Graeter and Hallie. The ice on which he lay began to tilt, and suddenly he was sliding toward the crevasse that had swallowed Bacon and her machine. Just before he dropped in, another, smaller crack appeared.

The glow of his headlamp showed him grabbing its edge with both mittened hands. The whole section of ice swung down beneath him, like a giant trapdoor on hinges, finally stopping just short of dead vertical. All Hallie could see of Graeter was the bright glow of his headlamp showing above the edge of the fracture.

She ran toward him and, fifteen feet from where he held on, dropped to her belly like a baseball player sliding headfirst. Spread-eagled to distribute her weight as widely as possible, she pulled with her hands and pushed with her toes. Her own headlamp showed Graeter's black mittens—all she could see of him from her prone position.

"Graeter," she yelled. "Are you secure?"

"Barely." He sounded breathless but uninjured. "I kicked little holes, but my boot toes could slip out at any time."

"Do you know how deep it is?"

"No. And I don't want to look."

Could be a hundred feet, she thought. Or a thousand.

"I'm going to ease forward until I can grab your wrists."

"Are you *insane*? I could pull us both down. You back off and wait until some people get here with ropes."

"Can't wait. You'll lose your grip or the ice will break. They probably don't even know anything happened. And you have the radio."

She knew that a proper crevasse rescue involved belays and ropes and pulley haul systems, but there was no time for those niceties here. And what was the option? Let the man hang there until he dropped? She inched forward some more, reached out with her right hand, and gently closed her fingers around his left wrist. Two layers of gloves and mittens did not help, but the base of his thumb and the heel of his hand flared out like small handles, helping her hang on. She repeated the move, clutching his right wrist with her left hand. "Okay. Go ahead and kick new toeholds and try to step up."

She felt the pull increase on her left hand as he picked up his right boot and began kicking a new cavity. "Good as it'll get." He kicked another. "Here goes."

She felt him stand, slowly and gently, on that precariously poised right boot toe, felt him repeat the motion with his left, and then he had gained a foot. She could visualize the placements: a half-inch of boot sole pressed into the shallow concavities he had kicked. The only thing saving him was the extreme temperature. When it was that cold, friction could not generate enough heat to liquefy the ice's microsurface. Instead of the slick ice that would have been there at warmer temperatures, this was more like sandpaper.

"Go again," she said.

She waited, feeling her hands starting to numb. He kicked, again and again, then the agonizingly slow process of putting weight on each toehold and standing. But it was working. She could see his headlamp and most of his face. A crack opened up behind Hallie's feet, and the ice surface on which she lay lurched, tilting down toward the crevasse. The angle was gentle yet, and she didn't slide forward, but she knew that their combined motions and weight shifts could trigger a collapse and send them both plunging into the void. There was no time for him to finish coming up as he had been.

"Do you know how to do a mantle?" she asked.

"No."

"It's a climbing move. Put the palms of both hands on the edge of the crack right in front of your chest and push yourself up as far as your waist. Then you can flop forward and you'll be out of there."

"What the hell" was all he could manage.

She held on to his wrists as he leaned forward far enough to place his forearms and elbows on the sharp edge of the crack, with his palms on the ice right in front of his sternum.

He took a deep breath. "Here goes."

She felt his forearms clench as he pushed down. Slowly his body rose until his waist was even with the edge of the crevasse and he could go no higher. Gently he folded over, gasping, laying his chest and belly flat on the ice, so that only his legs were still hanging over the side.

Elbow-crawling, he dragged himself forward, an inch at a time. When he moved, Hallie moved with him, wriggling back. Slowly they put distance between themselves and the crevasse edge. Five feet, ten, thirty, a hundred. Both breathless, they stopped and lay on their bellies. Hallie knew that Graeter's brain was digesting the fact of its continued existence. It was like watching someone wake up from a trance.

Directing his headlamp to one side, to avoid blinding her, he said, "Son of a *bitch*. Nineteen years in the Navy and I never got that close." He took a deep breath, exhaled. "Think it's safe to stand now?"

"Yes."

They got up and walked back to Graeter's snowmo, brushing themselves off. Hallie was considering how lucky both of them were. Her own reaction had been instinctive, and she did not regret it. But inside all the layers, she felt her hands shaking, and it was not because of the cold. Before either she or Graeter could speak, two big men wearing black Dragger parkas and tool belts roared up on snowmos.

"What the hell happened?" one asked Graeter.

"Bacon's machine broke through," Graeter said. "Is anyone else coming?"

"I don't know. We were headed to the machine shop when that dozer's lights just disappeared. We figured it went down."

"Is that you, Grenier?" Graeter asked.

"Yeah. And Lange. So Bacon is down in the crack?"

"Yes," Graeter said. He reached for his radio. "Graeter, emergency to comms. Bacon's Cat went into a crevasse. We need Search and Rescue out here now. Tell them to look for the snowmo lights."

"Comms copy. Will do."

"How long will that take?" Hallie asked.

"Fifteen minutes to muster. Thirty to dress and collect gear. Another five to get out here, if the snowmos start right away. Say an hour."

"Too long." Hallie was staring at the crevasse.

"Is what it is. There's a SOR protocol for crevasse rescues."

"Mr. Graeter. She could be bleeding down there. In shock and pain. We can't wait that long."

"We don't know if she's alive. And we don't have a way to get anyone down there."

There is always a way. She looked at the two Draggers' tool belts and saw that they both carried big, twenty-four-ounce hammers with long, curved claws.

"We do have a way to get down," she said. "Give me those hammers. They'll do in a pinch for ice tools."

"Negative on that," Graeter said.

"What?" Hallie wasn't sure she had heard right.

"I said negative. SAR is gearing up. We'll wait and do this according to the regulations."

"You can wait if you want," Hallie said. She stepped forward, pulled the two hammers out of their metal-loop holsters, and started toward the crevasse.

"Dr. Leland!" Graeter snapped. "I gave you an order. We will wait. Did you hear me? *We will wait.*"

"You do that," she said.

19

HALLIE WALKED TO WITHIN FIFTY FEET OF THE EDGE OF THE CRE-
vasse. She got down on her stomach, feet toward the abyss, and
started inching backward. At the edge she dug the claws of both hammers into the surface, using them like the picks of ice tools, and lowered herself down.

The ice wall fell at about a seventy-degree angle. A romp with
proper ice tools and twelve-point crampons. With the hammers and
bunny boots, doable, but delicate.

"*Rockie!*" she yelled.

No answer.

She kept down-climbing, punching one tool lower, than the other,
kicking toeholds with her boots. After forty feet her forearms were on
fire and she was gasping for breath, but it was working.

She smelled diesel fuel, looked over her shoulder, and her headlamp beam caught machine twenty feet lower. It had come to rest
where the crevasse's walls converged. She heard Bacon's radio crack-
ling and nearly shuddered with joy; in her haste she hadn't asked for
one. Graeter probably wouldn't have given it to her, anyway.

Hallie descended to the Cat and stepped onto its track, near the front of the machine. She walked back toward Rockie, who was still held in place by her seat belt, bent forward at the waist, arms hanging between her knees. There was frozen blood on Rockie's face mask, and more on the Cat's deck and dashboard.

"*Rockie.*"

No response.

With gloves and mittens on she could not feel for a pulse, but she could see that Rockie was still breathing.

The radio crackled again.

"Graeter. Can you copy me down there?"

Hallie unzipped one of Bacon's pockets and found the radio. "This is Leland. I'm on the dozer. Rockie is alive, but injured and unconscious. I don't know how badly. Can you drop a litter down here?"

There was a silence. When Graeter spoke, he sounded very angry. "No. The goddamned thing broke."

"You only have one?"

"They both broke. Cracked like window glass. It's too cold for fiberglass."

She thought for a minute. "Lower one end of a good rope down here. Eleven-mil or bigger. Keep lowering until I tell you to stop."

As Hallie probed the darkness with her light, she saw holes in the crevasse wall. They reminded her of the mouths of small caves, but with angles and lines. No straight lines in nature, as the saying went. Odd, finding them down here. At some point, flowing water must have bored them, as it bored much more slowly through stone to make terrestrial caves. But . . . neat lines? Then she thought: Old Pole. They must be part of the buried complex. She briefly considered trying to carry Bacon out that way, then decided there were too many unknowns. A rescue hoist would be better.

A few minutes later she grabbed the end of a rope. She waited for about twenty extra feet to come, then radioed for them to stop. "Don't do anything until I call again," she added.

Hallie folded the rope back on itself to make a ten-foot doubled length. Then she tied a double figure-eight knot, called "bunny ears" by climbers because of the two single loops at the knot's end. She dressed the knot so that each loop was big enough to fit under their arms. She worked the rope over Rockie's shoulders, down past her hands, and pulled it up under her armpits. She unfastened Rockie's seat belt, then put the other loop on herself, making sure that the rope was secure under her own arms as well.

After a final check of the rope and loops, she keyed the radio.

"We're both on rope. You need to bring us up very slowly and very smoothly."

"Copy that," Graeter said. For a few seconds, nothing happened. Then Hallie felt the rope grow taut, and was thankful for all the layers of clothing, which prevented it from cutting painfully into her armpits. She and Bacon were lifted away from the D9 and rose slowly up through the crevasse.

Hallie held Bacon facing away, keeping her own back to the crevasse wall, acting as a cushion between the unconscious woman and the ice. She knew that this was not the best way to bring up someone who might have suffered spinal injuries, but there was no choice. It seemed to take a long time, but finally they were approaching the lip of the crevasse. Hallie radioed their position and had the haulers slow down even more. This was going to be the hardest part. She had them raise her and Bacon in small increments until she could hook her butt over the lip. Then, holding the inert woman against herself with one arm, she radioed the haulers to bring them on back.

They came across the ice smoothly, Hallie on her back, Bacon lying between her legs and against her chest. When they were out of the danger zone, Search and Rescue team members stabilized Bacon with a cervical collar and eased her onto a backboard. A big Pisten-Bully snowcat, like those used at ski areas, had traveled out. The SARs loaded Bacon onto the machine's back deck, and it headed toward the station.

Hallie turned to the two Draggers, Grenier and Lange. "I'm sorry about your hammers, guys. Didn't have enough hands to bring them up."

"Hell with the hammers. They're NASI's," Grenier said. "You're a Beaker, right?"

"Yep," she said. "Microbiologist."

"A Beaker," Lange said.

"A Beaker," Grenier said.

They looked at each other.

"Goddamn," Lange said.

"Son of a bitch," Grenier said.

Then they stepped forward, slapped her on the shoulder, said, "Good job," and headed to their snowmos, looking back as if still having trouble believing.

It felt good. She was tired from the crevasse work but sparking with adrenaline and the elation of having saved another human.

Graeter stood off to one side. The face mask kept her from seeing anything but his eyes. Hell hath no fury, she thought, like a martinet disobeyed. Her roster request would have to wait.

He came toward her and planted his feet, and she braced herself for a tirade. Or worse. She moved one hand toward the right pocket of her Big Red.

"You should not have come on that cracked ice to help me. And you should not have gone down into the crevasse for Bacon."

The elation drained away, leaving exhaustion, hunger, thirst, and cold. She opened her mouth to reply, but he held up one finger, then lowered it to point directly at her.

"I'm glad you did. I owe you. *We* owe you."

Overhead, the southern lights flared green and purple. He turned on his heel and motioned for her to follow.

20

BACK IN HER ROOM, HALLIE SLUMPED IN THE DESK CHAIR. THINGS were happening too fast. Emily's killing. Two dead women. Graeter's close call. Bacon's closer call. Even so, the hardest thing of all was one that had *not* happened: she still had told no one about the murder. *Could* not tell anyone.

She checked for email, found none, used the room phone.

"Agnes, Hallie. I'm still not getting any email. Is yours working?"

"On and off," Merritt said. "Apparently there was a solar event yesterday. Medium-sized coronal mass ejection. It's been really screwing up comms. I wouldn't worry too much. Things usually settle down in a couple of days."

In a couple of days I'll be out of here, she thought, but she said only, "Thanks."

She wondered about sharing the secret with Graeter. She would not even be considering it if she had not caught, out on the ice, a glimpse of something human beneath his spiky carapace. But you didn't have your life saved every day, and it might have been nothing more than adrenaline and endorphin intoxication. She would wait.

She had to meet with the one they called Fido, and that was becoming more urgent with each hour that brought her closer to the dive. She called comms and asked them to page him.

She fetched herself a cup of chlorinated coffee and sat at a table by one of the windows to wait. Because it was light inside and so dark outside, she could see nothing through the glass. Leaning back, she gazed up at the strings of lights. More appeared to have burned out since her first visit to the galley. It was hard not to put her arms on the table and fall asleep right there, like napping in elementary school.

A man at a nearby table was eating a hamburger and French fries, washing the food down with gulps of milk. She watched him chewing. *Listened* to him chewing. And chewing and chewing, mouth mostly open, making sounds like horses walking in mud. Finally he swallowed, took another bite, and started chewing again, jaws working away beneath glazed eyes. She felt herself getting mad, understood, dimly, that the Pole was wearing her down already, eroding her patience. She felt like getting up and smacking both of the man's bulging cheeks between clapping hands to make him swallow.

He must have felt her staring, because he glanced up suddenly and stopped chewing. They looked at each other for several seconds. He turned away first and closed his mouth. Her anger drained, and she felt both guilty and stupid.

It was not a big leap from those feelings to Bowman. At once the biggest and the most gentle man she had ever known. And the fiercest, when he had to be. The previous year, she had seen him, armed only with two knives, kill three Mexican *narcotraficantes* carrying AK-47s. They had been taking her to a jungle camp where torture, rape, and eventual death would have been her certain fate.

So what would she and Wil have done if she *had* been pregnant? What kind of father would Bowman make? For that matter, what kind of mother would she? Hallie thought him probably better suited temperamentally for parenting. He was patient, good-hearted, and gentle—with her, at least. Having grown up on a ranch, he loved horses with a passion matching her own.

During their year together, they had visited friends with small children. She'd worried that they would be afraid of the giant Bowman. But when he got down on the floor they climbed all over him, draped themselves around his neck, hung from those long arms. Like dogs and horses, she thought, picking up something adults had lost the ability to sense.

A man who resembled a street person wandered into the galley. He was vacant-eyed and shambling, his face a mask of dark stubble, in a stained shirt and green Dickies work pants. He had the chocolate complexion of an East Indian. She waved him over, stood.

"Dr. Muktapadhay?"

"Yes."

"I'm Hallie Leland. I'm so glad to finally meet you."

They shook hands, and his felt to Hallie like an assembly of bird bones. "You had me paged," he said.

"Twenty minutes ago," she said. "I tried your room earlier, but you weren't there. The lab was locked."

"You were lucky I heard it."

"Sorry?" she asked.

He dropped into a chair, put his hands in his lap, stared.

"Would you like some coffee? Something to eat?" she asked.

She could almost hear gears scraping in his brain. "No coffee. It hurts my stomach." His voice was hoarse—Pole throat—and too much time elapsed between his words.

"I'm sorry to hear that. Look, can we dispense with formalities? I'm Hallie. Is it okay if I call you Fido?"

"No! *Please* do not use that term."

"I'm sorry. I thought that was your first name. I heard other—"

"My name is Fida." *Feeda.* "Fido is my Pole name, and I despise it. Some people think I look like . . . Goofy."

"The cartoon dog?"

He glared at her.

She had to admit there was a resemblance. The man had large, ovoid eyes, slightly buck front teeth, and the angles of his face slanted toward the end of a long, muzzle-like nose.

"Look." He held up a hand. "I have four fingers."

She understood that he was differentiating himself from three-fingered cartoon characters.

"I am sorry, Fida. Did I get it right that time?"

"Yes. Thank you."

"So I assume you know why I'm here."

"To replace Emily."

"To help retrieve biomatter from the cryopeg, actually."

"Uh-huh."

"I'm with CDC, not NSF, but I have the same skill sets that Emily did, and I could come here on short notice. No notice, to be honest."

"Short notice," he repeated. The outburst about his name had kindled some attention, but now he had gone off again to some other place in his head, staring past Hallie's shoulder.

"I'll need a briefing on your work. We have to get this dive done before I fly out for winterover."

"We can talk later. I am very tired."

"I'd also like to talk about Emily," she said.

That brought him back. "I do not want to talk about Emily."

"I can understand that. But let me explain. Emily and I were good friends at one time. So her death causes me pain, too."

He looked at her more closely, nodded. "But not here."

"You mean, in the galley?"

"Yes."

"Why not?"

"Come on. We will go someplace else."

He was already shambling away, and she had no choice but to follow.

His room smelled like spoiling food and dirty laundry. The bunk mattress was bare, and a wadded parka served for a pillow. Snickers wrappers and Pepsi cans littered the floor.

"I am sorry for the way this place looks," Fida said. "I just cannot seem to get around to cleaning. I am not spending much time here these days, anyway." He shoved books and papers off his desk chair. "You can sit here."

She did, and he approached as though he were going to kiss her, but at the last minute put his lips close to her ear and whispered, "Do you have your cellphone?" Then he put an index finger over his mouth and extended the other hand palm up.

Hallie gave him the phone. He powered it down, wrapped it in aluminum foil, and stowed it in a steel toolbox.

"Why did you do that?" She was whispering, too.

"We can speak now," he said in a normal voice, slumping against the bunk frame.

She had actually thought her cellphone would be useless here but had been told that NSF had installed a special system for the Polies' convenience. They'd given her a Pole chip on arriving. She would turn it back in when she left.

"You think my phone is bugged?"

"You can install a program just by calling. It can record audio, take pictures, even video. Without you knowing. And send those to someone."

"Nobody has called me."

"I tried to call you twice. Sent you an email, too."

"You did?"

"Yes."

"I didn't get calls from you. Or from back home. No emails, either. I should have by now."

"Possibly there is something wrong with your phone."

"And my terminal, too?"

"I do not want you to think . . . never mind." His eyes went out of focus, came back. "I am sorry. What is your name again?"

"Hallie Leland. I knew Emily very well at one time. We worked together at a CDC lab."

"Emily did not call me Fido." He peered at Hallie. "Now I remember. She was very fond of you. She did climbing and things with you."

"Lots of things. On one climb she saved my life. I wouldn't be here if not for her."

"She was an easy person to like." His eyes filled with tears.

"I can't think of a better epitaph." She managed to keep tears out of her own eyes. "I was told Emily died of a drug overdose. I find that hard to believe."

He glanced at the door, licked his lips, caught her gaze and held it. Hallie knew he was taking her measure. She had long ago come to trust what her gut said about people, and it was telling her that this man was exhausted, overworked, pained by grief, burned out maybe—but trustworthy. In his eyes, she thought something changed, a softening and relaxing, that might suggest that he found her to be, also.

"I do not think Emily died of a drug overdose either."

"You don't?"

"No."

"What do you think happened?"

"I believe that somebody killed her."

21

HALLIE'S BREATH CAUGHT.

Fida, seeing her reaction, held up both hands. "Wait. I know how I look. How I sound. And I am very tired. You may think I am not completely normal. But I—"

"Stop. I agree with you."

He blinked, gaped. "You do? Why?"

"You said it first. So you tell me. Then I'll tell you what I know."

He nodded. "Two things. I do not think Emily used drugs. And it could have been because of Vishnu."

That stopped her. "The Hindu god of creation?"

"Those of my faith call him 'the great preserver.'"

"I'm not following you."

He took a deep breath, let it out. "The extremophile Emily found in the cryopeg is a superhalophile."

"Survives in sodium concentrations that would kill anything else. What kind of salt are we talking about?"

"Thirty-six percent, salt to water, by volume."

She found that hard to believe. "Even *Salinibacter ruber* doesn't live in anything over twenty-five."

"You are right. And you know of course that Rube is the most extreme halophile ever discovered."

"Yes." She was thinking about the implications of diving in such water. One thing at a time. "What exactly is Vishnu?"

"It has existed down in that freezing, absolute darkness for eons."

"What could it metabolize?"

"Carbon dioxide."

That was not unheard of. "When he was at Stanford, James Liao put genes from four other bacteria into cyanobacteria. The new organism consumed carbon dioxide."

"This is different."

"How?"

"Their consumption was microscopic."

"And Vishnu?"

"Vishnu may consume more CO_2 by orders of magnitude than anything known to science."

It took Hallie a moment to consider the implications of that. Carbon dioxide was soluble in water. Oceans, in fact, were the planet's great "carbon sinks," absorbing up to half of all carbon dioxide in the atmosphere. She knew that at some future date—sooner rather than later, the way things were going—the oceans would reach supersaturation with CO_2. When that happened, earth would start the long, hot slide toward a dead Martian end.

"Do you know the concentration of CO_2 in ocean water?" Fida asked.

"Depends on whose research you're reading. But about ninety parts per million, give or take."

"Care to guess what the concentration is in the cryopeg?"

"Tell me."

"About ten parts per million."

"Wait. That's ocean water in there, right? Because the whole continent is just frozen ocean miles thick."

"Yes.

"I don't get it."

"Do you know how old that ice down there might be?"

"No idea."

"It formed during the Eocene. Paleobiologists worked with pollen in the ice cores to confirm that."

"Fifty million years back, then?"

"Close enough. Do you know what the atmospheric CO_2 concentrations were then?"

"High."

"*Very* high. Palm trees grew in Wyoming. Crocodiles swam in Hudson Bay. You have to have a Florida climate for that. There was no polar ice. No ice *anywhere,* for that matter. The CO_2 levels were more than thirteen hundred parts per million."

"Today they're what, about three hundred and eighty ppm?" Hallie said.

"That is right. So you see what this means."

She was beginning to. "What's the CO_2 concentration in the cryopeg's deep ice?"

He grinned for the first time since they'd met. "About thirteen hundred ppm."

"And you say the water is just ten ppm?"

"Yes. We tested and retested because we couldn't believe it at first. But that's it."

"I give up. Enlighten me."

"It's Vishnu."

"The halophile?"

"Yes."

"It's metabolizing carbon dioxide from the water? At that volume?"

"Yes."

"My God. It must be huge."

"Emily said it reminded her of a coral reef system. Stretched far beyond the reach of her lights. It could go for hundreds of feet."

It took a moment for Hallie's thoughts to reorder themselves. "Do you realize the implications here?"

"Wait. It gets better."

"How could it?"

"Because there is more. The sample we worked with not only metabolized carbon dioxide; it produced a combustible by-product unlike petroleum distillates at the molecular level."

"Different how?"

"The by-product, when burned, gave off emissions seventy-five percent lower than petroleum fuels."

"This could stop climate change. If it burns clean at practical volumes."

"So you understand. Yes. It could slow global warming and supplant petroleum fuels at the same time. Of course, we are far, far away from that kind of application. At least the possibility exists, however remote."

"Vishnu was a good name for it."

"I thought so."

"You looked happy a few moments ago. Not now. I'd think you would be bouncing off the ceiling."

"I think it might have killed Emily."

She was stunned. "You mean the extremophile itself?"

"No. We employed the strictest biosafety protocols, and we worked together. If Vishnu had killed her, I would not be here, either."

"Then I don't understand."

"Someone who feared Vishnu."

"Who wouldn't welcome a discovery like this?" But even before Hallie finished the question, she knew the answer, so obvious that she felt stupid for asking.

"The richest people on earth are those who produce petroleum fuels. The second richest are those who sell them."

Her first thought: He *is* disturbed. Paranoid. "Let me be sure I understand what you're saying. Somebody from the petroleum industry killed Emily."

"What is fundamental to the scientific method? Process of elimination. By that, I cannot discover another reasonable explanation."

Too bizarre, she thought. "Are any of the scientists down here connected to Big Oil?"

"None that I'm aware of. But someone else is."

"Who?"

"The station manager works for NASI. Which is owned by GENERCO. Do you know it?"

"Global Energy Corporation. They had that huge North Sea oil spill last year."

"Petroleum interests all over the world. And if ever there was a man who followed orders, it is Graeter."

"I don't know, Fida. It seems a stretch."

"*Does* it? He is unstable, to begin with. And taking one life to preserve billions—maybe trillions—in profits? I think they would do that like squashing a roach."

A part of her kept thinking, No, too outlandish, a crazy conspiracy thing. But then she started remembering. A corporation had engineered her dismissal, in disgrace, from BARDA on trumped-up charges several years earlier. A corporate mole had killed three people, and almost killed her, on the Mexican cave expedition. And Bowman had told her things.

The more she thought about it, the more she had to admit that Fida's suggestion was not impossible. *One life for billions in profits. Maybe trillions.* Wasn't even really improbable. Sad, but true. The way things were. It was what it was. Business as usual. All those palliatives used to make the truth less ugly. And tolerating it less execrable. So now there was only the obvious next question:

"You realize the implications?"

"Of course. I might be next."

"Who else knows about Vishnu?"

"We told only Agnes Merritt, as we were required to. But she gives Graeter regular reports on research projects, so he would know as well."

"Anybody else?"

He shrugged. "Most research projects here are restricted-access. This one surely is. Reports to Merritt are supposed to remain confidential. But . . . who can know for sure?"

"I'm worried that she might be in danger, too."

"And now she is not the only one."

"Who else?"

"You."

"Oh. Right." She hadn't thought about that.

"So now you see why I did not want to talk in the galley."

"Yes." All through their conversation, her feeling about Fida had been growing. Now she looked directly at him. "I don't think Emily was killed."

"What? But you just said—"

"I *know* she was."

"How could you?"

"I saw it happen."

As she described the video, he broke down and wept, repeating something over and over again in Urdu. A prayer, she thought. He found a crumpled paper towel, blew his nose, wiped his eyes with the heels of his hands. "I am sorry," he said. "I am not very strong-feeling these days."

"You should have seen me after I watched that video."

"And you could not tell who the killer was?"

"No. Only that it was a man."

"But why?" he asked. "Why would anybody want to do that to her? I mean, even if someone wanted to kill her . . . why that way?"

"No normal person could do something like that."

"So it could have been Graeter."

Could it? Graeter was a stickler for rules, certainly, and irascible. But a psychopath? From what she had read, psychopaths who killed were more often charming, able to deflect suspicion for decades, in some cases. That was hardly Graeter. But again: *make no assumptions.*

"What do you know about triage?" she asked.

"I believe it is used in war and disasters to prioritize victim treatment."

"Can you think of any way triage could be related to the station?"

"No," he said, without hesitation.

"I found something else in Emily's room. A video diary." She recounted Emily's narrative about somebody named Ambie and triage.

"This Ambie person said triage was coming soon? To this station?"

"Remember that this was all coming from Emily, and you know what shape she was in then. But I do think that's what she meant."

"A disaster is always possible here," he said thoughtfully. "But it sounds like he might have known one was coming. Could that be why he was so afraid?"

"This is going to sound bizarre, but . . ."

"I think we are already beyond bizarre."

"Suppose there's secret research here. Something called 'triage.' If this man Ambie got drunk and blew the cover, he might have good reason to be afraid."

"It is possible. Even with research, one has time on the hands down here. So I read some of the history of NSF. It was conceived by Franklin Roosevelt, and national defense was a big part of its reason to be in those early days. Have you talked to anybody else about this?"

"No."

"Wise. The killer might still be here."

"Yes."

"Any man in the station."

"With a head and two arms," Hallie said.

"When did you decide it wasn't me?"

"When you said Emily had been killed. The murderer wouldn't have done that," she said.

"I am glad you trusted me."

"Me, too, Fida. This thing was getting heavy."

Neither of them spoke for a few moments. Then Hallie asked, "Can you tell me about the night she died? I know it's painful, but it could be important."

"Yes. We finished in the lab at five and went back to our rooms. Emily said she was going to Thing Night, though."

"What exactly is Thing Night?"

"You know that old horror movie *The Thing*? Where they find a creature from outer space frozen in the ice?"

"Sure."

"It became a tradition to watch the movie. Then to watch the movie and drink and get high. And then, over time, to have a great party called Thing Night at the end of every month."

"A blowout to let off steam."

"It's like Halloween and New Year's Eve and Mardi Gras all wrapped together. People dress up. There's a band. Free liquor and beer."

"And drugs?" she asked.

"Of course drugs. Everybody has them. They grow pot in the greenhouse, even. It is great pot, by the way." He blinked, coughed. "Or so I am told."

"Did you go to Thing Night?"

"For a little while. My religion forbids alcohol. The band was good, though too loud to bear for long."

"Did you talk to Emily?"

"No. But I saw her dancing with someone."

"Do you know who?"

"The Frankenstein monster. An excellent costume."

"That's him. Do you have any idea who it was?"

"There must have been twenty Frankensteins. Very popular with Polies."

"Did you see them leave together?"

"No."

"Was Blaine at the party?"

"I did not see him. But—" He shrugged. "The costumes."

"So he could have been a Frankenstein."

"Do you think he killed her?" Fida asked.

"No. She wouldn't have gone to her room with him." She thought for a few moments. "I'm going to call Washington."

"Maybe." They looked at the satellite schedule on his computer. "Comms down. Maybe later. Always maybe."

"There's no other way to communicate?"

"Just email, sat phone, and VOIP. All satellite-dependent." He eyed her thoughtfully. "Are you planning to use the station sat phone?"

"Yes. Why?"

"You have to go through Graeter. Calls are probably recorded. And monitored."

Hallie sat back in her chair, feeling squeezed again, the walls seeming to shift, pushed in by an avalanche of darkness.

She stood up suddenly.

"What is wrong?" Fida asked.

She breathed deeply, put a hand on the bunk. "I started to get a bad feeling."

"Like you were drowning?"

"More like buried alive."

He did not seem surprised. "Yes. It happens."

"Do you get used to it?"

"No," he said.

Hallie's watch beeped. "Damn. I'm supposed to dive soon. Where can I find you later?"

"Do a page."

"Don't you have a cellphone?"

"I do not carry it," he said, retrieving hers from the toolbox.

"How about here?"

"I would not be here if you were not, also. I do not think it is safe."

"Where do you go?"

"I walk, try to stay visible. Sometimes I go to Old Pole. It is too cold to remain there long, but it's the only place I feel safe now."

"I thought it was off-limits to all personnel."

"Exactly," Fida said.

22

"WELCOME TO OUR HUMBLE DIVE SHED," SAID AGNES MERRITT.

She and Hallie had ridden there on one snowmo, Guillotte on another.

"Its official name," Merritt continued, "is the Amundsen-Scott
Research Station Dive Operations Center, but that's a bit fancy for an
Army-surplus Quonset hut with a plywood floor." She glanced from
Hallie to Guillotte. "I heard about Bacon's Cat going through."

"Word travels fast," Hallie said. "It's warm in here. Well, warmer."

"Seventy below freezes up the dive gear," Guillotte said. "So we
keep it about zero. Balmy, yes?"

Several Draggers were working on compressors and other machinery. No one stopped for the new arrivals. Racks of double- and single-
tank scuba rigs lined one long wall. A workbench ran the length of
one short wall. Along the other short wall stood five-foot-tall cylinders of air, pure oxygen, and helium for blending Trimix and Nitrox
breathing gas mixes. Two blue argon cylinders provided insulating
gas for use with dry suits.

Sharing her secret with Fida had been a tremendous relief for
Hallie, but she was still walking around with the knowledge that a

murderer might be roaming the station. Any person in this shed, other than Merritt, could have done it.

Once, deep in a cave, her main headlamp had failed. Then, both backup lights. It was the first and only time that had happened to her. She never forgot what it felt like to suddenly lose all light, to know that twenty steps in any direction could send her over the lip of a pit or into a sump. It was paralyzing knowledge, and the feeling now was almost as powerful. In the cave, she had simply sat down and waited for another member of the expedition to come along with light. Here, that wasn't going to happen.

Regardless, the dive had to go forward. If she had not had the conversation with Fida and learned what Vishnu could mean, she might have called it off. But not now.

"We will go over to my, ah, office and talk through the dive plan." Guillotte pointed to a four-by-eight sheet of plywood on four saw-horses. Hallie was following him when she saw a burly man stumble and, to keep from falling, grab a rack of scuba tanks.

"Hey," she yelled. *"Don't do that!"*

The rack was already starting to fall. Hallie was closest, about eight feet away, and she reached it just before the whole assemblage, tanks and rack, tipped. She shoved it back upright and stood for a second, collecting herself. If an impact broke the valve head off a full scuba tank, the escaping gas, pressurized at thirty-two hundred pounds per square inch, would propel it like a lethal and unguided missile. Hallie had seen one, dropped by a careless customer in a dive shop, break clean through an outside wall and smash in the side of a parked car beyond. What it would do to human bodies in an enclosed space she preferred not to imagine.

When she realized that none of them were going to die, she turned to the clumsy worker, who was standing there looking far less guilty than she thought the moment required.

"You need to be careful around those things," Hallie snapped. "They can—"

She stopped. Bulky body, red face, boozy breath.

"Hey, it was an accident," Brank rasped. "Chill the fuck out." He took a step forward, his face contorted with anger, and she thought: *Him. He could have killed Emily.* But her own anger flashed then, and she planted herself in his path.

Instantly, Guillotte slid between them and put his hand on Brank's chest. "Go sober up," he said. "You have no business here drunk."

"Fuck yourself, Frogman," Brank said, shoving Guillotte's hand away. "I don't take no orders from you."

The two men stood glaring at each other, and Hallie wondered which would throw the first punch. Before either could, Agnes Merritt stalked over and stood on tiptoes to put her face inches from Brank's.

"You don't take orders from me, either. But if you're not out of here in five seconds, I'll have Graeter on you like stink on shit and you can kiss your fat Pole paycheck goodbye. *Forever.*"

Hallie was as surprised by Merritt's transformation as by its effect on Brank, who was already backing toward the exit. To Hallie, he said, "Ain't seen the last of each other, blondie," and slammed the door so hard the DOC shook.

"I cannot apologize enough for Brank," Guillotte said to Hallie. "He works for someone else. I do not even know why he was here." He looked at the door, then back at her. "But I promise you it will never happen again."

Hallie tried to sound settled. "At least no one got hurt. That's the important thing."

"Indeed," Guillotte said. "So. Let us plan your dive now."

"I'm curious. Why aren't you doing this dive yourself?" Hallie asked.

"I would love to, believe me. Two years before coming to Pole, I suffered a decompression accident diving a U-boat in two hundred and sixty feet of water. I was paralyzed from the waist down for several days. After many hours in the reco chamber I could walk. But as I am sure you know, there is no more diving after an accident like that. It would be suicide. So . . ." He drew an index finger across his throat. "I am done. *Finis.*"

"I'm sorry to hear that," Hallie said.

"Was hard at first," Guillotte said. "Okay now. Not good, but okay."

He pointed to a round hole, five feet in diameter, cut out of the plywood floor in the center of the hut. Two feet below the rim, black water sloshed. "They bore these shafts with big, hot-water drills. This one broke through about thirty feet down. So you descend in the shaft, and at that depth enter the cryopeg through its ceiling.

"Poor Dr. Durant made four dives before she found her thing at a hundred and five feet."

For twenty more minutes they planned the dive—route, distance, maximum depth, destination, bottom time, possible emergencies and resolutions. Then it was time to gear up. Hallie had brought her own critical components—first- and second-stage regulators, mask and fins, dry suit, thermal undergarments, computers, lights, assorted tools.

She shed all her ECW except her silk long underwear and, over that, black, expedition-weight polypropylene long johns. That got the Draggers looking up, but she quickly donned a Viking Arctic Plus insulated dive suit with booties, size medium, and over that another, size XL. Last, her red DUI CF200 crushed-neoprene dry suit. She preferred lighter, more flexible trilaminate dry suits. But when diving wrecks, with so much ragged metal, or in any environment with unknown hazards, she used the crushed neoprene. It was heavy, thick, and stiff but much tougher.

She put on insulated dive boots, gloves, and a fifteen-millimeter neoprene hood. After purging her suit three times with argon gas, a much more efficient insulator than air, she buckled two dive computers onto her left arm and a bottom-time calculator and compass onto her right. The compass would be no use here at the South Pole, but Hallie's donning protocol never varied. Two freeze-proof, submersible pressure gauges were clipped to D-rings on her left hip, and three high-intensity, handheld dive lights were fastened to D-rings on her chest harness. She clipped primary and backup dive reels to D-rings on her right hip and snapped an Envirotainer, a flashlight-sized, stainless steel cylinder she would use to retrieve samples of the extremophile, to another D-ring.

She was impressed with Guillotte's efficiency. As soon as she finished donning one piece of gear, she found him standing close by, next piece in hand. Experienced, skillful, attentive. Where an extra set of hands was required, he was firm and steady, not erratic and yanking. Overall, a manager she could trust. Very good to know for a dive like this.

She strapped on a rig with double steel tanks, each with one hundred cubic feet of capacity, equipped with her specialized Scubapro cold-water regulators. She put on her fog-proofed mask, and Guillotte secured her diving helmet with a headlamp that had a front bulb and single-bulb lights on either side. All told, she was now weighted down with close to 125 pounds of gear, so Guillotte supported most of the weight from behind, with his hands under the tanks, while she shuffled over to the shaft. Then he helped her sit on its edge. She pulled on fins and dangled her feet in the water. Even through double socks, insulated inner booties, and eleven-millimeter outer neoprene boots, she felt the cold.

They ran through the final predive checklist items. Guillotte raised a hand with thumb and forefinger circled. "Okay?"

His voice sounded distant through the thick hood. She returned his okay signal, placed both hands on the lip of the shaft, and eased forward and down into the water.

23

SHE VALVED GAS OUT OF HER DRY SUIT TO ACHIEVE NEGATIVE buoyancy, dropped to fifteen feet, hovered, and performed predive checks, testing both regulators, all her lights, both computers, her suit inflator and deflator valves.

She released more gas and sank down through the shaft. The hot water drill had left smooth walls that gleamed in her light. Dropping from the bottom of the shaft into the cryopeg, she stopped, got neutrally buoyant, and played her light over the ceiling. It was not, as she had expected, like the jagged, spiked roof of a cave. Instead, slightly concave and riddled with dish-shaped depressions, it reminded her of the surface of a vast golf ball.

She had thought that such high salinity would probably cloud the water, and indeed visibility was only about twenty feet. There was so much backscatter that her light beams looked like car headlights on a very foggy night. Her computers registered the water temperature at twenty-two degrees Fahrenheit. So much salt kept the water from freezing, but fluid that cold and saline had a molten, syrupy feel. At this temperature, the thick crushed neoprene of her dry suit became stiffer and more resistant, too, so every kick and hand movement required extra effort, which meant increased respiration. Gas management would be especially critical on this dive.

Emily had placed an ice screw in the ceiling next to the shaft bottom and run a guideline from that point diagonally down to the extremophile colony. Hallie tied her own guideline to that ice screw as well. It would spool out from her main reel as she descended. If she did not do that, and anything happened to the primary, fixed line, she would have no way to return to the shaft.

Circling the main line with her thumb and forefinger, Hallie started following it down. Even with all her layers, she was feeling the cold, and more than the whisper she had experienced on entry. Now it was more like standing in damp clothes in a brisk fall breeze. She looked at her computers for a depth check: eighty-three feet. Nothing compared to some of the extreme technical dives she'd done, but it was impossible to forget the thousands of feet of black water beneath her.

She descended slowly, keeping contact with the line, equalizing the pressure in her ears with each breath. It took her almost twenty minutes to reach the vertical wall of the cryopeg, where strange ice formations sprouted and flared in her light beam. They were not the sharp, spearlike shapes of cave stalagmites or stalactites but more like ornate coral growths. Some resembled giant mushrooms twenty feet long and other bulbous domes, but most were as random as snowflakes. Unlike cave formations, which were colored brightly by mineral deposits, everything in the cryopeg was blue. But not *just* blue. As she played her light over the wall and the various shapes, she saw the blues of sky, turquoise, berries, violets—everything from blue so light it looked almost white to the blue-black of a moonless night. Water this murky normally filtered out much of any color's intensity, even in strong light, but here, strangely, the colors were sharp and intense.

There was no perceptible current, nor any sediment to stir up, and the only sounds were the hissing and burbling of her regulator's second stage when she inhaled and exhaled. Then, suddenly, the extremophile colony blazed up in the bright spot of her headlamp. It covered the cryopeg's wall in a foot-thick layer of matter that resembled bright orange cauliflower with irregularly shaped yellow patches. The largest extremophile colony she had encountered in terrestrial caves had been no bigger than a refrigerator. This one stretched out on the wall and down into the depths, far beyond the reach of her light. There was simply no telling how large it might be.

Establishing neutral buoyancy, she detached the Envirotainer from its D-ring on her chest harness and opened its hinged top. Using a scalpel-sharp excavating tool, she removed some biomatter and placed it inside the container, which had filled with cryopeg water. The extremophile might resemble cauliflower, but it was much tougher. Slicing through it was more like cutting canvas. She rehung her tool, secured the Envirotainer's top, and reattached it to the D-ring. As she did so, she inadvertently hit the switch on her headlamp's waist-mounted battery canister.

She knew what had happened and wasn't alarmed. In fact, it was not unpleasant to hover there in complete darkness—except for the glowing displays of her computers. Any variation of pressure in her ears would tell her if she was rising or sinking. She rotated slowly a full circle, enjoying being one with this strange environment, and moved her hand toward her waist to turn her lights back on.

A faint, reddish glow began to come from the thing Fida called Vishnu. It wasn't limited to one spot but seemed to emanate from the entire mass. She felt her respiration and pulse increase. She didn't feel afraid so much as surprised. Bioluminescence was fairly common in the oceans, but she had not expected to find it down here. As she watched, the glow became brighter, then dimmed and went out completely.

Something touched her right knee.

She jerked her leg away, grabbed for her light switch, missed. The damned clumsy, three-fingered mitts.

She recoiled again, swiping one hand through the water in front of her knee while she fumbled for the switch with her other. Felt it, clicked it on, saw the beam shoot from her helmet. She swept it down toward her legs and spun 360 degrees, lancing the water with her light.

Nothing.

A computer alarm sounded.

She gasped involuntarily, sucked in a spoonful of freezing, salty water, spat it back through her regulator.

Calm down.

Breathe.

Think.

Act.

The computer alarm had been her turnaround signal.

One-third of her gas gone.

Time to leave.

Her right knee suddenly felt as if someone had stuck an ice pick into it.

She looked down. A tiny stream of bubbles was flowing from a pinhole in her dry suit. That ice pick was a needle-sharp stream of frigid water, driven by the pressure here at depth, squirting through her inner layers to her skin. How? Tough reinforcing patches covered both knees, so they were the last places a suit failure should have occurred. That was beside the point now. She could feel icy water beginning to accumulate in the dry suit boot on that side. The cold was so intense that it felt like her foot was on fire.

Thank God it was only a pinhole. Not common in professional-grade, $3,000 dry suits like hers, but not unheard of, either. This suit didn't have that many dives on it—fifty, maybe. It had seen hard use on deep wrecks, though. She might have damaged that knee on a previous dive, not punctured it completely but stressed it enough that failure would occur later. It would be uncomfortable, but not a true emergency. She had plenty of air and was already starting her return.

She headed back the way she had come, frog-kicking, reeling in her safety line. Halfway to the shaft's bottom, she felt the leak in her suit grow worse. Her boot was full of water, and her foot was completely numb. The feeling of being on fire was crawling up her leg. Soon it would go numb, as well.

She knew that this was how disasters began: with a single failure that led to two others, each of which led to more, a cascade of events feeding on itself. She forced herself to breathe evenly and slowly and swam faster. Eventually she spotted the ice screw, untied her line, and secured her reel.

The pain in her leg was excruciating, but she could not rise up through the shaft too fast. In warmer water, an ascent rate of thirty feet per minute would have been possible. Here, in water so cold, that might not give her tissues enough time to off-gas their nitrogen load, and nitrogen caused the bends, a buildup of gas in the joints that could cripple or even kill a diver. With no recompression chamber, she could not risk getting bent. To be on the safe side, she had decided earlier that ten feet per minute would be best. At that rate, it would take her three minutes to ascend to the top of the shaft.

Almost immediately her computers began to beep, signaling that she was violating her preset ascent rate. It had happened without her realizing it, prompted by anxiety. She slowed down, but recognized a new danger. As it filled with water, the dry suit lost buoyancy. Even completely flooded, it would not sink, because the water in her suit would have the same buoyancy as the surrounding water. But without the buoyancy of an intact dry suit to compensate, the weight of all her equipment *would* make her sink.

In addition to the dry suit, she was wearing a buoyancy-control device, which, when inflated, might get her to the surface. But buoyancy was not the worst of her problems. That was hypothermia. She knew that water conducted heat away from the body twenty-five times faster than air. If her suit flooded with twenty-two-degree water, she might well die from hypothermia before buoyancy became an issue. She was facing a Hobson's choice: ascend too fast and risk the bends or rise too slowly and have her dry suit flood. She checked her depth. Twenty-five feet. Two and a half minutes. It was going to be close, and painful, but she would make it. Probably.

Then two things happened in rapid succession.

A pinhole leak opened over her other knee.

Her helmet light went out.

24

NIGHT IN THE JUNGLE, AND BARNARD SAW THE BAYONET GLITTER-
ing gold in the AK-47's muzzle flashes. Stroboscopic bursts all up and
down the line, the smell of cordite and shit, salt sweat burning his
eyes. Rounds slapping mud, smacking tree trunks, a scream, curses.
A bullet nicked the toe of his boot, felt like a trap snapping on it.

He was pushing and pulling his M16's charging lever to clear a
stoppage, but it was solidly jammed, not a millimeter of travel forward or back, and the NVA soldier was coming at a dead run and
Barnard could not take his eyes from that shining bayonet and the
NVA was ten steps away, then five, and the bayonet came at his face
and Barnard started to scream.

Something woke him from the jammed-gun dream. He had it only
rarely now, but it came back when things were stressful in the waking
world. At least he wasn't sweating and gasping, the dream's occa-
sional aftermath. Lucianne still slept beside him. It was the soft buzzing of his cellphone on the bedside table that had awakened him
before the bayonet punched through his eye socket.

Wednesday, 3:54 A.M., the clock's luminous numbers said. Moving carefully, so as not to disturb Lucianne, he eased out of bed and went into the hall, closing the door behind him.

Normally, the ID window in his phone showed who was calling—name and number. Failing that, it said, "Private caller." Just now, nothing at all appeared. That was a tip-off in itself.

"We need to meet," Bowman said. "I've got something to show you."

Barnard knew Wil would not be calling like this without good reason. "It'll take me a few minutes to get dressed. Where are you?"

"Stay in your pajamas. Just make some coffee. I'm in your driveway."

Barnard examined the manila folder's label: "Christchurch medical examiner's report." They were sitting downstairs at Barnard's dining room table. Both had cups of fresh black coffee.

"None other."

"How in God's name . . ." Barnard began, then stopped. "I know. Don't ask."

"Give it a read," Bowman said.

Five minutes later, Barnard put the papers on the table in front of him. "Ketamine overdose."

"Self-administered. That was their finding. Do you see anything wrong with the report?"

"No. Their procedure looked three-P."

"What's that?"

"Sorry. 'Per proper protocol.' They performed a solid-phase extraction procedure using Bond Elut C18 for ketamine and norketamine detection in biological fluids and tissues. They analyzed and confirmed the drug using gas-chromatography and mass spectrometry. The procedures yielded ketamine levels of 8.1 and 2.9 milligrams per liter in heart and femoral blood, respectively. Anything above about 6.0 in heart blood would likely be fatal to an otherwise healthy adult."

"They also found alcohol in her system."

"Level just .038. That's not even a DUI." Barnard pushed the papers away from him. "Emily Durant using drugs? Unthinkable."

"But there was ketamine in her system."

"Know much about it?" Barnard asked.

"It's an anesthetic. Not much beyond that."

"Was an anesthetic. Today, a recreational drug. 'Vitamin K.' Some years back, it was used for monitored anesthesia surgery—twilight sedation. Colonoscopies, some plastic and dental work, minor ophthalmic procedures. That lasted until people started waking up."

"While they were being operated on, you mean?"

"Yes."

"Bad."

"Worse. Waking up during a colonoscopy is one thing. In the middle of a face-lift . . ."

"That happened?" Bowman asked.

"Yes. And wasn't even the worst of it."

"What could be worse than waking up while someone was carving you a new face?"

"Not being able to move or communicate about what you were feeling. Ketamine is a short-acting paralytic. So imagine being fully awake, paralyzed, in agony."

"You said it was being used as a recreational drug, though."

"Smaller dose levels produce euphoria and disinhibition."

"But they found no evidence of foul play," Bowman said.

"Absence of evidence is not evidence of absence. I don't believe Emily Durant died from an accidental overdose."

Bowman set his cup down. "Neither do I."

Barnard's head snapped up. "You don't?"

"I suspected it before. Now I'm sure."

"What *do* you think?"

"I think somebody killed her."

25

"WHY DO YOU THINK THAT?" BARNARD BLURTED.

"The postmortem found multiple injection sites on the body. Drugs and paraphernalia were in the room."

"Yes."

"Injection sites included the femoral vein and artery and the median cubital and cephalic veins of both arms. Typical addict injection sites. But there were also micropunctures under each breast. Not typical."

Barnard nodded, waited.

"Death from ketamine overdose seems beyond question."

"And?"

"The microwounds weren't injection sites."

"What, then?"

"It was torture, made to look like something else. This is a homicide. And a bad one, at that."

It took a moment for Barnard to grasp what he was hearing. Homicide was not a thing he had yet considered. And . . . *torture*? He became aware of a building rage, could feel his face flushing, his hands clamping into fists. He started to ask Bowman how he could know such a thing, but Bowman spoke first.

"Every wound site is close to a major nerve or nexus. Femoral, in the upper thigh. Solar plexus. Ulnar, on the inside of each elbow"

"You really think so?" Barnard was still struggling with the idea of torture.

"Yes. Whoever did it was good enough to avoid collateral trauma, which would have alerted a medical examiner." He paused, looked at Barnard. "Sorry to tell you this, but I would bet that a more thorough postmortem would disclose damage to the optic nerves and possible others."

"My God," Barnard said. "Whoever did this has to be insane."

A scientist, Barnard normally dealt with new information in a systematic, linear fashion: *If that is so, then this must follow; and if this is so, then it is reasonable to believe . . .* But a revelation like this defied such orderly dissection. The questions came tumbling out of his brain faster than he could articulate them. Why had this happened? Who had done it? How could they have done it without being discovered, in such a contained environment? What he finally said was "Criminal investigation is not my field. I'd better get on the horn to the FBI."

"Maybe not quite yet," Bowman said.

"Why not?"

"Let's think this through first. Who, and why?"

"Jealous scientist," Barnard said.

"Possible. Maybe she made a discovery that someone else wanted credit for."

"Or a jilted lover," Barnard suggested.

"More likely, I'd say. Hell hath no fury. And a place like that could magnify anger. If there are any cracks in a mind, a place like the Pole will make them worse."

"Or it could have been a stark raving lunatic," Barnard said.

"Yes. Somebody who was unstable before or became so after arriving. Now let's look at why."

"Another scientist might want to take false credit," Barnard said.

"A jilted lover would want revenge."

"And psychopaths just kill."

"Killing is one thing. Torturing is another," Bowman pointed out.

"Hard to see anyone but a psychopath torturing."

"For every psychopath, there are hundreds of sanctioned torturers. All wanting one thing: information."

"So they might have suspected Emily knew something she shouldn't." Barnard rubbed his face. "God. This is hard, Wil."

"I know what you're thinking."

"Hallie is down there, and I sent her," Barnard said.

"You had no idea. Have you reached her yet?"

"Tried email and sat phone both. Still no luck, so I did some inquiring. A NASA launch has preempted most of the station's satellite time. And there was a solar event, as well."

"I didn't get through, either," Bowman said.

"If *you* can't, it has to be a complete blackout. I guess now we call the FBI."

"We could try. But the Bureau is very buttoned up and brutally overtasked. The official report shows death from overdose. It would take a lot more than our suspicions for them to fly agents down there."

"Even if you talked to them?"

Bowman chuckled. "I play for a different team. Crosstown rivals. Coming from me could hurt more than help. Stupid, but how much in government isn't?"

"What the hell do we do then? If you're right about this, a murderer is running loose around the station. Unless he already flew out," Barnard said. He was feeling something close to panic, a sensation he had not experienced for a very long time.

"We have to go on the assumption that he's still there. Or she."

"So Hallie could be in danger," Barnard said miserably. "*Everybody* could be in danger. We should at least reach out for the station manager."

"He might be the one who killed Emily."

Barnard started. "How likely is that?"

"We have no way to know." Then Bowman was quiet for some time.

"What, Wil?" Barnard asked.

"I was thinking how long a ride it would be in the back seat of an F-35."

"I didn't know they had two-seaters."

"Prototypes for the Israelis."

"You could do that?"

"Yes. But it would take most of today for authorization, half the night for them to find a plane and pilot, eight hours for the trip, including travel time to an air base. They couldn't land in New Zealand. So Australia, then civil aircraft to McMurdo . . ." Bowman shook his head. "Not fast enough."

"What about contacting McMurdo?" Barnard asked.

"I did, before coming here. They can't communicate with the Pole, either. And it's too cold for planes to land there."

"So they're completely cut off."

"Yes." Bowman sat still, hands flat on the table, staring straight ahead, jaw clenched. Barnard recognized the look in his eyes, knew it had been in his own at one time. Trapped in a room with no doors and life at stake. Finally Bowman said, "How many scientists are down there?"

"Can't be many, this late. Why?"

"We'll keep trying Hallie. Meantime, let's put the scientists under a microscope."

"Why them?"

"More likely to know anatomy than a forklift driver."

"We don't have much time," Barnard said.

"Won't take much."

Barnard walked him to the door. "Wil—if anything happens to Hallie because of me . . ." He stopped, had to look away.

"I understand," Bowman said. "Believe me, I understand."

26

HALLIE COULD TELL BY THE INCREASING PRESSURE IN HER EAR-
drums that she was sinking. With miles of freezing black water beneath. If she went too deep, or her descent rate exceeded her equipment's
ability to counteract it, she would just keep going, accelerating all the
while.

She valved more gas into her dry suit and started to rise again. The
new pinhole grew more quickly than had the first. By now the water
was almost to her knee in one leg, over her foot in the other.

Twenty feet. Two minutes.

Losing buoyancy again, she valved still more argon gas into her
suit and started finning as well to keep ascending. She could feel her
hypothermia worsening—hard shivering now, her teeth beginning to
chatter.

Ten feet. She could see the bright circle of the shaft's top. Water
over her knee in one leg, up to mid-calf in the other. The pain threat-
ening to drive coherent thoughts from her mind. The only good thing
was that the higher she went, the more buoyant she became.

Finally breaking the surface, she saw Merritt and Guillotte standing by the hole. They would have been monitoring her bubbles, once she was in the shaft.

"I ha-ha-had a dry-suit failure," she stuttered. "Lower half flooded. Need help ge-ge-getting out."

Guillotte yelled for more men. With two holding each arm and him pulling on the tops of her tanks, they hauled her out. She flopped onto her belly. Freezing water flowed through the suit, soaking her torso.

"He-he-help me doff. Can't do myself. Too cold," she said, through shivers and chattering teeth.

When they finally peeled the drysuit off, she had to get out of the wet dive underwear. Extra sets hung from one wall. She went to them, turned her back to the men, stripped naked, and pulled on dry ones. She donned all the rest of her ECW gear and drank a full thermos of hot chocolate given to her by one of the Draggers.

Once Hallie had just about stopped shivering, Merritt asked, "What happened down there?"

"Very strange," she said. "Suit failure on both knees. I don't ever remember—"

Merritt spun on Guillotte. "You let her dive in a suit with *defects*? She might have died. We could never replace her now!"

Guillotte's cheeks reddened. "I inspected every piece of her gear. Including the suit. There were no visible defects."

"But there *were* defects!" Merritt snapped.

"Aggie, wait," Hallie said. "I don't think Rémy missed anything. I inspected the suit, too. I was halfway through the dive before it started leaking."

Merritt took a deep breath, stepped back. "Okay. Sorry if I flew off the handle. It's just that with Emily gone, we can't afford to lose you, Hallie. Can we, Rémy?"

"Of course we cannot."

"I have to get back to the station. Rémy, you can transport Hallie after you've secured her gear." Merritt turned and started for the door.

"Hey," Hallie said.

"Yes?"

"I got the extremophile. There's a biosample in the Envirotainer."

"Oh," Merritt said. "Right. Good work."

And she left.

27

AFTER RIDING BACK TO THE STATION WITH GUILLOTTE, HALLIE went straight to her room and fell asleep. The ringing phone woke her an hour later.

"It's Aggie. Have you seen Doc yet?"

"Not yet. The dive was—"

"Please do it as soon as possible. He's waiting to hear from you."

She hung up and lay there trying, without success, to sleep. The dry-suit failure had been frightening, but she'd handled worse diving emergencies. A good dive was one you walked away from, and she had walked, this time.

She wanted to hear from Wil so badly it was like a physical ache. To stay quiet this long, he must have been very angry. But, remembering the scene at the airport, she didn't think he'd looked angry. More sad than anything. Why would what she said make him sad? And what on earth had he meant: *There are things you don't know about me*. Really? After a year together?

That led her to wonder if there were things he didn't know about her. Important things, not who she'd dated in high school or why she disliked French food. No, she decided, he did know the important things. She'd held nothing back. Nothing had warranted holding back. Which made his own comment all the more mysterious—and troubling.

The next morning was Wednesday, the start of her third day at the Pole. She had set the alarm on her phone for seven. The station PA system woke her at six-thirty.

"Attention the station. Attention the station. All hands meeting in the galley at zero seven hundred. Repeat, all hands meeting in the galley at zero seven hundred."

"I called this meeting to talk about the recent fatalities," Graeter said, standing up front, near the serving area. Hallie had arrived early, hoping to see Fida again, but he hadn't appeared. Agnes Merritt sat with her, and Rémy Guillotte joined them just after Graeter started speaking.

"As I'm sure everyone knows, Dr. Harriet Lanahan passed away on Monday, Dr. Diana Montalban Tuesday. If anyone has questions or concerns, this is the time."

"How about, like, what the hell happened?" a gruff male voice asked from somewhere back in the gloom.

"Doc?" Graeter said.

Morbell came forward, wearing a white lab coat and the dark glasses. He seemed to shrink under scrutiny.

"Well. Ah, yes, I can offer something in the way of explanation. Wound dehiscence. Harriet Lanahan had an esophagectomy last year. Diana Montalban had undergone a C-section delivery two years earlier. I believe that their surgical scars ruptured—"

"Wait a minute," a woman from the audience interrupted. Short, red-haired, combative. "You're talking about incision sites, right? That's just skin and subcutaneous tissue. It wouldn't cause bleeding like that."

"As I was about to say," Doc continued, "major veins and arteries were involved in both operations. Some must have ruptured."

"Why now, and why two so close together?"

"Many kinds of stress can cause dehiscence. A condition called Ehlers-Danlos syndrome is sometimes at fault. Pole is cruel. I don't have to tell you that." He shrugged, held up his hands.

"I was a surgical nurse once upon a time," the red-haired woman said. "So I know about dehiscence. It almost always happens soon after surgery. This long after—very rare."

Hallie could see Doc's jaw clenching. Graeter stepped forward. He said, "All due respect to nurses, Doc is the physician here. Anyone else?"

For a moment no one spoke. Than another woman stood. She had very white skin, even for a Polie, and shining black hair, and deep purple circles under both eyes. "Yeah." She pointed straight at Hallie. "What about her?" Every head in the room turned to stare.

"What about her?" Doc said.

"She comes in and people start dying." She looked at Doc. "What about *that*?"

"I told you what I think caused the deaths. I don't believe Dr. Leland had anything to do with them."

"Would you be saying that if she was a Dragger?" the woman asked, and murmurs of agreement came from the crowd.

"Of course," Doc said.

"I'm not so sure," the woman retorted. "We don't—"

Graeter stepped forward. "Doc answered your question. Are there any more *reasonable* ones?"

The woman colored, but she sat without saying anything else.

"Thanks for coming," Graeter said. "Let's get back to work."

People started filing out through several exits. Hallie saw a number of stares directed her way. A few people whispered and pointed.

She left the cafeteria and headed for Doc's office, moving along in her bubble of light. She kept looking over her shoulder, unable to shake the feeling that someone was following her, but every time she looked, there was only the darkness.

28

DOC WAS WAITING IN HIS OFFICE WITH A STETHOSCOPE HUNG around his neck. There was enough light, barely, for her to see his strange pink eyes.

"No glasses?" Hallie asked.

"Here I can adjust the light," he said. "My condition is of the oculocutaneous variety. Too much light is not only painful, it makes everything I see look washed out and blurry. Like a badly overexposed photograph."

As Hallie's own eyes adjusted to the gloom, Doc took on a ghostly white glow. "I know what you're thinking," he said. "Someone who can't see must be a lousy doctor."

"Actually, I was thinking how hard you must have worked, given your condition, to become a doctor. And how admirable that is."

He blinked. "Oh." Clearly it was not the response he was accustomed to. "So how have you been feeling?"

"Exhausted. Sore throat. Some rumbling in the gut. Other than that, okay."

"Par for the course." He checked her pulse, temperature, blood pressure. While he was working, she looked around with something

like wonder. Even in the dim light she could see immaculate beige
walls, gleaming stainless steel cabinets, a gurney with crisp white
sheets. An exam area with a hospital bed and a privacy curtain.
Counters with neatly arranged trays of instruments, swabs, wipes.
Disposal containers for sharps and biohazards. The cream-colored
floor was clean and waxed to a shine. The room smelled good, too,
like alcohol and pine-scented disinfectant.

"My compliments," she said. "This is the cleanest place I've seen
here."

"We make sure it gets special attention." Agnes Merritt had been
sitting on a stool near one corner of the shadowy room.

"I didn't know you were here. Are you sick?" Hallie asked.

"No. I didn't want to get in the way. SORs require that a female
be present when another female is being examined by a male physician. We don't have any registered nurses, so sometimes I fill in. Don't
I, Doc?"

"Yes, yes. That's true. Agnes does help out on occasion." He directed Hallie to an exam table. Merritt followed. He drew the privacy
curtain.

"Dr. Leland, I'll need you to disrobe on top to your underwear,
please."

She stripped down to her sports bra. He asked the usual questions
and performed the usual checks, listening to her heart and lungs, per-
cussing her back and chest. After asking her to lie down, he palpated
her abdominal area.

"All just fine," he said. "I'll draw some blood and do a throat
swab. You can leave a urine sample on your way out."

"I get the blood and urine," she said. "But why the swab?"

Merritt answered: "People come here from all over. We like to
know what they bring in. It can help if there's a serious outbreak.
Right, Doc?"

"Yes, exactly," Doc said.

He directed Hallie to a blood-drawing chair against the wall, sat
in front of her on a wheeled stool. He arranged her arm correctly,
straight line from hand to shoulder, applied the rubber tourniquet

four inches above the draw site, tapped inside her elbow several times.

"Good veins," he said.

"I bet you say that to all your patients." She knew how trite that was, but she hoped to settle Doc down a bit. He had seemed nervous when she'd arrived and had become more so as the exam had progressed. His hand was unsteady as he swabbed the draw site with an alcohol pad. When he brought the syringe toward her arm, he couldn't make the proper alignment, needle parallel to vein. He sat back, took a deep breath.

"Are you all right?" Hallie asked.

"Sorry. Too much coffee this morning, on an empty stomach. Let's try that again."

He got it on the second try. He filled three Vacutainers, slipped the needle out, and covered the venipuncture site with a cotton ball and a piece of medical tape. Merritt, Hallie noted, had watched the whole draw very closely.

"Just one more thing and we'll be through," Doc said. He examined her eyes and ears, then put a tongue depressor into her mouth. "Say ahhh."

She did.

"Say ahhh again and look up this time. Here comes the swab."

She did that, too, and with his other hand he stuck the swab's cotton tip down her throat. *Way* down her throat. She had performed throat swabs herself and knew that the tip was supposed to contact the tonsillar columns on either side of the uvula. Doc's swab went deeper. She gagged, violently. He pulled the swab out and secured it in a sterile container. "Quite a gag reflex you have there," he said.

"My gag reflex is actually minimal," she said.

"How would you know?"

"I'm a technical diver. Stuff gets down there. I know. You went pretty deep with that."

"We go deeper here at Pole because some pathogens thrive only beyond the tonsillar/uvular region. Can't have them slipping through the net, can we?"

She stood up. "Are we finished here, Doctor?"

Merritt walked over. "Glad to have that out of the way." She patted Hallie's shoulder.

"I can give the urine sample now," she said.

Doc and Merritt exchanged glances. Merritt waved a hand. "You know what? Enough for one day. Go grab a coffee. Or rest."

Halfway to the galley, she stopped. Something was bothering her about the exam, and she couldn't decide what. The procedures Doc had performed had been just like those done by countless doctors throughout her life. His hand had been shaky for the blood draw, but that wasn't it. What, then? She started off again, still wondering.

A male Polie came shuffling toward her in his own little pod of light. He was tall, with a long, rust-colored beard, and he was bent over a smartphone, texting.

She got it. Doc had not recorded any of the data produced by his exam. Not on paper, not in a computer. Merritt hadn't written or recorded anything either. Then why in hell would they do an examination?

There was only one answer.

They didn't care about the results.

Then what *was* the reason, if not obtaining data from her?

Only one answer: doing something *to* her.

29

THE INFIRMARY, WITH ITS THREE HOSPITAL BEDS, WAS, FOR REA-
sons Hallie could not imagine, halfway down the corridor from Doc's
office. Another human factors decision, perhaps—to ensure that
medical officers got enough exercise shuttling back and forth.

"Graeter stopped by and told me what you did," Bacon said. She
reached out the hand that was not in a cast, and Hallie took it.

"You'd have done the same for me."

"Tried like hell, anyway."

"Well, ya look like ya coulda been a contendah," Hallie said.

"I goddamned well feel like it." The accident had left Rockie with
a concussion, a fractured left wrist, a broken nose, a cracked rib, and
a gash across her forehead that Doc had used five stitches to close.
Both eyes were black and puffy. "I was lucky. If the Cat had flipped
and fallen on me, I'd be a stain in the snow." Bacon sipped water and
set the glass back on her bedside table. "So you really climbed down
into the crevasse using *hammers*?"

"I got lucky, too. The wall wasn't dead vertical."

"Amazing."

"Do you feel up to talking just a little?"

"Sure. But Doc gave me a shot. I might doze off right in your face."

"What happened out there?"

"Wish I knew. I was heading out for the grade. I got a nosebleed and everything started to spin."

"That must have been scary."

"If I'd had time to think about it. Next thing I remember, waking up here."

"I know you'd been sick. *That* sick?"

"I didn't think so, or I wouldn't have been on the Cat."

"When did it start?"

"My Pole cold, six months ago. This new thing, last week."

"Anything else?"

"Some Polarrhea. Comes and goes. So to speak."

"You saw Doc yesterday morning?"

"Getting to be a regular customer."

"Really? Why?"

"I went in last week."

"What was wrong?"

"Nothing with me. He needed to update my Pole medical file."

"Do you remember what he did?"

"The usual. Weight, blood pressure, blood and urine samples, throat swab."

"How soon after that did you get sick?" Hallie asked.

"Hadn't thought about it. Couple days later. Maybe the next day." She shrugged. "All the people going to that office . . . not surprising."

"This may sound strange, but can you think of anyone who might have wanted to hurt you?"

Hallie had expected surprise, but Bacon just nodded. "Sure. Couple of Draggers I blew off at parties. A few Beakerholes who think they know more about Cat work than I do. Oh, and one rebuffed lezzie."

"Mad enough to sabotage your machine?"

"Cat was fine. It was me. I just passed out."

"You said you knew Emily Durant."

"Liked her, too. She didn't have her head up her ass, like some Beakers." Bacon stopped. "Present company excepted. But the last month or so . . ."

"What happened?"

"She stopped talking, never smiled, got Pole eyes—just staring off at nothing all the time. Used to be, she'd say hi when we met and talk. Then it was like she looked right through me."

The same thing Merritt had told her. "Why do you think that happened?"

"Too much ice time. Look, I know where you're going with this. I was surprised as hell when I heard she OD'd. She never struck me as the drugging type. Down here, you get so you can spot the weird ones. Boozers, gamblers, sex addicts, S&M freaks."

"How would you spot *them*?"

"They walk funny. And wince every time they sit. All that paddling and whipping."

"Ah. I knew Emily Durant well. And I cannot believe she was into drugs."

"How long since you'd seen her?"

"Several years."

"A good while. And she'd been at Pole a year," Bacon said.

"Merritt told me that, too. But still . . ."

Hallie looked around. It was like any hospital room back in the world, except smaller, dimmer, and colder. Adjustable bed, rollaway tray, one chair, a bathroom, wall cabinets. Even a television monitor hanging from the ceiling.

"Can you think of anyone down here who would have wanted to hurt Emily?"

"No. But there are a lot of Polies I don't know. Why?"

How far to go with Bacon? Ease into it. "If you don't buy the overdose story, which I don't, then what's left?"

It took a second, but Bacon understood. "Jesus. That is some heavy shit, Hallie."

"Do you know anything about Vishnu?"

"From World Religion 101. Some Hindu god, right?"

"Right. But connected to the station?"

"You lost me."

"Emily and Fida had identified an extremophile. Vishnu was what they called it."

"A what?" Bacon asked.

"Sorry. An organism that survives in extreme environments. Like subfreezing, supersalty water."

"Oh. And what's special about this one?"

"They thought it might save the earth."

Bacon laughed, winced, touched her ribs. "Yeah, right." Then, watching Hallie: "Wait. You mean, *really*?"

Hallie gave a quick explanation.

"So you think somebody might have killed her over that stuff?"

Hallie told Bacon about the link between NASI and GENERCO.

Bacon shook her head, wide-eyed. "Do you think things like that really happen?"

"I know they do," Hallie said.

"Graeter killing Emily." Bacon rubbed the cast on her wrist, shook her head. "The man can be a world-class asshole. But murder? I don't know. He's more like . . . wounded. Lot of scar tissue over that man's heart."

"You may be right. What about triage?"

"What about it?"

"Do you know anything about it down here?"

"It's probably part of disaster planning. Why?"

She explained what she had seen in the video log.

"You think that guy might have killed her?"

Bacon's voice trailed off. Hallie heard a soft buzzing in her ears, and the room slowly faded.

Bacon's laugh brought her back. "Hey. I'm the one who got the shot. You took a little trip."

"Did I?"

"Classic microsleep. See it all the time here."

Hallie rubbed her face. It had happened before. One second she was there in the room, talking, and then she was gone, and then something snapped her back awake. "I'm sorry, really. Don't mean to be rude. I just—"

"No worries. We've all been there."

Come at this from a different direction. "Can you think of anyone at Pole who could be a killer?" she asked.

Bacon didn't frown, look shocked, or even surprised. She nodded. "Sure. That's easy. Let's see. I'd start with that asshole Brank. Then there is—"

Bacon stopped talking and stared at Hallie. One arm went to her throat. She frowned, coughed, tried to speak. Her face began to swell. A rash erupted, bright red, as if someone had slapped her, hard. Her wrists puffed up, and the rash appeared there, too. The facial swelling grew worse. Bacon's head was thrown back, mouth open, and her chest heaved as she struggled to breathe.

Hallie grabbed the receiver off the wall-mounted phone, hit 0, and, the instant the comm operator answered, yelled, "Emergency in the infirmary. Rockie Bacon is choking. I need help NOW!"

Bacon began to convulse, her body's response to a lack of oxygen and a buildup of carbon dioxide. Her lips and fingertips turned cyanotic blue, and her face had swollen so badly that Hallie could barely see her eyes. Foam bubbled at the corners of her mouth. She fell back against the pillow, her chest heaving against a closed airway.

Hallie looked around for something she could use to perform an emergency tracheotomy, but there was nothing in the room. The door burst open and Doc rushed in.

"What happened?"

"She can't breathe. Can you do a trach?"

He stood there staring, not speaking, frozen. Hallie had never seen an albino flush. His face turned red, pinched in on itself, and Hallie thought he was going to cry.

"Doctor!" she snapped. "We need—" Bacon's body stopped convulsing, went limp. "Get me a kit. *I'll* open her airway." She smacked his shoulder.

That brought him back. He ran out and returned in thirty seconds with gloves, a scalpel, a hemostat, an endotracheal tube, and an ambu bag. He jumped onto the bed, straddled Bacon, bent her head back, made a vertical incision just beneath the thyroid cartilage, rotated the scalpel 360 degrees to create a circular opening, used the hemostat to control the trachea, and pushed the endo tube through. He rotated it to secure the tube's flanges inside the trachea, attached the ambu bag, and started pressing it to inflate Bacon's lungs.

Under normal circumstances, the bag should have compressed with very little force. Doc squeezed, squeezed harder, and then with so much force that his face reddened again.

"Nothing's going through!" he said. Holding the bag in his left hand, he started punching it with his right fist.

Hallie touched his arm. "The swelling must have closed her trachea all the way down."

"Shit," the doctor said. "God damn it to hell." He let go of the bag, struggled down off the bed, and buried his face in his hands. Hallie realized that he was crying. Rockie was not coming back. She pulled the sheet up, covering Bacon's grotesquely swollen face, and helped Doc sit in the room's one chair. She had never seen a physician go to pieces like that.

"I can't take any more of these," he sobbed. "I took an oath, goddamnit."

Agnes Merritt came into the room just at that moment.

"Rockie's dead," Hallie said. "Some kind of allergic reaction. She asphyxiated."

But Merritt was staring at the doctor, who was still crying. "What happened to him?" she asked Hallie.

"I think he needs some rest."

"Did he say anything?"

"What?" The question Hallie would have expected was what Doc had done. Why would Merritt care what he'd *said*?

"Did he *tell* you anything?"

"Just that he couldn't take any more of these. I think it's safe to assume he meant people dying."

Merritt actually appeared relieved. "Come on, Doc, let's go back to your office." Merritt was stronger than she looked. She lifted him bodily from his chair and guided him out to the hall. To Hallie she said, "Graeter's been notified. He should be here any minute."

After Merritt left, Hallie realized that the chief scientist had not even glanced at Rockie's body.

30

WEDNESDAY AFTERNOON, THREE P.M. SHARP, SIXTH FLOOR OF THE National Science Foundation headquarters, new and gleaming, lush with huge potted plants and bright with vast expanses of glass. Not having to keep secrets has its advantages, Barnard thought.

"Dr. Donald Barnard. I have an appointment with the director." Barnard was surprised to see a young man of East Indian descent behind the executive assistant's desk in the director's anteroom. When he had come up, executive assistants were secretaries, and secretaries were women. Like Carol, who was about his age, in his own office. But these were different times, even in Washington—perhaps especially in Washington, where failure to be politically correct could scuttle careers.

"Dr. Barnard, of course. Just give me one moment, please."

The young man's voice made Barnard think of soft chimes. He passed through the door behind him, reappeared in less than a minute. "I'm so sorry to have kept you waiting, sir. Please go in."

He held the door for Barnard and closed it behind him. A short, trim man with dark skin and close-cut black hair—another East Indian, Barnard guessed—came toward him, hand extended.

"David Gerrin. So pleased to meet you."

31

THE NSF BUILDING'S ENTRANCE LOBBY WAS EQUIPPED WITH BIG revolving doors of the kind more commonly found in New York City. Barnard disliked them. He had once seen a darting child's leg broken by such a door, whose infrared stop sensor was four inches higher than the top of the child's head. Nevertheless, he had to admit that being trapped and spinning like a gerbil in a treadmill was probably a more fitting end to the meeting just concluded.

Outside, gray drizzle was freezing into stinging sleet, forming a dangerous sheen on pavements and sidewalk. Barnard turned right and walked west on Wilson Boulevard, then turned right again onto North Stuart Street. He had not gone twenty steps when a gray Toyota Camry double-parked in the street abreast of him. The car had surprised him the first time he'd ridden with Bowman, whom he'd half-expected to show up in an armored, machine gun–toting Aston Martin. Barnard had said something about it, and Bowman had laughed. "Invisibility is the best armor of all," he'd said.

Barnard got in. "Back to BARDA."

———

Earlier that morning, at about ten, Barnard had been surprised to see Bowman in his office so soon after their four A.M. meeting. He had been more surprised by what Bowman brought.

"Thirty-two scientists at the South Pole now," Bowman reported.

"More than I would have thought."

"Not a problem. I had some people create and analyze a deep-source data mass. Information from birth to present day for every one of the scientists. *Tons* of terabytes." He grinned—looking, Barnard thought, like a wolf.

"They did that for you so quickly?"

"When they call, I'm there for them. Works both ways. Every human life is a collection of data. Ninety-nine percent mediocre—in the statistical sense of remaining within certain parameters. Think of a seismograph readout—an endless line of one-inch oscillations. Then something extraordinary—Krakatoa, say—makes the needle jump. A life graphs like that. Long stretches of small squiggles, then a spike.

"Anomalies move the needle. An A student fails. Good credit tanks. Doctor visits increase suddenly. Thirty-year marriage ends in divorce. Cadillacs after Hondas. On and on. Algorithms digest a year in nanoseconds. It's like panning for gold. You keep washing out the dross and—maybe—end up with something that glitters."

"And?"

Bowman bared his teeth again. "And we found some things. Whether fool's gold or real remains to be seen."

"Let's hear it."

"After the initial screening, three scientists were left in the bottom of the pan. Dr. Alston Sinclair, an astrophysicist. For some years, a man with whom he had had a homosexual affair had blackmailed him. Then the payments had suddenly stopped."

"Do we know why?"

"The blackmailer died."

"Murdered?"

Bowman shrugged. "The death occurred while Sinclair was at the Pole. Police ruled it an accident."

"Doesn't sound like the kind of wrinkle we're looking for."

"Next is Dr. Elaine Graydon. Biochemist and a rising star in her field. Until she left the Harvard faculty in mid-semester and later went to the South Pole."

"People don't usually jump that ship," Barnard said. "Do we know why?"

"Got caught having an affair with a dean's wife. Very messy."

"Ugly, but not really sinister."

"Number three is a genetic virologist named Maynard Blaine. Works for a biotech startup called Advanced Viral Sciences."

"What stuck out about him?"

"He left a teaching job at Rutgers several years ago to go with AVS. Doubled his salary. Blip. Then his travel changed. Blip. He's a bachelor. Before leaving Rutgers, he took one vacation every year, and it was always some Club Bed–type cruise. After changing jobs, no more Love Boats. Instead, he went to Bangladesh's capital, Dhaka, twice; New Delhi twice; Lagos, Nigeria, once. Blip, blip, blip."

"Not vacation spots."

"Filthy, overcrowded, disease-ridden, and dangerous."

"Sounds like you've been."

Bowman only smiled. He said, "Where did he stay? Who did he meet? Credit card use? And a lot more."

"And?"

"He met three men on each trip. One is a retired geneticist from England named Ian Kendall. Another is a French medical doctor, Jean-Claude Belleveau, who practices in New Delhi, of all places. And the third is an epidemiologist."

"Name?"

"David Gerrin."

Barnard gaped. "Director of Antarctic Programs."

"None other. You'll want to keep that appointment," Bowman said.

32

AFTER BARNARD LEFT, DAVID GERRIN SAT BEHIND HIS DESK AND
gazed at a large, framed photograph of Dhaka that hung on his wall.
Barnard had asked about it. Once they learn where I came from, he
thought, they all ask the same things. Is that rush hour? How many
people live there? When do the typhoons hit? What are the slums
like?

From television news they knew about the storms, floods, and
famines, epidemics, genocide, death tolls in the hundreds of thousands. Some recalled a concert to raise funds, very famous musicians
and entertainers. So many years later, though, not many knew much
beyond its name.

We were so poor, Gerrin thought now, staring at the picture, reflecting on Barnard's visit. Not poor as they understand the term in
this country. The poor here live like royalty by comparison. They
walk into some office once a month and are handed money, free and
clear. They do nothing for it. *Nothing.* Unimaginable for a Bangla-
deshi.

He recalled sitting beside his mother—these were his first
memories—in a vast, steaming, stinking dump that stretched as far as

he could see. That was his world. There was simply no way to tell people here about the smell: rotting food, putrefying flesh, burning shit. And *hot*. One endless compost heap. She had to keep picking him up so that he would not be burned. When she found anything edible—apple cores, fish bones, moldy bread—she ate half and made him eat the other half.

They lived in Karail, Dhaka's worst slum. Perhaps the world's worst. He pissed and shat in any open space, as the urges struck. Most water was life-threatening. He and two brothers and two sisters and his mother slept underneath an abandoned truck trailer. The trailer itself was full of others. He did not remember his father, who died of typhoid when he was still an infant. They scavenged clothes from people who were dead or dying. They ate dogs and cats when they could catch them. He saw people eating corpses.

He remembered his mother dying from malnutrition and dysentery when he was eleven. She had grown too weak to move, had lain in her own filth, blanketed with flies, unable to eat or drink at the end. After, both sisters were taken away by men who, he learned later, raped ugly women to death and sold pretty ones to pimps. He watched from a hiding place while a gang killed one of his brothers for the clothes he wore. They did not want to soil the shirt and pants with blood, so they strangled him with a soft rope. The second brother disappeared one night while he slept, and Gerrin had not seen him since.

Hunger never left him. His body ached constantly. There were times when his bones felt like they were on fire. He became covered with sores that would not heal, and living scabs of flies covered the sores. He passed blood from all his orifices and walked about nearly blind some days, barely able to think with a starving brain. Much of the time he was too weak to defend himself, and people took advantage of him constantly. He did the same to others who were even weaker.

To survive, he did horrible things. Even now he had nightmares about them. Many people would rather die than do the things he had done. Others had the will but lacked the wits. He had been born with unusual intelligence. Pure luck of the draw, as they said here. The brain in his head kept him alive.

A year after his mother died, he broke into a black Mercedes-Benz. He would never forget the silver circle with the three-pointed star that was a few inches from his face as he slid under the car. He had learned how to defeat alarm systems from beneath. He smashed a window, let himself in, and was looking for anything of value when a huge hand wrapped around his neck and pulled him out. The man held him up in the air with his feet dangling. He was that skinny, and the man was that strong. He had very white skin and a reddish beard so perfectly trimmed that each hair was clearly visible, like a nest of wires.

He expected that the man would beat or maybe kill him. It happened all the time to thieves who ventured out of the slums. No one knew or cared.

"Tell me why you broke into my car," the man said.

No one had ever asked him such a question. Lies would earn him a beating. He told the truth as clearly as he could: He was starving to death. His parents were dead. His sisters and brothers, too. He began to describe his life.

The man set him down and listened. Anger changed to mild interest and eventually became attention. The way he spoke, how his eyes worked. He did not know it then, but he understood later: intelligence recognizes itself.

Finished, he simply stood before the man and waited, watching his hands, because when they clenched into fists he would curl up into a ball and take the beating lying down. But they never turned into fists.

"I want you to come with me," the man said.

They drove in his car to a place like an orphanage. It was that but, as he learned later, full of children who were, like him, extraordinarily intelligent. So began his journey out of Karail, from which only one in ten thousand escaped.

Here, in the beginning, he had told people about that time of his life. But seeing faces contort with disgust and pity was as unpleasant for him as hearing details about Karail was for them. So he'd learned to keep it short and, if not sweet, at least devoid of horror.

Thus he had not told Dr. Donald Barnard any of that, though he'd sensed that Barnard might have listened with more attention and less revulsion than most. Gerrin was no stranger to the land of nightmares, and he thought that Barnard had seen and probably done some of the things that black dreams are made of. He looked about the right age to have fought in Vietnam. Intelligence was not the only thing that recognized itself.

Barnard's reason for coming seemed genuine: a decent man's desire to know how a valued former subordinate had died. But surviving a place like Karail instilled an exquisite sensitivity to threat. Something felt odd about Barnard's interest in someone so far removed from him by time as well as work.

He'd pretended not to know who had been sent to replace Durant, and felt confident that the lie had passed unnoticed. Deceit had been another essential survival skill in Karail. It was, as they said here, like riding a bicycle. Once learned, it stayed with you forever, ready to be retrieved as needed.

But of course he knew exactly who had been sent to replace Durant. That person had been chosen with great care. Emily Durant had been the only female scientist at the station who, before winterover, would be returning to North America. She'd made her own death inevitable after becoming suspicious and asking too many questions about Triage. Her death was not the problem, at least not by itself. But it meant that one entire continent would be left uncovered when Triage launched. And after everything they had done, all the planning and testing, the money spent, risks taken—that was simply unacceptable.

33

HALF IN A DAZE, HALLIE WALKED ALONG THE CORRIDOR OF LEVEL 1, heading for Fida's room. Two women were coming the other way. Both wore overalls, black bunny boots, and heavy wool work shirts. She saw one of the Draggers turn and say something to her companion. After that, both of them gave her hard stares as they approached. As soon as they passed, she heard one say, making no effort to whisper, "That's her. She's the one."

She glanced over her shoulder and saw that they had both stopped and were standing there, watching her go.

She understood. The only new arrival in weeks, she might have brought in some pathogen that was responsible for two inexplicable deaths. Now three, although they wouldn't know that yet. What was it they called such a person on the old sailing ships? A Jonah. One who brought inexplicable misfortune to ship and crew. And one who sometimes disappeared, just as inexplicably, when seas were heavy and the sky held no moon.

It wasn't hard to understand how Polies, like sailors at the mercy of natural forces, could harbor superstitions. But there was nothing she could do about that now. She knocked on Fida's door, softly at first and then, when she got no answer, harder. Down the hall a door flew open and a woman's face popped out. She was pale and had dark, arched eyebrows. The bags under her eyes were so severe that it looked like there were black circles around them. It was the same woman who had pointed her out during the all-hands meeting. "You want to stop that fucking noise, please?" the woman said. "People're *trying* to sleep."

"Sorry."

The woman started back, then stopped, peering around the door, recognizing Hallie. She shook her head but said nothing more and disappeared into her room.

Hallie needed to talk to Fida. There were too many complications flying around in her head. It might not be saying much, given his condition, but she thought he was the best person to help her sort them out. She wasn't exactly sure what that said about her own condition.

She tried the laboratory where Fida and Emily had been working, and where she had secured the halophile sample, but he wasn't there, either. In addition to everything else, they needed to decide what to do with the new biomatter. He had said that their other samples had survived as long as they were kept in water taken from the cryopeg but died soon after removal. She didn't want to repeat that mistake.

She called and had Fida paged. Once again she went to the cafeteria and sat at a table with a cup of chlorinated coffee to wait. After fifteen minutes she grew impatient, and after thirty she started to worry.

She knocked on Graeter's door, heard a growl that sounded something like "Enter," and went in. She saw that he had replaced the woman's picture on his wall with a fresh one, which, as yet, showed only a few punctures. Six darts lay neatly aligned on the right side of his desk. A stack of forms sat in front of him.

"Mr. Graeter, we need to talk."

"Can it wait? You can't imagine the paperwork required when someone dies here. And three?" He shook his head.

"No. Look, I'm a microbiologist. You know that. You're probably an engineer by education. You think in numbers and angles. I think in pathogens and infections."

She at least had his attention. "And?"

"You know that old saying, 'Once an incident, twice a coincidence, three times a pattern'?"

"Heard it somewhere, yes."

"Well?"

"You think the three women's deaths are somehow connected."

"I think it would be wise to assume they are and see where it leads."

"That's your take on what happened. Mine is different."

"What is it?"

"Pole kills in lots of ways."

What the hell is wrong with these people? she wondered. "That's pretty much what Merritt said. But it sounds to me like you both are trying to explain these deaths away. I understand the reasons why you might want to do that. But wouldn't it be wise to at least consider other possibilities?"

"I am considering them. I had Doc look into what happened, as you know. He can't do much, but it's all we have until conditions change and planes can land. You heard his statement about Lanahan and Montalban. His preliminary opinion is that an allergic reaction caused Bacon's death."

"And you buy all of that?"

He looked up sharply. "Did you go to medical school?"

"I don't buy it. Bacon had been here almost a year, right?"

"I'm not an allergist. Neither are you, last time I checked. Doc is running some blood tests."

"Did he say what kind? How long they would take?"

"What difference could it make?"

"Is he doing anything else? Growing cultures?"

"Jesus. I don't know. Can you grow cultures from blood samples?"

"Are all the bodies down in the morgue?" she asked.

"You don't need to worry about them."

"I'm worried about what they might have left behind up here."

"I have no reason to believe there's danger to anyone else," Graeter said.

It was like talking to a post. "You don't know there is *not* danger to anyone else. Three people are dead."

His head jerked up. "I definitely do not need you to remind me, Ms. Leland."

She let the "Ms." pass this time. "Mr. Graeter, I am not trying to get under your skin or tell you how to do your job."

"Really? Because it feels like you're doing both."

"Others might die."

"Nobody else is going to die. Jesus Christ. The bodies are quarantined and frozen. Doc has reasonable explanations. What do you have? Some crazy Andromeda strain bullshit? You haven't been down here three days and you want to tell me how to run my station?" His voice had been rising, and his face reddening.

None are so blind, she thought. Might not be the best time to point out his, but too bad. "You could be compromising the safety of the entire station. You need to think about that."

She nodded at the three framed photographs on his desk.

His hands balled into fists, stretching the skin, pulling open healed cracks that started oozing blood and fluid. She was sure he was going to slam both fists down onto the desk top. Instead, he opened them slowly and laid his hands flat, palms down. Took a deep breath, let it out. "We're finished here. If you have a problem with my actions, you can file a complaint with NSF."

34

"I WON'T DO THAT, AND YOU KNOW IT."

He picked up a dart and started running his thumb over the point. More calmly, he said, "I have a station full of Polies who have been here a year or longer. Some are okay, but a good many are right on the edge. You've seen them wandering around like zombies. An announcement about some killer germ could destabilize this population."

Should I tell him? She wanted to. *Needed* to. But not yet. "Could I have a look at the station personnel roster?"

He stared. "Why?"

"I'm looking for a name."

"Personnel information is confidential."

She'd been expecting that. "Can you look at it for me, then?"

"What's this about?"

That, too. "Emily was seeing somebody whose first name started with A-M."

"And?"

"I'd like to know who it was."

"Why?"

"He might know something about how she died."

"We know how she died."

"You think you do. I'm not so sure."

"Sherlock Holmes in a dress. You're beginning to show signs of paranoia. Are you aware of that?"

"I'm not paranoid, Mr. Graeter. And I'm not wearing a dress."

"You know what I meant."

"Isn't a deputy U.S. marshal required to mount an investigation of something like this?"

He rubbed his forehead, took a deep breath. "That marshal stuff is mostly bullshit. More a formality than anything."

"You said you were trained and sworn, though."

"Two days of classroom work and two hours on the range. They called it LOST, believe it or not."

"What?"

" 'Limited Operation/Situation Training.' Translation: just enough to satisfy the bureaucrats."

"But still. If a crime—"

"First a killer germ loose in the station. Now Emily Durant was murdered?"

"What have you got to lose by humoring me for five minutes?"

She had been choosing her words very carefully and watching Graeter's reactions as she might have watched a copperhead on the desk in front of her. If he was the one, *something* would show on his face, in his voice, his eyes.

"Leland . . ." He shook his head but then turned around, looking over his shoulder to make sure his body blocked her view. "What was it, again?"

"Ambie. Probably short for a name like Ambrose. Ambert. Ames. Amos. Can you look for first or last names beginning with 'Am'?"

"Do you know why I'm doing this?"

"No."

"That's too bad. I don't, either. Thought you might be able to enlighten me."

"Wow." The genuine surprise in her voice drew a look from him.

"Wow what?"

"You do have a sense of humor."

"It's usually broken. Slips out at odd times."

"I can see that."

"Listen. Need to say this. When I'm wrong, I'm wrong. I'm sorry I yelled at you."

"No need to apologize. Men are prone to such outbursts when they can't think of anything better to do."

He gave her an incredulous look, shook his head. "When was this?" he asked. "I mean, when was she supposedly seeing whoever this supposedly was?"

"They hooked up just after Thanksgiving."

"For the record, I hate that expression. Sounds like railroad cars."

"You know what? I hate it, too. Consider it deleted from our communications."

"The station would have been fully staffed then," he said. "It's going to take me a few minutes to read through all these names."

"Wait. You don't have to do that."

"How else?"

"Use the Find function. It'll take half a second."

"Where's the Find function?"

"What program is that?" she asked.

"Excel."

"Up in the right corner of your screen, there are the words 'Find' and 'Select' with little binoculars beneath them."

"I see it."

"So just pull that down and type 'Am' in the search box."

"Son of a bitch. That's neat."

"What did it find?"

"Kramer. Liam. Quamber. Ramirez. Sam. William. Yoaman. A few more like that. But nothing that would shorten to Ambie."

"Damn it."

"I'm just the messenger here, Leland. Maybe Ambie was short for something else."

"Like what?"

"I don't know. Ammo. Amber. Ambient."

"I guess you're right." She would have to work on it later.

He swung around to face her. "Will there be anything else?"

"As a matter of fact."

"My turn: how did I know you were going to say that?" he said.

"I came to see you about Fida."

"What about him?"

"I can't find him."

"Can't find him? What's that mean?" Graeter asked.

"He's not in his room and not in the lab. Didn't respond to a page. Is there any place where he might not hear it?"

"No."

"If he was outside, though?"

"SORs require anyone going outside to carry a radio," Graeter said. "And a page would be broadcast over that. Maybe he's sound asleep."

"I knocked hard on his door."

"Wait one." Graeter had comms page Fida and direct him to call the station manager immediately. Nothing happened. He said, "Here's what I think. He's lying around somewhere stoned out of his gourd, listening to Ravi Shankar on headphones." He sighed, stood. "But let's have a look."

At Fida's door, Graeter knocked loud enough and long enough to bring the same irate woman out of her room.

"Help you?" Graeter said.

She glared, but closed her mouth and slipped back in.

Graeter took from his pocket a single key, attached by a small chain to a spent rifle cartridge. "GGM," he said.

"What's that?"

"The great grand master key. Opens every door in the station. There's only two. I have one and so does Merritt."

Inside, Graeter's nose wrinkled. "Been down here too long. This is what happens. People stop taking care of themselves."

"We talked yesterday," Hallie said. "He was aware of it."

"Being aware and doing something about it are two different things."

"So if he's not here, where would he be?" she asked.

"I can't think of a place where he wouldn't hear a page."

"The Underground?"

"PA system goes down there," Graeter said.

Old Pole? she thought, but she said nothing.

"Maybe he was out and didn't take a radio. Or didn't have it turned on."

Graeter shook his head. "First, SORs forbid egressing without a radio. Second, we're in Condition One. It's eighty-four below and blowing with whiteout. Nobody leaves the station."

"This morning it was seventy and calm."

"We're surrounded by thousands of miles of ice. Fronts zip in and out like hockey pucks. There's a saying: 'If you don't like the weather, wait a minute.'" Hallie had heard that about Alaska, too, and Colorado. But it was even more accurate here. "Why don't we check the lab again?" he said. "SORs forbid headphones for this very reason, but sometimes . . ." He shrugged.

Halfway to the door, Hallie had a thought. "Hold on a second." She moved the mouse of Fida's computer. The monitor, which had been in sleep mode, illuminated. "Look at this," she said. On the screen a document was open, with these words:

I AM JUST GOING OUTSIDE AND MAY BE SOME TIME.

"Oh God," she said, thinking, Why would he do that? Then she thought: He wouldn't. For a moment she felt torn loose from her surroundings, assailed by horror and fear, nauseated and dizzy. She reached for a wall to steady herself.

"What?" Graeter asked.

"I know that quote."

"Care to enlighten me?"

"Ever read about the Scott polar expedition?"

"I know they died coming back from the South Pole," he said.

"Four starving, frostbitten, and exhausted men, trapped in their tent by a storm. One, Oates, was in agony. Desperate for relief and to leave food for the others, he said those exact words and walked off into a blizzard. His body was never found."

"Son of a bitch. Fida took a penguin," Graeter said.

"What?"

"It's an expression. Sometimes a penguin will walk away from its flock, off into the wasteland," Graeter said. "Certain death. No one knows why they do it, but it's a documented phenomenon. People do, too. Less often, but it happens."

"He was clearly crisp," Hallie said. "But I didn't think he would do something crazy like this. What now?"

"We have to assume he's gone out," Graeter said.

"And?"

"There's a missing person protocol. Search inside and outside simultaneously, two different teams. I'll start the inside now."

Hallie headed down the hall. Graeter locked Fida's door and trotted after her. "Where are you going?" he asked.

"To get my ECW gear. I want to help search."

Graeter grabbed her elbow. "Negative. Nobody egresses in Condition One. That's the SOR."

She pulled free. "We need to search now."

"Not in Condition One."

"I won't stand by while a man might be out there freezing to death."

"That's not your decision to make."

"The hell it isn't." She walked away.

When she was out of hearing, he keyed his radio.

A few doors down, the angry woman stepped out of her room.

"Hey," she said.

"Hi." Hallie kept on going.

"*Wait* a sec. I'm sorry I was rude before. I want to talk to you."

Hallie stopped, turned. Over the woman's shoulder, she saw Graeter's back. He was still talking on his radio. "I'm sorry. There's something I have to do. It's really important." The woman didn't need to know that one of her close neighbors might have just committed suicide.

"I have something important, too." The woman's face was reddening. "It will just take a minute."

"Sorry. I'm in Room A-237. Come see me later." Hallie hurried on.

"Asshole," the woman called.

"Dr. Leland."

Hallie was almost to her room when someone spoke from behind. She turned and saw two big men approaching. One wore a Dragger's dirty Carhartt overalls and black boots. The other was tall and powerfully built, with a white lab coat on over jeans, a blue shirt, and a red sweater.

Dragger and Beaker, she thought. I wonder what brings these two together. But she had a pretty good idea.

"I'm Ben Lowry, biochemistry," the Beaker said. He was clean-shaven and had huge hands. She could see him as a forward for Duke or UNC. His voice was flat.

"Jake Grenier. Diesel mechanic," the Dragger said. Hallie recognized him.

"You were out on the ice. When Rockie's Cat went down."

"Yep. You did good out there, Doc."

"Thanks. What can I do for you, gentlemen?"

"Not make any trouble, would be a good start," Lowry said.

"Excuse me?"

"We'll be escortin' you to your room," Grenier said.

She took a step back, her face hardening, anger kindling. "I don't think so."

"Zack Graeter called," Lowry said, tapping the radio in his coat pocket. "We're on the station security team."

"It's for your own good, Doc," Grenier said, and she heard real concern in his voice. "You can't imagine what it's like out there right now. Flesh freezes solid in seconds. Cracks like glass if you tap it. You can frostbite your lungs. *Eyeballs* freeze, for Christ's sake."

"That's exactly why somebody has to go after Fida."

Grenier said, more gently, "Look, it warms up a little, I'll be the first on the ice with you. But nobody's goin' out now."

She must have looked unconvinced, because Lowry said, "I'm told you go on expeditions. Mountains and caves and such. Done a bit of that myself. Alps, Andes, some others. Cardinal rule: Don't make more victims. Am I right?"

He was correct, and she knew it. "Okay. What will happen when it warms up?"

"A Search and Rescue team's gonna be staged and ready to roll," Grenier said. "We plan and practice for this, Doc. Ain't a bunch of Boy Scouts fallin' over ourselves down here."

"After you," Lowry said politely. "We'll just see you to your room and leave it at that."

"How long do you intend to keep me confined here?"

"Until dinner hours in the galley, Zack Graeter said. Just enough for you to cool down, was the impression I got."

"How do you know I won't go out anyway? After you leave?"

"Because I'm going to ask you to give me your word of honor that you won't. Unless there's an emergency of some kind, of course. Otherwise, we'll have to post a Polie here, and that would be a shame because with wintcrover coming, we all have way too much to do." He put out his hand. "So: word of honor?"

She sighed, then shook.

35

"BRANK!" GUILLOTTE EXCLAIMED, WALKING INTO THE STATION'S grimy weight room. Though Guillotte's expression and tone were friendly, Brank took a step backward. He and Guillotte had not spoken since the incident in the dive shed. Guillotte came forward.

"I am sorry for what happened," Guillotte said. "We should not let Beakers get between us." He winked. "And besides, what is the harm in a little drink, right?" He took a flask out of his gym bag, uncapped it, drank, offered it to Brank.

"What is it?"

"Something special. You will like it."

Brank sipped, gingerly at first, then took a real swig. "Good shit," he said, licking his lips. "Where'd you get that?"

"Some friends in France make it special. I keep a supply."

Brank handed the flask back. He wore black sweatpants and a red tank top. A big man, six-two and 220, and strong, but a coat of bear-like fat covered his muscles.

"So," Guillotte said, extending a hand. "Put that behind us?"

Brank looked suspicious, but only for a second. He shook. "No problem, man. It's forgot."

"Do you mind if I work out some, too?"

"Hey, more the merrier," Brank said. He picked up fifty-pound dumbbells and started pumping out a set.

Guillotte pulled off his gray sweatshirt. Underneath, he was wearing a sleeveless black tank top that was stretched skin-tight over his torso. Brank glanced over, one lifter checking out another; then the two got down to work. Guillotte put on an old pair of fingerless gloves, started with push-ups and sit-ups and dips, then put four 45-pound plates on the bench-press bar, for a total weight of 225.

"Would you spot me for this? I am going up twenty pounds now."

"Yeah, sure." Brank was unable to contain a smirk at so little weight. He stood at the head of the bench and kept his hands several inches beneath the bar as Guillotte pushed it up off the rack, balanced it over his chest, and started his reps. After ten his arms started to shake and the bar's ascent slowed.

"C'mon, c'mon," Brank urged. "You got another one in there, *push it out!*"

Guillotte grunted and heaved and got the bar back in place on the uprights. He panted a few times, stood up, massaged his pecs and arms, got some water. Two minutes later he was ready again.

"Watch me close on these," Guillotte said. "I am feeling shaky."

"I got you," Brank said. "Go for it."

Guillotte managed nine, and half of the tenth. Brank had to help him get the bar back into place. Guillotte stood, red-faced, breathing hard. He patted his chest, grinned. "On fire here." Brank nodded. He did not seem impressed with the weight. "What are you putting up now?" Guillotte asked.

"Two sixty-five," Brank said.

"You shit me? No way. Two *sixty-five*?"

"Fuckin' A, man. Want to bet?"

Guillotte looked doubtful. "How much?"

"Shit, I don't care. Twenty bucks."

"Yes, I bet that. Go ahead. I spot."

Brank looked smug as he added twenty pounds to either end of the bar and locked down the collars. "Watch now, see how it's done. You got me?"

"I got you. Go for it."

Guillotte positioned himself at the head of the bench. Brank started to push the bar up off its rests, then stopped.

"Wait a second," Brank said. "How many reps?"

"What?"

"How many reps I got to do here?" ·

"Six."

Brank grinned. "Piece of cake." He got the bar up over his chest, lowered it, raised to full extension, and kept going. By the fourth rep his face was scarlet and he was holding his breath on the lifts, rather than exhaling. His whole body shook with the sixth rep's effort. Just before he set the bar back on its pegs, Guillotte said, "A hundred says you do not have one more in you."

Brank tried to look back at Guillotte. "Done," he gasped. He moved the bar over his chest and started lowering it. His face was the color of brick. Guillotte put his hands on top of Brank's.

"I got it," Brank said.

Guillotte pulled back, so that the bar was directly over Brank's face. He began to press down.

"*Don't!* What the fuck are you—" The bar touched the bridge of Brank's nose, and he stopped talking.

"*Frogman?*" Guillotte said. "You insult me, and my country? Big mistake, fat fuck." He pushed down again, but not very hard. Two hundred and sixty-five pounds did the work. There followed the brittle snaps of cracking bone and a very brief scream.

36

CAROL HAD BROUGHT COFFEE, COLD DRINKS, AND ROAST BEEF
sandwiches to Barnard's office. They drank the coffee, left the rest
alone. Barnard removed his pearl tie tack and handed it to Bowman,
who plugged its stem into a digital voice-stress analyzer the size of a
laptop computer.

"How does it work?" Barnard asked.

"The unstressed human voice produces sounds within a known
range, measured in hertz units. Deception causes involuntary sound
anomalies called Lippold tremors. Higher vocal frequencies, in lay
terms."

"And it can work from a recording?"

"Oh yes." Bowman opened a program, and two windows of equal
size, separated by a black horizontal line, appeared on the computer
screen. A thin orange line ran straight across the middle of the top
window's white background.

"That will show his voice as any audio recorder would," Bowman
explained.

The lower screen displayed a green line against a black background. Above and below the thin green line were red lines. "This is where we'll see evidence of the Lippold tremors. If the green response display passes beyond the red lines, there is deception."

Bowman fast-forwarded past Barnard's meeting with the young male assistant in the outer office.

"David Gerrin. So pleased to meet you."

"Donald Barnard. Thanks for seeing me, Dr. Gerrin."

"I am happy to."

"Look at that." Bowman paused the audio. The green line had swelled beyond both red lines. "He's not happy to see you at all."

"Doesn't mean much. He could be thinking about lunch or his mistress or any one of a thousand things I was keeping him from."

"Let's keep going." Bowman started the recording again.

"So, I saw your confusion and will explain. This name, David Gerrin, does not fit with my appearance. It is not the name I was born with. That one has so many syllables, even fellow Bangladeshis find it difficult."

"Good move."

"Would you like something to drink, Dr. Barnard?"

"No, I'm fine."

"So. You are the director of BARDA."

"Yes." Pause. "That's an interesting picture you have," Barnard said.

"The one over the credenza?"

"From Bangladesh?"

"The capital city, Dhaka. Where I grew up."

"Is it always like that? So many people, I mean? I don't see how traffic moves with them in the streets like that."

"It doesn't."

"Is that rush hour?"

Gerrin laughed. "That was ten in the morning of a Sunday. Think of Times Square at a rush hour that never ends. Dhaka is always that way."

"What was it like when you were growing up?"

"It was very bad. Not like now, of course. Now it is simply unimaginable. But bad enough, I can assure you."

"Have you been back? Recently, I mean," Barnard asked.

"I attended a U.N. conference there not long ago. But I know your time is valuable. We should discuss your reason for coming. Unfortunately, I was not able to obtain a copy of that report."

"Why would he lie there?" Barnard asked. Bowman stopped the recording.

"Either he didn't try, or he has it and doesn't want you to know."

"But why wouldn't he?"

"He's afraid you'll find something wrong with it."

"Goddamned right. Emily Durant was no drug user," Barnard snapped.

"Let's keep going." Bowman started the recording again.

"So you have no idea how she died?" Barnard asked Gerrin.

"None whatever."

"The New Zealanders wouldn't give you the report?"

"I did not make the inquiries myself. An assistant . . ."

"Look at that," Barnard said.

"All lies."

"But I can tell her to press on," Gerrin said.

"And another," Barnard said.

"Might I ask the reason for your interest?" Gerrin continued.

"Emily Durant worked for me at one time. I was shocked to learn of her death."

"Oh yes. I believe you did mention that," Gerrin said, but he sounded puzzled. "It was unexpected, indeed. Sadly, that happens not infrequently at the South Pole. Utterly inhospitable. Have you been?"

"Yes, once. You?"

"Oh no. I'm a warm-weather person."

"Did you know Emily?" Barnard asked.

"*Know* her? Personally, you mean? I'm afraid not. She was, well, you know—a researcher. But you did, apparently?"

"Yes," Barnard said.

"Why did she make the change from there to here?" Gerrin asked.

"There's very little churn at BARDA. Twenty years from now she might have found herself still a GS-13."

"Of course. Even scientists like money," Gerrin said.

"So you don't know how she died?"

"You asked me that a few moments ago."

"Did I? Sorry," Barnard said, and the screen showed the degree of that deception.

"Not to worry. But no, I have no idea how she died."

"Holy shit," Barnard blurted. "A *huge* lie."

"Shouldn't there have been an autopsy report by now?" Barnard asked Gerrin.

Audible sigh. "Everything goes through the New Zealand medical examiner's office, not famed for speed. Then to their police. Then to State. Then to us. Perhaps."

"The only thing slower than one bureaucracy is two," Barnard said.

"Well put," Gerrin laughed. "How does your scientist like it down there? Have you heard from him?"

Bowman stopped the audio. "What's he lying about there?"

"I don't know," Barnard said.

"Can't be the first question," Bowman said. "Has to be something in the second."

They both stared at the screen. Barnard spoke first: *"Him."*

"What?"

"He knows the replacement is a woman."

"Why would he lie about that?" Bowman asked.

"He doesn't want us to know that he knows the replacement is a woman. Goddamn, Wil. What the hell is going on here?"

Bowman hit Play.

"Her. Hallie Leland," Barnard said to Gerrin. "Does the name ring a bell?"

"No. Not even a tinkle."

"One of the biggest lies yet," Barnard said.

"Have you heard from her?" Gerrin asked.

"No. Have you had *any* word from down there?"

"Not for several days. NASA preempted a lot of satellite time. And there have been solar disturbances."

"So that's the truth, at least," Bowman said.

"Do you know what Emily Durant was working on?" Barnard asked.

"Specifically? Not off the top of my head."

"Look at that. Amazing," Barnard said.

"Ha, ha. I love that expression," Gerrin joked. " 'Off the top of my head.' Where on earth do you suppose it came from?"

"I'm sure Google could tell you in a flash." Irritation was audible in Barnard's voice.

"I could have one of my people look into the details of Dr. Durant's research."

"Son of a bitch," Barnard said to Bowman. "He had no intention of doing that."

"Could I ask for one other favor?" Barnard said to Gerrin. "When you do learn more about Emily's death, could you read me in?"

"The moment I know something, your phone will ring."

"Nor that," Bowman said.

Several minutes of small talk.

Sounds of bodies moving.

"It was nice to meet you, Dr. Barnard," Gerrin said.

"Even that was a lie," Barnard said. "Asshole."

Bowman turned off the machine. Neither man spoke for some time. Then Barnard said, "Why would he tell so many lies?"

"Why would he pretend not to know the replacement was a woman?" Bowman asked. "And deny knowing her name?"

"He lied when I asked if he knew how Emily died," Barnard said. "So he must know what happened to her."

"What else?" Bowman asked.

"He lied when I asked if he knew her. So he did know her."

"Yes. And he knew the replacement was a woman."

"And he knew her name."

Barnard had been hungry before. Now he looked at the plate of sandwiches. His appetite had disappeared.

"Why in hell would he lie about *that*?" Bowman said.

Again neither man spoke. Bowman picked up one of the roast beef sandwiches Carol had brought. Thick whole wheat bread, crisp lettuce, slices of tomato and Bermuda onion, Dijon mustard. All the sandwiches were overstuffed with rare, red beef. As Bowman held the one he had taken, blood dripped onto the coffee table. He put the sandwich back and sat there staring at the red drops. He took one of the white cloth napkins Carol had brought and wiped up the blood. His expression changed. He looked up at Barnard.

"This is not about the science."

"What do you mean? They told our director that it was a critically important research project."

"It's not about the research."

"What then?"

"They didn't care about research. It's not about the science. It's about the replacement. This is all about Hallie Leland."

37

LOWRY AND GRENIER HAD SEEN HALLIE TO HER ROOM SHORTLY
after two P.M., which left three hours until dinner in the galley. She lay
awake for two, dozed briefly, woke again. She swung down from the
bunk, booted up the station computer, and checked for email. Nothing.

A knock. Agnes Merritt.

"How did you know?" Hallie asked.

"My business to know. For the record, I gave Graeter hell. He
claimed it's for your own good. Bulldoo, but he's in command. Tell
me about Fido."

Hallie described her meeting with him the previous day. Then:
"He told you about Vishnu. Why didn't you tell me?"

She had thought Merritt might look uncomfortable. Not one bit.
More like bemused. "I wasn't trying to hide anything. Remember I
said to talk to Fido about the research? I knew he'd get it right."

Reasonable, Hallie thought. "What about Graeter?"

Merritt shrugged. "He's with NASI. That's part of GENERCO.
Oil is what they do."

"So they might be afraid of something like Vishnu."

"Conceivably."

"Fida thought Graeter might have killed Emily."

Merritt looked skeptical. "Graeter's bitter and angry. Hates women, for sure. But killing Emily? I don't know." Her tone and expression said she could not completely discard the possibility, either.

"Did anything change after you told him about Vishnu?" Hallie asked.

"He got friendlier, now that you mention it. That did strike me as odd at the time. Now I'm thinking he might have been trying to divert attention. A smoke screen." She shook her head. "This is crazy. But telegraphing intentions is the last thing a killer would do."

"So you do think he could have killed Emily? Because of Vishnu?" She felt something move down in her belly. Not a pain, exactly. More like pressure. She thought of Diana Montalban. "And might be involved in Fida's disappearance."

"I can't believe we're even talking this way."

"I'll take that for a yes."

"A maybe."

"Can you communicate with NSF?"

"Not until comms are back up."

"Do you have a secure line?"

"You mean like CIA spook stuff? It's hard enough getting hamburgers and gasoline at Pole."

"Can't go out because it's Condition One. Can't fly. No phone or email. Aren't people talking about these deaths?"

"Of course. Graeter's dog-and-pony show in the galley didn't help. Might have made things worse. A good many people think he's covering something up."

"I got some very dirty looks in the hall earlier. They must really believe I brought a pathogen in."

"Some definitely do. Not sure how many."

Hallie's gut spasmed suddenly, like a fist clenching, then released. She remembered Diana Montalban bleeding to death on the floor of the galley. Another spasm, this one bad enough to make her wince and grunt.

"What's wrong?" Merritt asked.

She needed to keep going. "Just a cramp. So about Graeter . . . ?"

"Nothing to do until comms are up."

"Any idea when flights might start again?"

"The cutoff is sixty and ten. We're about twenty degrees away from that now. I hate to even think this, but winterover might have come early this year."

"And winterover lasts eight months, right?"

"Yes."

She thought about eight months trapped in the most escape-proof prison on earth with Polies dropping dead, going crazy, boozing and drugging, maybe killing one another, and possibly with some deadly pathogen floating around the hermetically sealed station.

In for a penny . . . "Agnes, do you know anything about triage?"

A frown, then a split second of hesitation, both of which could have been evidence of a struggle to remember some long-forgotten fact. Or of something else. "It's an emergency medical technique. Sorts out who gets treated when. Or not at all. Why do you ask?"

"I was just curious. Maynard Blaine mentioned something about triage when we were having coffee." That, of course, was a lie, but detectives told lies to get at the truth, didn't they? "He sounded pretty excited about it. Before I could ask him anything, he was paged and had to rush off."

"Blaine told you that? When?"

"Yesterday. He just wandered over and sat down. You know how he is." She gave a sly wink, and just then something serious happened in her lower regions.

"I have no idea what he was talking about." Merritt looked confused, and very displeased.

"Could it be the name of a research project?"

"No. I would know if that were the case."

The conversation had dead-ended. "It was really nice of you to come all the way down here, Aggie."

"Got to watch out for my Beakers." Merritt glanced at her watch, stood. "Five o'clock. You should be out soon. I'll probably see you at dinner."

Merritt left. Hallie waited a minute to let her clear the corridor. She had given Lowry and Grenier her word, but this qualified as an emergency if anything ever did. She stood, gasped, and sprinted for the women's room.

38

THE ONLY BENEFIT FROM A POLARRHEA ATTACK WAS THE AMPLE
time for contemplation it afforded while working itself out. She was
still carrying around a secret that, she felt even more sure now, could
get her killed. With Fida gone, she was back where she had started,
unable to trust anybody, not one person.

Certainly not Blaine. He had lied to her about Emily, and that was
the first strange thing about a visit that had kept getting stranger from
that moment on. Why would he do that? Only one reason that Hallie
could think of: he had some connection to Emily's death. Stranger
things had happened. She knew about John Wayne Gacy and Ted
Bundy and all the charming psychopaths who seemed like perfect
neighbors while they were torturing and butchering and eating their
victims. But Maynard Blaine? He struck her more as a clumsy
Lothario than a sadistic murderer.

What about Graeter? Earlier, she would have put him close to the
top of a suspect list. But then he had agreed to look through the personnel roster. Still, he might have known that no men at the station
had names beginning with "Am." She hadn't been able to see the
computer screen, so he might have lied about it, too. But she really

didn't think so. She had seen flashes of humanity there. He was hiding from something, which Hallie thought was probably guilt over the sailors' deaths. And though he despised the philandering ex, he might feel guilty for that as well—a husband who'd left his wife stranded and increasingly desperate.

What about Brank? A definite possibility. And so many other men that she did not even know. In the end, she found herself asking this question: *Who do you trust when you can't trust anybody?* The answer came quickly: *Not who. What.* And the what was science. You could always trust the science.

She was about to finish up when the door swung open and two women entered. They settled into adjoining stalls.

"So what do you think?" one said. Her voice was so rough it could have been a man's. Pole throat.

"I think it's her." That voice was more normal.

"Me, too."

"Question is what to do about it."

"That is the question. But you know what?" man voice asked.

"What?"

"There's a lot of answers to that question in a place like this."

"Y'all talkin' 'bout that new Beaker?" Hallie roughened her own voice, exaggerated the southern accent. Probably not necessary, since she hadn't spoken with these women before. Better safe than screwed, though.

"Who's that? I didn't know anyone else was here."

"No worries—it's me, Braden. Fuckin' Polarrhea. Y'all think she's carryin' some kinda germ?"

"Facts is facts. She comes in, women start dying." Man voice sounded angry and afraid.

"She'll be flyin' out Saturday though, right?"

"If planes fly. Tell you this: no fucking way I'm winterin' over with a killer germbag. Not just me, neither. She'll go out, one way or another."

"Who'd you say that is over there?" the other woman asked.

But Hallie had already finished and slipped through the door.

———

She was still technically under house arrest, or whatever they called it here. She hoped that Graeter had not made any general announcement about her confinement. If he hadn't, the only people who would know she wasn't supposed to be wandering around were Graeter, Grenier, Lowry, and Merritt. She would risk running into them. What could they do, anyway, other than put her back in her room? It did not feel good to break her word, but she rationalized that another, much bigger emergency requiring her attention trumped that. Graeter might be in denial, but something very bad was happening in this sealed-off, isolated pressure cooker they called the station.

Back in her room she pulled on a heavy fleece sweater and a parka. She stuffed a wool cap, gloves, spare dive knife, and headlamp into various pockets. She went down to the lab to gather certain items and moved on, still getting used to walking in a bubble of light. She passed a woman who didn't even look up, then a man who was texting. He gave her only a quick glance. She could not keep from looking back at them after they passed, and doing the same thing more often as she walked.

At the air-lock doors to the Underground, she made one last check, saw no other light pods coming behind, and pushed through, sure that she was alone and had made the trip unobserved.

39

IN THE UNDERGROUND'S MAIN CORRIDOR, SHE TRIED EDGING ALONG flat against one ice wall, hoping she might avoid triggering the lights, but they came on anyway. Nothing she could do about it, so she moved as quickly as she could to get away from the entrance.

This would have to be done fast, and not only to avoid detection. She had not wanted to risk going all the way to the ECW room at the station's other end. Stepping from fifty-four degrees in the station to sixty below in the Underground almost took her breath away, but now she knew enough not to gasp.

Dive knife in hand, she slipped down the main corridor, praying that she could remember the route Graeter had taken when he'd escorted her around down here. The first right turn was easy, then down a secondary corridor about twenty yards, not worrying about lights now, past one corridor on the left and into the second. A long way along that one, then down a narrower passage, then around the heavy black curtain.

Once in, she switched on her headlamp and unzipped a body bag. Harriet Lanahan still had on the clothes she'd died in. Blood had frozen into a thick, red carapace on her chest. Her face looked like white wax. There was no frost on her—the humidity was too low for that. Hallie was thankful that someone had closed her eyes.

She had never feared dead bodies, even badly damaged ones. But these bodies were different. They evoked a childhood terror from some very deep place, unspeakable, nearly irresistible—a fear that these bodies might rise and take her back to their own realm. It was hard not to jump and run.

She put on the surgical mask and gloves she had taken from the lab, removed from her pockets plastic bags and oronasal swabs. She inserted one swab deep into Lanahan's right nostril, past the turbinates and up into the ethmoid sinuses, until she felt hard resistance. She rotated the swab shaft between shaking fingers, then carefully withdrew and bagged it. She repeated the process in Lanahan's left nostril, then took samples from Montalban and Bacon. The nasal blood was frozen, but she was hoping that the bodies had not been here long enough for the cold to have killed all of the pathogens present. Looking down at the three dead women, she said, "I'm sorry I had to do that. But I think you would have wanted me to. Thank you all."

She closed up the bags and left the morgue, felt her fear slipping away. By then she was shivering so hard she had to clamp her jaw shut. How ironic it would be, she thought, to survive the cryopeg only to freeze here.

On the way in, she had used the dive knife to scratch a small arrow at every corner where she'd needed to turn. In less than five minutes she was standing in front of the air-lock doors.

The lab where Emily and Fida had worked was on Level 1, Pod A, behind the air-lock door with the warning sign. It was kept locked, but Merritt had given her a key when they first met. Hallie had seen dozens of microbiology labs just like it, except most were bigger. Rows of white wall cabinets, two stainless steel sinks, a workbench with a ventilator hood. On a central bench rested an autoclave, a

centrifuge, microscopes, racks of test tubes, Bunsen burners, dessica-
tors, incubator cabinets.

In the time it had taken her to reach the lab, her body heat had
begun to soften the tiny red ice clusters on the swabs. She set out six
petri dishes with red agar growth medium and used a sterile wire inoculating loop to transfer matter from the cotton-tipped sticks, swiping them back and forth in three separate sections on the surface of
each dish. "Making a lawn," it was called.

Since she wasn't sure what she was trying to grow, she didn't know
the optimal incubation temperature. Many pathogenic bacteria liked
eighty-six degrees Fahrenheit, so she set the lab incubator for that
and waited for it to warm up.

Nothing would happen right away. Bacteria typically took from
twenty-four to seventy-two hours to colonize growth media. Hope-
fully any pathogen in the blood samples would be a fast grower. She
walked down to the far end of the lab to examine the Vishnu sample
she had retrieved. It rested in a thirty-gallon tank full of cryopeg
water that Guillotte had collected while she was diving. The tank itself resided in a chest freezer, the only way to keep the water as cold
as it had been in the cryopeg. Nothing about the organism had
changed, which she took as a good sign.

At the door, with her hand on the light switch, she paused, then
decided to double-check the incubator temperature setting. As tired
and brain-weak as she was, it would have been easy to get it wrong.

She peered through the glass window.

"*Damn!*" She actually jumped back a step.

Stripes like bright yellow pencil lines had appeared on the red agar
in all the dishes.

By the time she finished in the lab, it was okay for her to be seen
walking around. Hallie came to the place where the corridors di-
verged. One led to Merritt's office, the other to Graeter's. Merritt or
Graeter? She stopped, leaned against a wall, waited out a dizzy spell.

Merritt had been right: it was getting worse. On top of everything else, her throat was sore, and not just from the first day's frostbite; the discomfort felt deeper and more painful, like the onset of a strep infection.

Where had she been going? It took her several seconds to remember. She looked both ways down the intersecting corridor. Left would take her toward Merritt's office. Right to Graeter's.

40

She went to the comms office and asked. "He's out on the iceway," the comms operator said. "Some landing lights are out."

"I thought it was Condition One."

"Yeah. But planes won't land without those lights working right. Gotta be ready for them."

"Did he take someone with him?"

"Nope."

"When will he be back?"

"Couple hours, I expect."

"As soon as he gets in, will you tell him to call me, please? It's important."

"Sure will, Doc." All Draggers called all Beakers "Doc," she had learned.

"Thanks."

"Um, ma'am?" He looked at the comms office door, then back to her. His face was partially hidden by his long, lank brown hair and the requisite Pole beard. But underneath all the hair she saw that he was very young. He had large, fanlike ears, bulb cheeks with blemishes, a receding chin, and a squashed-looking nose. And fear in his eyes. "Can I ask you something?"

"Sure."

"These women that died?"

"Yes."

"What do *you* think happened?"

"Rockie Bacon was sick and had a bad accident. I don't know about Harriet Lanahan or Diana Montalban."

He paused, looked uncertain, then went on: "You think there's something down here? Some germ?"

Reassuring lie or frightening truth? She decided on a little of both. "I don't know that. But I do know that only women have died."

He lowered his voice. "People are saying you brought something."

"Is that what you think?"

"Don't make much sense to me."

"No. Why not?"

"*You* aren't dead."

"There is that."

"Tell you one thing. This is my first tour at Pole. And my last."

"Can't say I blame you."

"Ask you something else?"

"Sure."

"Doc Fida took a penguin?"

"It's what they're saying."

"You don't think so?"

"I didn't know him well," she said.

"*I* knew Doc Fida."

"You don't use his Pole name?"

"He didn't like it. I could relate. One they gave me? Neuman. As in, Alfred E."

Hallie understood. Beautiful people sought their kind. So did those at the other end of that spectrum.

"He was a little weird. *Everybody* gets a little weird down here. But him just up and taking a penguin? Doesn't compute for me."

"You know what? Me neither."

He seemed relieved to hear that he was not the only one.

"Good talking with you," Hallie said.

"You, too."

She started away. His voice stopped her. "Hey, Doc?"

"Yes?"

"Strange people down here. A lot of 'em are scared shitless. Do well to watch your back."

41

THE ALTITUDE, DRYNESS, AND POLARRHEA HAD LEFT HER DEHY-
drated. She had no appetite for solid food, but she needed liquid:
juice, water, coffee—well, maybe not coffee just yet. She headed for
the galley, thinking that she had not had such an unbroken run of bad
luck for as long as she could remember. She was still thinking that
when she came off the serving line with two big glasses of apple juice
and her luck suddenly changed. Maynard Blaine was alone at a corner table, twirling spaghetti around a fork. She sat across from him.

"Aren't you supposed to be locked up or something?" he said.

"It's prime dinner time. Why aren't there any people here?"

"They're afraid. Don't want to be with other people." He forked
up a ball of spaghetti dripping with marinara sauce. "Especially not
with you. I heard Graeter put you under house arrest. How come
you're out?"

"How come *you're* here, Maynard?"

He shrugged. "I hate my goddamned room."

"No, I mean, how come you're still sitting here with me?"

"I think it's probably bullshit, what they're saying."

"That I brought in some exotic germ?"

"Yes." He stopped twirling spaghetti, looked more closely at her. "Maybe I was wrong, though. You don't look so good."

"Aw, well, thanks for the compliment, Embie."

He looked as if she had slapped him.

Polarrhea had turned out to be productive in more ways than one. Maybe there really was something to high colonics, after all, she thought. Ambie wasn't short for a name beginning with "A-M." Emily's Georgia accent had made it sound that way on the video log. She had been saying "Embie." Short for M.B. And those were the initials of Maynard Blaine.

"What did you call me?"

She leaned forward, lowered her voice. Not really necessary, because only one other table was occupied, and that man was well out of hearing. But she wanted to make an impression. So she hissed just one word:

"Triage."

He rose too quickly and spilled spaghetti sauce on his shirt. He stood there, staring down at the bright red blotches, seeming to have forgotten all about her.

"Sit *down*," she snapped. "We can do this right here, just the two of us, or with Graeter."

He sat.

The fury she had been holding in made her voice shake. "You told me you barely knew Emily. I know you were sleeping with her. Why did you lie?"

He glanced around, leaned forward. "Please lower your voice."

"It is low. But it's about to get louder. Talk to me."

"Would you want to be known as the jilted boyfriend of a scientist who died under suspicious circumstances?"

She sat back. That was reasonable. Why hadn't she thought of that? Pole brain. But too soon to let it go. "Other people must have known about the two of you, though."

"We were discreet. Rarely ate together, no public displays of affection, all very professional."

"Why?"

"I didn't care one way or the other. She wanted it that way."

"Do you know why?"

"She was afraid if word got around, it could hurt her chances for more grants."

"Who would have cared?"

"Graeter and Merritt both file performance reports on everybody here. In case you haven't noticed, women are not his favorite people. Women who sleep around are beneath the bottom of his shit list. She thought he would ding her big-time for it."

"Do you know anything about Vishnu?"

"Yeah. It was the stuff Emily found in the cryopeg."

"What did she tell you about it?"

"Not much. Ate carbon dioxide like a champ, I think. What's that got to do with anything?"

"Talk to me about Triage," she said.

Hallie had read the expression "the blood drained from his face," but she had never actually seen it happen. His mouth opened halfway, but nothing came out. Finally, not looking at her, he said, "About what?"

"I'll be back with Graeter, Embie." She stood up.

"Please don't call me that. And sit down. *Please*," he whispered.

"The last time."

"It could be the end of my career if it goes farther than this table."

"Could be the end of more than that if you're involved with Em's death."

She had to lean forward to hear. "I'm engineering a new virus that can immobilize enemy combatants without killing them. 'Humane warfighting' is what it's called."

"By whom?"

"The project originators."

"You'll have to do better than that."

"You know how picornaviruses have those really long, multifunctional, untranslated region fives? My work focuses on a ribosome entry source in one of those regions that's very susceptible to protease manipulation. I want to stimulate the protein synthesis in infected cells, which should increase their pathogenicity and give it a neuro-logical affinity."

"Why in God's name would you be doing that at the South Pole?"

"There's no place for it to go."

"To go? You mean, if there's a breach?"

"Yes."

"So you're using the whole station as one big BSL-4 containment lab."

"Jesus, no. I told you that before. My lab is biosecure. And Triage isn't supposed to kill people, anyway. Just immobilize them."

"Isn't supposed to. But you're not sure about that, or you wouldn't be working down here. You just told me that."

He didn't agree, but neither did he deny it. Hallie's stomach clenched again. The churning and rumbling in her gut was clearly audible.

"Polarrhea," Blaine said. "Lucky you."

"Is there any chance your pathogen could have breached containment and killed those women?"

"No way in hell."

"How much experience do you have working with Level Three and Four pathogens?"

"Enough. Or I wouldn't have been picked for this project."

"What's the first step in donning a Chemturion BSL-4 biosafety suit?"

"Take a piss."

That was right. "Who's running this operation?"

"NSF."

She was about to laugh in his face, but then she remembered what Fida had said about NSF's national security origin.

"I know it sounds crazy," he protested, trying to regain some composure and control. "But there it is." He shrugged. "How did you find out?"

"Believe in ghosts?"

"What? No."

"You should. Emily told me everything."

"Bullshit."

"Like how you mixed Stoli and beer and Ecstasy at the New Year's Eve party. Got drunk and high and babbled on about things you shouldn't have. And like how she dumped you, but you kept hanging around, stalking her. I could go on."

He stared, speechless.

"Let me ask you something else. And keep in mind that I might already know the answer to this question. Just seeing how many lies you're telling. What did you dress up as for January's Thing Night?"

"A Walking Dead."

She waited, holding his eyes.

"Really. I swear. A zombie."

"Can anybody verify that?"

"I don't know. The costume was really good. Part of it was a rubber mask over a lot of my face."

"Do you work with a partner?"

"In the lab? No. Security."

"Have you ever been down into Old Pole?"

He looked at her like the Pole might already be depriving her of certain faculties. But when he spoke, he sounded hugely relieved to be talking about something other than Triage. "Yes."

"Tell me about it."

"What does that have to do with anything?"

"Humor me."

"Creepiest place you could possibly imagine. Like something straight out of the old Thing movie. The walls and ceilings are collapsing. Everything is fifty years old. Stinks. No lights. It's like a labyrinth. You can get good and lost down there."

Sounds just like a cave, she thought. She loved caves. "If it's so bad, why go there?"

"There's old booze, for one thing, stashed in odd places. But mainly, it's fucking *different*. You can't imagine what it's like after you've been here eight or nine months. Your mind shrivels up. Day after day, nothing changes. Old Pole is new, odd as that sounds. Different. Scary. You go down there to make sure you're still alive."

"Even though you could get killed."

"That's maybe the point, I think."

"How do you get down there? Through the Underground?"

"Not anymore. There was a tunnel, but Graeter found out about it and had it blocked."

"So?"

"There's an equipment shed a quarter mile from the station. Off to the right, about a forty-five-degree angle from the main entrance. The shaft is behind, out of sight of the station. There's a plywood cover and snow on top of that. Why do you want to know? Are you thinking of going down there?"

She recoiled. "God, no. You couldn't drag me down to a place like that. No way in hell. I was just curious. The way people talk . . ." Her stomach moved again, a feeling of viscous churning.

Blaine heard it, said, "You'd better hurry. That stuff can be explosive."

"I learned that." She stood. "We're not done. Be here when I get back."

She pointed at his shirt. "That looks like blood."

She left him scrubbing the red spots furiously with a handful of napkins.

42

"WE NEED TO TALK TO GERRIN," BLAINE SAID. HE HAD COME
straight to Merritt's office after being grilled by Hallie. She had called
Doc and Guillotte, who were on their way.

"The non-gov sat link they use is supposed to be secure. But every
call is like a submarine's periscope going up."

"She *knows,* goddamnit," Blaine said.

"She knows something. I'm not sure how much."

"She asked me straight out about Triage. You said she asked you,
too."

"You fed her the story Gerrin gave and we all rehearsed. That was
good. I pretended ignorance. She believed me. Do you think she believed you?"

"Not really." He hesitated. "I don't know. Maybe. Did you hear
about Brank? It had to be goddamned Guillotte. The last thing we
needed was another death."

"He has his uses, you have to admit."

"I've never liked Guillotte. There's something wrong with him."

"He's French," Merritt said. "There's something wrong with all of
them."

"No. He's a psychopath. There's something wrong with all of *them*."

"*Stop* that," Merritt said. "It makes you look like an old woman."

"What?"

"Wringing your hands."

He looked down. "Didn't realize I was doing it."

A knock on the door. Guillotte and Doc came in. Blaine related the conversation with Hallie Leland. Merritt told them about her own.

"Maynard thinks we should call Gerrin. I'm on the fence. Let's hear your thoughts."

"Do it," Doc said, his voice unsteady. "Damn the risk. It feels like things are starting to—"

"Will you take those goddamned glasses off?" Blaine interrupted. "This is a serious discussion."

"It hurts my eyes," Doc said. "You know that."

"Stop it," Merritt said.

"Leland may not know everything," Blaine said. "But she knows enough to suspect that there's a lot more. And she doesn't strike me as the type who gives up easily."

"No," Merritt said. "She isn't. But Maynard, Gerrin will want to know what went wrong. It will be his first question."

"The answer is that nothing went wrong." Blaine's voice got louder. "I engineered a picornavirus that carries a strep bacterium payload. Not a big deal, actually. The *real* challenge was genetically engineering the streptococcus strain to have affinity for ovarian cells."

"He's not going to care about that," Doc said. "He will want to know why three women died here after I swabbed their throats and drew blood with contaminated instruments. *I* want to know that myself."

"Keep your voices down, both of you," Merritt said.

"You know what he is going to think, Maynard," Guillotte said. "That you fucked up the genetics."

"Something else killed those women, I tell you," Blaine protested. But it was too quick and too loud.

"I hope you can do better than that for Gerrin," Guillotte said.

"Do you want to know something? That man scares me. *Me*. There is something in him. A huge anger. Like a grenade about to explode."

"Do you think we should call, Rémy?" Merritt asked.

He shrugged, appearing more concerned about a hangnail. "Call, do not call, makes no difference to me either way. But here is something else. I followed Leland down to the morgue a little while ago."

"What?" Merritt snapped. "Why? What did she do?"

"I am not sure. There is a heavy curtain. I did not want her to know I was there."

She looked at each of them in turn. "That's it, then. We call. What is wrong with that woman?"

"There are some people who cannot help themselves," Guillotte said.

"From doing what?" Blaine asked.

"The right thing." Guillotte shook his head.

"I'll make the call later tonight," Merritt said. To Guillotte: "How much longer can you keep comms interdicted?"

"Four hours. Eight, at most. Even these engineers here will figure a work-around at some point."

"This was never about killing women," Doc said. He was hugging himself.

"We need to kill *her*," Guillotte said, finally pulling the hangnail out with his teeth. He didn't wince. Blood oozed from beneath his fingernail.

"That's Gerrin's decision," Merritt said. No one spoke after that.

Guillotte left first, with Doc right behind him. Before Blaine made it through the door, Merritt said, "Maynard, stay here for a bit. There's something I'd like you to do."

43

AFTER ANOTHER LONG MEDITATION IN THE WOMEN'S ROOM, HALLIE hurried back to her own. There were things she needed to do: talk to Graeter, check the cultures, look in on Vishnu, try to get a couple of emails out. She started on an email but fell asleep in the middle of writing it. She was still sitting there, arms folded on the keyboard, head on her arms, when someone started hitting her on the head. She woke and realized that there was indeed hammering, but on the room door rather than her. Then a shout, louder than the hammering:

"It's Graeter. Answer the door!"

"Coming!"

"Weather's eased," he said when she opened the door. "We're going out to look for Fida. I thought you'd want to come." He started away, said over his shoulder, "Meet me in front of the station in twenty."

"What day is this?"

She expected a strange look, but he must have been accustomed to such questions from Polies. "Wednesday. Little after ten." He turned to go.

"Mr. Graeter—wait."

Before she had gone to sleep, there had been something she'd wanted to tell Graeter. Maybe quite a few somethings. She fought to pull the things up from memory. Got one of them. "I need to show you something in the—"

"Not now. The goddamned pope could be coming in and he'd have to wait. Search and Rescue takes priority over everything."

Thirty minutes later, Hallie stood beside Graeter's yellow snowmo. She had brought her Leatherman tool, which had all kinds of uses. Left the dive knife behind this time. Around them, operators sat astride six other growling machines, their headlight beams streaking the solid dark. Shimmering green and purple lights flowed across the sky.

"I know how to drive a snowmobile. Another machine would increase the probability of finding him," she said.

He appeared to give that some thought. "Not a bad idea, but SORs say no. Hop on."

He checked the emergency box contents, then sat in front of her, pumped his raised fist twice, and snowmo engines screamed as operators fanned out in all directions. Leaving the station, he had explained the protocol: "For a Search and Rescue like this, the station is divided into grids assigned to specific team members. We do regular SAR drills, so a searcher gets to know his grid like a good cop on the beat. That's the theory, anyway."

Hallie wore full ECW gear, including a face mask, and Graeter's body in front of her on the snowmobile broke the wind, but she felt the cold seeping in anyway, despite the fact that it was "just" seventy-two degrees below zero. She hesitated to think what the windchill factor was on a snowmo going thirty miles an hour.

As SAR leader, Graeter had no assigned grid. He parked at the end of the iceway, where they could see most of the station and the surrounding area. For an hour they watched the snowmobiles' headlight beams slashing the dark, stopping, flashing off as team members searched buildings and open spaces. One after another, they began radioing back reports: "Block B2 complete. Nothing found." When the last transmission ended, Graeter said, "God damn" and walked away, his back to Hallie and the station.

"Mr. Graeter." She started after him, caught up, touched his shoulder. He turned. She could see only his eyes. Long experience underwater had taught her that eyes were not just windows on the soul. They were remarkably reliable indicators of a person's mental state. They showed panic even before a victim knew it was coming, and when that happened they looked like thin glass pushed out of shape by a strong wind. Graeter's didn't look like that. Instead, they looked immeasurably sad.

"Drive that thing back. I need some time," Graeter said.

"Sure."

But she didn't leave immediately. She sat on the snowmo, watching him, the phrase "taking a penguin" echoing in her mind. Graeter stood there, staring out into the wasteland, for a long time, then headed back toward her. She had been trying to decide what to tell him about first, Emily's murder, or the bacteria cultures, or Maynard's confession. About halfway back, he caught a boot toe on a sastrugi ridge and stumbled, surprising her because until then he had been sure-footed and agile. Seeing it, she thought that the other things could wait. There was enough to deal with here. Neither Maynard nor the bacteria were going anywhere, after all.

He stood beside the snowmo, still looking out and away.

"Go ahead, take it back," he said. "I'll walk to the station."

She stood, nearly as tall as he, and looked him in the eye. "You were not responsible for Fida's death—if he is dead. Nor Emily's, nor the other three. There might have been more, if not for you and your SORs."

When he answered, his voice had less rasp than she had yet heard.

"*Everything* here is my responsibility, Leland. Every leaking pipe, rusting beam, fuel shortage, sore throat, plugged toilet, broken light, flat tire, power outage. When I go to sleep at night, I hear old faucets dripping and sad people crying." The words came faster and faster until they just stopped, and Hallie understood that such things and a thousand others must have gnawed at Graeter's brain every waking minute and invaded his sleep as well. It was the first time she had seen them take over and come flying out, but now he regained control.

He raised a hand, possibly intending to touch her shoulder. She might have flinched, or he might have thought better of it. The hand dropped.

"Go ahead and take that thing back," he said. "I'll be all right."

44

"DAVID, IT MUST BE UNGODLY EARLY THERE IN D.C.," IAN KENDALL
said.

"A little after midnight." Gerrin was sitting at the desk in the study
of his modest home in the Virginia suburb called Vienna. He lived
alone, had never married—had not avoided women, just the entan-
glements of matrimony. He was looking at Kendall and Belleveau's
video-call images.

"Shortly past nine-thirty in the morning in New Delhi," Jean-
Claude Belleveau said. "This must be important."

"There are complications." Gerrin described the deaths of Lanahan, Montalban, and Bacon. Merritt had told him about Leland, as
well, but he didn't mention that part of their problem.

"Is there reason to believe they were related to Triage?" Kendall
asked.

"It can't be ruled out," Gerrin said.

"This is not good," Kendall said. "How long before winterover
flyout?"

"Tomorrow," Gerrin said. "If the temperature allows."

"God in heaven," Belleveau said. "What does Orson think about the deaths?"

Gerrin sighed. "He is afraid. And that makes me afraid. I have worried about him from the beginning."

"It was not easy finding a physician sympathetic to our cause and willing to spend a year at the South Pole," Belleveau said.

"He might well be afraid," Kendall said. "It was his swabs and needles did the work, didn't they?"

Belleveau said something in French. Then, in English: "How *could* this have happened?"

"Conjoining picornavirus and streptococcus was not child's play, Jean-Claude," Gerrin said.

Kendall waved a hand dismissively. Like most Englishmen, he was slow to anger, but once aroused, his temper was fierce. The glow was beginning. "Please, David. Joining bacteria and viruses is nothing new. Fischetti and Schuch discovered new symbiotic relationships between *B. anthracis* and viruses back in 2009. Even before that, Chisholm and Zeng at MIT figured out that viruses were manipulating genes in both *Synechococcus* and *Prochlorococcus* for their own benefit. Conjoining was not the challenge here. It was altering strep's genetic sequencing to produce ovarian-cell affinity. If Blaine bollixed that and those bacteria are attacking other cell types . . ." He shook his head, unable to find a term of adequate gravity.

"Blaine knows his work," Gerrin said.

"Victor Frankenstein thought he did, too," Belleveau put in. "Trite to say, but true nonetheless."

"David, we are talking about three dead women." Kendall sounded more disturbed with each sentence.

"Four, actually," Belleveau pointed out.

"Of course you're right," Kendall said. "But the first wasn't from Triage. What else do we know?"

"Morbell says that two women exsanguinated. The third suffered some kind of allergic reaction that closed her airway."

"What about the people at the station? What are they saying?"

"He told them that one woman's death was almost certainly a result of throat surgery. Another had had a difficult cesarean delivery. The third, he's supposed to be running tests on her blood to detect allergies."

"Killing was never part of our plan. *Never.*" Kendall's face was red.

"None of the mice died," Gerrin said. "Nor any of the dogs or cats or chimps, I remind you." He paused, held up his hand, let seconds pass. "My friends, we have seen the future. In my country alone, every year half a million children under the age of five starve to death. Stop and really think about that. *Starve. To. Death.* We witnessed dogs eating corpses in Lagos, and we know people are eating them there and elsewhere. Fifty years from now, or likely sooner, the earth's population will exceed fifteen billion. Those estimates of nine billion that governments throw out, by mutual agreement, are useful only for preventing panic. There will be famines, resource wars, terminal climate change. People will be eating one another raw. The human race has become a pathogen that will destroy itself and kill this planet in the process. You *know* all this."

"How many women has Morbell inoculated at this point?" Belleveau asked.

Gerrin closed his eyes, thought. "Thirty-six. No, thirty-seven, counting Leland. What are you thinking, Jean-Claude?"

"If three out of thirty-seven die, that is roughly eight percent, correct?"

"Yes." Gerrin saw where Belleveau was going. Not a destination he wished for, but he could think of no good way to derail the conversation.

"Bear with me," Belleveau said. "Approximately half the women on earth carry the Krauss gene—about one and a half billion. The plan was for Triage to infect only those."

"Yes," Gerrin said, unable to keep the irritation out of his voice.

"Eight percent of one and a half billion is one hundred and twenty million," Belleveau said, with finality.

"David," Kendall said. "My God. I can't even begin to imagine that." There was an audible tremor in the older man's voice.

Not in Gerrin's. "I must remind you that we don't *know* Triage caused their deaths."

"But we goddamned bloody well have to assume it did, don't we now?" Kendall shouted. "This was never part of what we were about. God in heaven."

"I do not think he is listening to us anymore," Belleveau said. To Gerrin: "We need to discuss alternatives. What happens if we decide to stop now?"

"We would have to remove the women," Gerrin said.

"Remove? To where?" Belleveau asked.

"I believe he means 'excise,'" Kendall said. "That was the word you used for the first one, wasn't it, David?"

"Not possible," Belleveau said. If Kendall now sounded horrified, Belleveau sounded appalled.

"It is possible, actually," Gerrin said. "A plan for that contingency has been in place since the beginning. An accident. No connection to us."

"You never told us anything about that," Kendall said.

"No. But such a plan was essential."

"What would happen?" Belleveau asked.

"There are options depending on a number of variables. The most likely involves an accidental explosion. Earlier in the year it would not have worked because people were living outside the station. Now everybody is in that one place, so . . ."

The silence stretched. Kendall said, "Someone would have to survive, though, wouldn't they? I mean, whoever made this happen would presumably not want to take his own life in the process."

"That has been accommodated," Gerrin said. "Our security asset will facilitate the explosion. He will wait at the runway, believing a plane will retrieve him."

"Believing?"

"Yes."

"So there will be no plane?"

"No."

"But excising the women means excising the men, as well, does it not?" Belleveau said. "I'm sorry. I cannot accept this. I will not be a part of it." He sat back and crossed his arms, his expression grave.

"There are only two options, Jean-Claude," Gerrin said. "This, or take the greater risk."

"That's not correct, actually." Kendall sat forward, new energy in his voice. "There is another option."

"No," Gerrin said. "There is not."

"Yes, there is."

"What do you see that we are missing, Ian?" Belleveau asked.

"We *tell* the people they are infected. Not just the women. Everybody. Quarantine them long enough to find a countermeasure."

No one spoke for some time. Then Gerrin said, "We might as well walk into the International Criminal Court and confess."

"No. Listen to me," Kendall said. "Morbell could announce that he has identified the pathogen that's making people sick. Say it was in the blood samples he's already obtained. Nothing about having created it. Nobody would know where it came from. The people would believe that, wouldn't they? The station could be placed under strict quarantine. No one comes or goes until a countermeasure is produced."

"They would all have to winter over. Are their facilities adequate for such research?" Belleveau directed the question to Gerrin.

"Yes," he said. "Some things at the Pole are skimped on, but science is not one."

"Well then. Wintering over is the best possible containment, isn't it? They could involve other government labs. Even private industry, if they saw fit, couldn't they?" Kendall asked.

"It is even possible—remotely—that an existing antibiotic might prove effective," Belleveau mused. "It won't against the viral component, though."

"The viral component is of no consequence," Kendall said. "That is simply the carrier. It's the streptococcus payload that Blaine engineered to destroy ovarian cells. We don't know what antibiotics might work against it."

"Do we know what antibiotics they may have on hand down there?" Belleveau asked.

"Stockpiles of amoxicillin, ampicillin, and ciprofloxacin sufficient to deal with infections during winterover," Gerrin said. "Protocol for any serious illness before winterover is evacuation to McMurdo and Christchurch."

"Too bad they don't have clindamycin or lincomycin. Effective against strep," Belleveau said.

"But *this* strep? We don't know, do we? We could get lucky, though," Kendall mused. "They might be able to air-drop things, even if they can't land. That's been done in previous emergencies, I believe."

"I think this is our only option," Belleveau said. "David?"

They both looked at Gerrin. For several moments, he said nothing. Then he drew a long breath and nodded.

"Yes, of course you're both right. As you said, Jean-Claude, we've never been about killing breeders. Just sterilizing them."

"Thank God," Kendall breathed. "For a moment there I thought . . ." He let the sentence trail off.

"What is our next step, then?" Belleveau asked.

"I will communicate our decision to Merritt," Gerrin said. "She will inform the others." He paused. "You see, Jean-Claude? God is listening to us, after all."

45

THE LAB HALLIE HAD USED WAS NOW LOCKED, BUT MAYNARD
Blaine had a key. Merritt's key, actually, one of the two GGMs that opened all doors. Graeter had told Merritt that he was leading the SAR team out to look for Fido and taking Leland. A two-hour process, at minimum. That would be more than enough time.

Most labs at the station were similar in size and shape—rectangles twenty feet wide and twenty-five long. The equipment varied from discipline to discipline. Blaine passed through the lab's small outer office and had no trouble finding what he was looking for. Emily had told him that they kept the extremophile tank in a freezer to replicate the cryopeg's water temperature. It was toward the rear of the lab, flush against one wall.

Lifting the freezer's lid, he saw the thirty-gallon glass tank that held the sample Leland had retrieved. He looked down into the water, which wasn't clear like normal aquarium water—but then, this wasn't a normal aquarium. The water was hypersaline, and so much salt would have an almost colloidal effect, accounting for the cloudiness.

He could see the thing down on the bottom of the tank. Leaning over the surface of the water, he sniffed and was surprised at how it smelled. Not like the cold, salt tang of the Maine ocean, nor the smoother, softer scent of warm bodies like the Caribbean. This was entirely different. The closest analogue he could pull out of memory was model airplane glue.

Then it changed. Right while he was looking down into the water, the scent altered in a matter of seconds to something much stronger and sharper, a vinegary, ammoniac smell that stung his eyes and nose. He jerked back.

What the hell? But then he understood. He had just exposed the tank to much warmer air. And much different. They had filled it with cryopeg water only the day before. The stuff hadn't seen light or fresh air for, what, fifty million years? No wonder it reacted oddly. Maybe it was the solutional equivalent of spoilage, like cut apples turning brown when exposed to oxygen.

In one pocket of his lab coat he carried a ten-milliliter syringe with a two-inch, fifteen-gauge needle. The syringe was filled with a 10 percent solution of sodium hypochlorite—the great nemesis of micro-organisms. Whatever you had that needed killing—bacteria, viruses, fungi—good old $NaOCl$, also known as chlorine bleach, got the job done. It terminated the worst of the worst—Ebola, smallpox, plague—with equal aplomb. He had no doubt it would work against this stuff they had fished out of the cryopeg. There was no way on earth it would ever have had contact with a modern compound like sodium hypochlorite. Easy as killing a baby.

He used a flashlight to see the specimen more clearly. Bright or-ange with yellow spots, texture like cauliflower, about the size and shape of a zucchini squash. How had Leland brought back so much? And why? The retrieval container Emily had shown him hadn't been much bigger than a large cigar tube. On her trip, Leland must have wanted to make sure they had enough for multiple experiments.

He took the syringe from his pocket and pulled off the needle's plastic tip protector. Then he leaned over the tank again. The ammo-nia reek was worse. He held his breath, but he had to keep his eyes open to see the extremophile, and they burned as if he had been slic-ing onions. He put his right hand in the water—and gasped. It wasn't the dull, blunt pain cold water usually caused. This *burned*. He almost dropped the syringe. He would have to do this very quickly or his hand would become too numb to use.

He injected chlorine solution into the biomatter over and over. When he finished and pulled his hand out, he could barely feel the syringe in his slow-moving fingers. He rubbed his hands together until some feeling returned to the right one. He closed the freezer and stood for a few seconds by the inner lab door, surveying the area to make sure he was leaving no evidence of his visit.

Satisfied, he switched off the light and left, locking the door behind him.

46

HALLIE DROVE HALFWAY TO THE STATION, STOPPED, TURNED
around to look. She could just make out Graeter's figure, a smudge
blacker than the dark purple background. If he decided to take a
penguin, she would go after him, but then what? Lasso and hog-tie
him with line from the emergency kit and haul him back in? Not
likely. If that happened, she would have to rely on her powers of per-
suasion. With Graeter, she suspected, they would be less than compel-
ling. But she didn't think he would do that now.

After ten minutes she saw him heading toward the station. She
waited long enough to believe that he would come all the way, then
started the snowmo and drove on back.

She secured her ECW gear and was walking along the corridor to the
stairs when she heard footsteps behind her. Turned, saw the woman
who had been angered by her loud knocking on Fida's door, the
snow-white face and black-circled eyes. Two other women were with
her. Anyplace else, Hallie would have thought it unusual for three

women to be out and about after midnight. Here, where work went on around the clock, she did not.

"Hey," she said. "Talk to you for a minute?" Friendlier voice, hint of a smile. Maybe she wants to make peace, Hallie thought.

"Jan Tolliver," the woman said, hand extended.

"Glad to meet you. Look, I—"

The woman grasped Hallie's hand. Hard. "Why don't we talk in there," she said. The three women herded her toward a door before she knew what was happening. Tolliver was small and slender. The other two were neither. One was white, the other black. The white woman had curls sticking up from either side of a very broad, curved forehead. Hallie thought of a musk ox. The other woman was black, just as big, hair clipped close to her head. Ox and buffalo.

One woman opened the door, and they pushed her through the entrance. Tolliver followed them in, shutting the door. Hallie jerked her arms free.

"You should have talked to me when you had a chance," Tolliver said.

"What the hell are you doing?" she snapped.

"Take it easy," Tolliver said. "We just want to ask you some things."

"Not like this." Hallie started toward the door. Ox moved very quickly for a woman of her size, setting herself between Hallie and the exit. Hallie turned to face Tolliver.

"What do you want?"

"When did you get here?" Tolliver asked.

"None of your goddamned business. Get out of my way."

"Answer her question," Buffalo said.

"Who the hell are you?" Hallie said.

Hallie's knees buckled and her vision filled with silver sparks. Buffalo had hit her with the heel of one hand on the side of the head. It had happened so quickly that Hallie felt the effects first, realized what happened only afterward, like a soldier being hit by a bullet, then hearing the sound of its firing. Tolliver and Ox grabbed her, helped her stay upright, waited for her head to clear.

No cut or visible bruising, Hallie thought. Smart. She's hit people before.

The black woman said, "Women are dying. Answer her when she asks you."

"You're in a world of trouble," Hallie said. Her voice sounded strange, distant, louder on one side than the other.

"Three witnesses against one? Not likely," Tolliver said.

Hallie always thought in terms of odds and probabilities. She would stand a good chance against one woman. Three, bad gamble. "I got here Monday."

"The last flight in or out since then," Tolliver said.

"Yes."

"How'd you feel coming in?"

"Like hell. I'd been traveling for four days."

"She means, were you *sick*?" the black woman said.

"No, I wasn't sick."

"How many airports did you come through?"

She thought back. "Five, counting McMurdo."

Ox turned to Tolliver. "See? She could've carried anything in."

"You seriously think something I brought killed the women?"

"Nobody was dying before you got here," Buffalo said.

Any reason is better than no reason, Hallie thought. I'm the easiest X factor.

"Tell us why it didn't happen that way," Tolliver said.

"That's easy. Harriet Lanahan died a few minutes after I came into the cafeteria. Something happened to her before I arrived. There's no way I could have been the vector."

"I wasn't there. That true?" Buffalo asked Tolliver.

"Yes."

"Still . . ." Ox said. Midwestern accent. Big healthy farm girl. Just Hallie's luck.

"That's not all," Hallie said. "No microbe on earth could transfer, colonize, and kill that quickly. Smallpox takes a week. Ebola symptoms can surface after two days, but it takes a week or more to kill a victim. The only one of those women I had contact with was Rockie, and she died from some kind of allergic reaction."

"What do you think?" Buffalo said to the other two.

Ox shrugged, watching Tolliver.

"I think she's full of Beaker bullshit," the smaller woman said.

"All right then." Ox pinned Hallie's arms behind her.

"I don't know," Buffalo said. She looked as if she were about to ask Hallie a question. A quick metal-on-metal sound and the door opened. Ox let Hallie go, stepped back. A man came in. Hallie recognized Grenier.

"How're you doing, Jake?" she asked.

Perhaps sensing something in her voice, or picking up on body language cues, he looked from woman to woman. "Everything all right here?"

For a second no one spoke. Then Hallie said, "We just wanted a little privacy. Some woman-to-woman talk." She gave him a knowing wink.

"Why are you here?" Tolliver asked him.

"Somebody said snowmo tracks were in this storeroom." He glanced around, not completely satisfied.

Hallie waved. "Good to see you again."

"You too, Doc." He studied the scene one more time, then nodded. "I guess they were wrong about the tracks."

When he was gone, Hallie said, "I understand how you feel. And I should have stopped and talked to you, Jan, but I thought my lab partner was in serious trouble." She paused, looked at each woman in turn. "It's not me. Something is going on here. I don't know what, but I'm trying to find out." The air in the room loosened, a sense of threat dissolving.

Buffalo looked at the other two. "I think we're done."

"Yeah," Ox said. She threw Hallie a sheepish look.

Hallie rubbed the side of her head, grinned. "Quick hands," she said to Buffalo.

"I'm from Philly. Boxed a little."

"How'd you do?"

"Eight and three before I quit," she said, pride showing in her eyes. "No money in it, though." She looked at Tolliver, said again, "I think we're done," and headed for the door. To Hallie: "Really am sorry about that." Ox followed Buffalo out.

"We're good," Hallie said. At the door she looked back. Tolliver was still standing, arms crossed over her chest. Hallie waved. Tolliver didn't wave back.

47

"ARE YOU ALL RIGHT?" GRAETER ASKED.

"Yes. Why do you ask?"

"Your eyes look a little funny."

"Bumped my head," she said.

"That'll do it." He was sitting behind his desk, six darts aligned perfectly on its top. She had come up after her talk with the women. He looked even bonier than the first time she'd seen him, his eyes sunk more deeply into their sockets, the circles under them darker. When he leaned forward and put his elbows on the desk, she saw a slight tremor in his hands. He clasped them together.

"I think he's gone," Graeter said.

"I don't understand this," Hallie said. "I talked to Fida just yesterday. Or maybe the day before. Not sure, exactly. He was tired—exhausted, really—and looked awful, but not a whole lot worse than others I've seen down here."

"What did you talk about?"

"Emily. He was taking her death hard."

"Anything else?"

"Sure. We talked about their work. This extremophile they found in the cryopeg."

"Anything else?" She hesitated, and he saw it. He leaned forward. "Look. I know you think I'm a prick. That's okay. I am, a lot of the time. But you *can* trust me."

She returned his gaze.

"Come on. Do I strike you as the devious type?" he asked.

At first, he had come across as a martinet with a big shoulder chip. And maybe devious. That was then. "No. Since we're speaking seriously for the first time, you strike me as a man being chased by something. I think it's probably guilt, but that's just a guess."

"You heard that from Merritt, right? Did she say why *she's* at Pole?"

"She said she was a scientist who'd moved on to administrative work."

"True, as far as it goes," Graeter said.

"I'm not following you."

"Think about it. The Beakers doing research here have a lot to gain—notoriety at the very least, and maybe even some real money if their work gets noticed by Big Pharma or other deep pockets. But not Merritt."

"She seems to like her work."

"Merritt had a good job with WHO," Graeter said.

"The World Health Organization."

"Right."

"You said 'had.' What happened?"

"Scuttlebutt said she went off the deep end about birth control. Publicly criticized people high in the Bush administration. And the Catholic Church. Even the U.N. That got her fired."

"Why should that make her untrustworthy?"

"Not that. Her firing was news for a few days. But she could have walked right into a cushy professorship. Instead, here she is, working at Alcatraz on ice for seventy-five grand a year. Something doesn't add up." He folded his hands, looked at her. "Goose and gander, Dr. Leland."

She got it, but hesitated. Had Merritt asked that her comments about Graeter stay strictly confidential? No. Even so, Hallie bridled. But Graeter had been honest with her. Fair was fair.

"Okay. She said you'd been down here too long and were, um, disturbed."

It was the first time she had seen him laugh. Not much of a laugh, more a gargly snort, but clearly he was amused. "Disturbed. Ha. Was that it?"

"No."

"Well?"

"She mentioned an accident on a submarine. And what happened after."

The amusement faded, but, to Hallie's surprise, it was not replaced by anger. Sadness loosened his clenched features.

"Is it true?" Hallie asked.

"It's true."

"The part about the captain and your wife?"

"True. All of it."

"Did you have any children?"

"No, thank God. Sea duty wasn't conducive to raising a family." He looked down at his raw, red hands. What was it he had said? Could still play. Just not allegro anymore. She wondered what other things he could no longer do. Or feel.

"Mr. Graeter, I'm sorry for the boys on your sub. And for you. My father was West Point, sixty-six. He led men in combat in Vietnam and lost a good many. He's in Arlington now, but they walked with him until the day he died. The hurt never stopped."

"No. It never does." He took a deep breath, rubbed his eyes, and looked at her in a way she had not seen before. "A goddamned Army brat. I should have known."

She thought, My God. How about that? *Beat Navy.*

For a moment he just stared. Then he grinned and said, *"Beat Army."*

"Do you know about Vishnu?" she asked.

"Buddhist god of something or other, right?"

"Hindu god of preservation."

"Whatever. Why?"

"Agnes Merritt said she'd briefed you about what Emily and Fida were doing."

"She said they found something growing down under the ice and brought samples back to the lab."

"Nothing else?"

"I asked her if it could blow up or catch on fire or poison anybody. She said no. That was all I needed."

"She didn't describe the actual research? Tell you why they were calling it Vishnu?"

"I didn't need to know that. Not my job. Merritt runs the Beakers and science. I run the station and keep people alive. Paragraph, period, end of story."

She laughed.

"What's funny?"

"It's period, paragraph, end of story."

"A period goes at the end of a paragraph last time I checked. Right?"

"Yes, but—" She laughed again.

"What's funny *now*?"

"The fact that we can be here amid all the crap that's been happening, arguing about the correct wording of a trite phrase."

"What's that mean?"

"It means we could be more alike than either of us has cared to admit."

He looked at her with narrowed eyes. "You may be right."

"Did you know that NASI is owned by a petroleum corporation called GENERCO?"

"Why wouldn't I?"

"Do you think GENERCO would have problems with Vishnu?"

He let slip a half-grin, wiped if off. "You mean, because it eats carbon dioxide and pisses fuel?"

She gaped. "You knew? All this time?"

"Christ, Leland, a captain has to know crap like that. And for the record, no, GENERCO would not have a problem with it. Those people aren't stupid. They put money—very quietly—into solar and hydrogen some time ago. They see what's coming just like the rest of us."

"You pass," she said.

"What?"

She had made a quick calculation. He needed to know about Emily's death. But Emily was gone, and nothing could change that. It was more important for him to know about what was down in the lab first, because it might be putting a lot more people at risk.

"Never mind. I'll explain later. Right now, there's something I have to show you."

"What's the yellow stuff?" he asked. The microbial colonies had grown larger, occupying more space now than the red agar.

"I don't know yet. But it's growing faster than anything I've seen."

"How did you do this?"

She told him about taking samples in the morgue and starting the cultures here. She expected him to offer some SOR-based reprimand, but he just nodded and said, "Guts and smarts—I like that. You're just full of surprises." He peered at her, then back at the dishes. "So it's unusual for something to grow like this?"

"Normal time for cultures to become visible to the naked eye is twenty-four hours, minimum. I saw them after a few minutes. And it's more than doubled since then."

"You don't know what it is, though."

"No. But isn't it reasonable to believe it had something to do with the women's deaths?"

"Yes. And that means we have to assume it's dangerous."

"Absolutely." She saw him staring at the dishes. "It's safe here. The cultures are sealed, and the incubator cabinet provides a second level of containment. I isolated the swabs and gloves and the other things I used."

"Good to know. Can you analyze it, or whatever, to see what we're dealing with?"

"*We*, Mr. Graeter?"

He looked surprised for just an instant. "Yes, we. You're the expert here. I'm strict, Leland, but I'm not stupid. So what do you do?"

"Analysis is mostly performed with scanners and computers now. I doubt either are here. So we'll rely on biochemical testing."

"What does that involve?"

"A long series of eliminative, identifying tests—oxidase, indole production, coagulase test, MR-VP test—"

"Okay, enough. The more important question is, how long will it take?"

"Starting from scratch, with what I have here to work with, twenty-four hours minimum. But didn't you say that Doc was working with blood samples?"

"So he told me."

"If he'd come up with anything, he would have called you, right?"

"Or risk getting my foot up his ass," he snapped. "Sorry. Navy talk."

"Forget it. My father spoke Army. For the tests I'll run, it could be sooner. Or later."

"Should we tell everyone?"

"Understand that I come from a facility where all information is closely held. Need-to-know is the first commandment."

"That BARDA place."

"Right, that BARDA place. So I can sound a little paranoid. If it were up to me, I wouldn't."

"Rationale?"

"I was remembering your comment about destabilizing an already fragile population. All those T3s walking around chatting with themselves. It's one thing to tell people they're locked in with a possibly lethal unknown pathogen. Much better if we can say, '*And* we have a countermeasure.' There's always a chance that it's treatable—staph, strep, whatever."

"Information could get out of here, too. Just imagine—CNN breaking news: 'Killer Superbug Devastates South Pole, Threatens Planet,'" he said.

"Which they would do."

"In a heartbeat. If it bleeds, it leads. Suppose some people aren't infected? If we wait, carriers could make healthy ones sick, right?"

"They could do that even if we tell them. Right now, we don't know who to quarantine."

"What about Merritt?"

"It's your call, obviously. But I think she falls into the need-to-know category. She is the chief scientist, after all."

"Yeah," Graeter said reluctantly. But he recited, " 'In the event discovery is made by any personnel of any condition that might reasonably be construed to constitute a threat to all or part of the station and/or personnel, such discovery shall be communicated to the senior and/or acting senior officials immediately.' "

"SORs, right? Memorized?"

"Most of them. Would you explain it to her, though? You speak Beaker."

"Sure. I'll set the tests up, then go see her."

"Do it." He started out.

She'd made her decision, held up one hand.

"Wait. There are some other things you need to know. I saved the worst for last."

She told him about Emily's murder, Blaine's confession, and Triage.

He reached for one of the bench tops. His other hand clenched into a fist, white-knuckled, new cracks opening, fresh blood seeping. "God *damn* it to hell," he said. "If I could find the bastard who did that, I would shoot him myself."

"Are you sure yours is the only gun here?"

"Reasonably." Then he shook his head, as though clearing cobwebs after a hard punch. "Let me say this out loud to make sure it's straight. The man who tortured a woman to death is walking around my station."

"He might have flown out after he killed her. But I don't think so."

"Why not?"

"He probably killed Fida, too," she said.

"So he's still here. Or they are."

"Yes. It could be a team effort, for all we know," she said.

"You're right. Wait a minute. You said you saw that video on Monday?"

"Yes."

"And now it's"—he glanced at his watch, shook his head—"two A.M. on Thursday. Why in hell did you wait so long to tell me?"

"Think about it. The killer could have been any man in the station."

"You thought it might be *me*?"

"The way you were when I got here?" She shrugged.

"Yeah, okay." He nodded, rubbed the side of his face. "What changed your mind?"

"You did," she said.

"Huh. Imagine that."

"How many men are still here?"

He closed his eyes, remembering. "Thirty-two. Eighteen Beakers, fourteen Draggers."

"We could question every one of them," she said, thinking out loud.

"Even at just half an hour per man, that's seventeen hours. More if you figure in time for breaks, bathroom calls, eating."

"Did your marshal training include interrogation techniques?"

"We barely got past Handcuffs 101."

"So neither of us is a trained or experienced interviewer. From what I saw on the video, the killer looked trained and experienced, both."

"Easy for him to slip past us," he said.

"Sure."

"We could try a lineup," he said. "Put every man in the station through it. See if we recognize anyone."

"We'd have to figure out some way to do it looking down on them from above," she pointed out. "The video never showed a straight-on shot. What about McMurdo? Or the New Zealand Police?" she asked.

"SORs say—" He interrupted himself. "For some reason, that sounds ridiculous."

"Maybe, but it could be important. What do they say?"

"Crime reports go through McMurdo to New Zealand's national police and our State Department."

"Not like nine-one-one. So no immediate help."

"I'll call as soon as comms are up, of course. But the killer may be loose in the station. Accomplices, too."

"Infection at every level," she said.

"What?"

"I was just thinking. A microbe of some kind almost certainly killed the three women. So there's infection at the microscopic level. And a much bigger infection is killing people at the macro level."

"Only a microbiologist would see things that way," he said.

"Maybe. But there is still the question: what do we do?"

"I could make an all-hands announcement or call a meeting," Graeter said. "Just put it out there for everybody to hear. See what happens."

"I don't like that," she said.

"Why?"

"A lot of them already think there's a killer supergerm loose. Then they hear that some psycho murderer is running around? Talk about destabilizing."

"What would you do?" he asked. "If you heard an announcement like that?"

"I'd grab the nearest weapon. It would be very hard to stay rational."

"So maybe we can't do anything right away," he said. "But we should at least tell Merritt."

"We should, you're right."

"Could you, when you talk to her about the other things?"

"I can. What are you going to do?"

"I'm going back to my office and make sure my gun's in working order."

48

THE SAT PHONE HUMMED, SIGNALING AN INCOMING CALL. MERRITT glanced at the door to her room one more time, making sure it was locked. She answered, said her name, waited.

"How copy?" Gerrin asked.

There was always garbage noise on the sat phone calls down here, sounds like wind blowing through canyons and gravel crunching. But she could understand him. "Clear."

"We discussed the situation."

"And?" Merritt asked. Before Gerrin could continue, there was a knock. "Who is it?" Merritt called.

"Hallie Leland. I need to talk to you. I tried your office, figured you would be here." Merritt heard her try the locked door.

"Can this wait until the morning. I just got to sleep."

"I think we should talk now."

Merritt mouthed a silent curse, then whispered into the phone, "Make it quick. Someone's at my door."

Gerrin didn't need much time for what he had to say.

She let Hallie in. "Are you catching something? You're starting to look like the rest of us," Merritt said. She had thrown a robe over her red long johns.

"Maybe the dreaded Pole cold. I'll be okay." She explained how she had obtained material from the women in the morgue and was culturing it in her lab.

Merritt flushed. "You didn't notify me."

"I didn't want to put you on the spot."

"So you're running standard biochemical screens?"

"Yes." Hallie explained the tests she'd set up. "Can you think of anything I missed?"

"Microbiology isn't my field. How soon will we have results?"

"Tomorrow is my best guess. Is the winterover flyout happening?"

"Not unless the temperature goes up by about twenty degrees."

"Is that likely?"

"It's a weird time of year here, very unstable atmospheric conditions. So it could happen. I'd say fifty-fifty."

"But there's something else. Two things, actually."

"What?"

"Vishnu's dead."

Setting up the biochemical tests had not been complicated. They were the kinds of things she had first done as an undergraduate in the microbio labs. The procedure was exacting and required strict attention, though. It also required biosecurity gear—such as it was here at the South Pole. Hooded Tyvek suit, booties, mask. And, though she would be working in a biosecure "glove box" made of quarter-inch, high-impact acrylic plastic, she put on surgical gloves as well.

It had required almost two hours of delicate and tedious work: inoculating a series of oxidase test slides, Enterotubes, and Oxi/Ferm tubes, securing them in incubators. She had discarded her security gear in biohazard containers, then ventilated and sterilized the lab.

Before leaving, she had gone to the freezer to check on the Vishnu sample. It had not grown since her last viewing. In fact, it looked dull brown and mushy, like a rotten apple.

"What the hell?" she had said. "Gods aren't supposed to die."

"Same thing that happened before," Merritt said. "You're sure?"

"Positive."

"Done deal, then," Merritt said, glancing at her sideways. "What a shame."

"We have to get some more."

Merritt looked up. "What?"

"I'll dive again."

"Is that a good idea? Not feeling well? And after what happened last time?"

Don't dive sick: it was one of the first contraindications beginners learned. But that was under normal circumstances. Hallie waved Merritt's concern off.

"I've done worse. And this is too important. I'll use one of the station's dry suits, and we will leak-test the hell out of it first. Do you think we could get Guillotte down to the dive shed at around four?"

"You're sure about this?"

"This thing could have unimaginable potential. You know what Emily and Fida learned. There's nothing more we can do with the bacterial cultures right now."

"You're right. Okay, go do what you need to—eat, drink, rest, whatever. I'll collect Guillotte, and we'll meet you in the shed at four."

"I'll be there." Hallie could see that Merritt assumed they were through. "There's something else I need to talk to you about."

Merritt's eyes narrowed. Hallie could hear her thinking, *What now?*

"It's about Maynard Blaine."

"Did that peabrain hit on you again?"

"No. But I made him tell me about Triage."

Funny, Hallie thought. She looks like Blaine did when I told *him*. Merritt's shock quickly changed to confusion. "About what?"

She recounted what she had learned from Blaine. "Did you know anything about this secret research he claimed to be doing?"

"Nothing." Merritt was rubbing her hands as if trying to get something sticky off them. "NSF should *never* have done that without telling me. Damn them. Damn *him*. Blaine lied to my face."

"Seems to have a knack. He lied to me, too," Hallie said. "And probably to Emily."

Merritt looked disgusted. "The bastard. I'll try to sort this out. Maybe we'll get comms back up. You can rest a bit. Sound good?"

"The rest part does," Hallie said. "But there's one more thing you need to know."

49

"LELAND TOOK BIOSAMPLES FROM THE BODIES IN THE MORGUE. She's culturing them in her lab now."

Merritt had called the others to her office. Guillotte had not come yet, but Blaine and Doc were there.

"Oh God," Doc said. "It feels like things are coming apart."

"It feels like *you're* coming apart," Blaine said.

"If she gets viable colonies, and figures out what it is, we're finished." Doc put his face in his hands.

"That's not the worst of it," Merritt said. "She knows that Durant was killed."

"*What?*" the other two screeched in unison. "How could she know that?"

Merritt explained about the surveillance camera.

"God *damn*," Blaine said. "Why would she have put a camera there?"

Merritt frowned at such a stupid question. "Simple. She felt afraid. Wanted to know if anybody came into her room while she wasn't there." Merritt looked directly at Blaine. "Thanks to you."

"You fucking *idiot*," Doc blurted. "This is all your fault."

"It is very important to keep calm," Merritt said.

"You didn't put Triage in those women." Doc's chin was quivering.

"I am not going to sneak back into that lab again," Blaine said. "They might have put a camera in there, too. Maybe Guillotte will do it, but I won't."

"I said to relax. You won't have to."

"Why not?"

"Because she's going to dive again."

"Why would she do that?" Blaine asked. The answer dawned on him before Merritt replied. "That's why you wanted me to kill the extremophile."

"Insurance," Merritt said. "Just in case."

"What did you do?" Doc asked.

Blaine explained about the chlorine.

"It worked," Merritt said. "She *insisted* on diving. I didn't even have to bring it up."

"Her last dive?" Blaine said.

"If Guillotte and I have anything to say about it." Merritt nodded.

Doc frowned. "I'm not sure I like the diving accident. They could—"

"It's perfect. Diving accidents happen all the time," Merritt said. "And in a place like this . . ."

"That freezing, hypersaline water will preserve her body better than embalming. They'll find—"

"Do you know how deep that thing is? Thousands of feet. They won't find anything."

"She works for an agency of the U.S. government," Doc said. "There will be an investigation and—"

Merritt cut him off: "There is *always* an investigation. They never care what actually happened. It's about covering asses. Making sure it was somebody else's fault. This is *government* we're talking about."

"But are we really sure this is the best course? With three recent—"

"Even better. *We* write the accident report. Everybody was sick. Maybe it got her while she was underwater. She was tired and disoriented. I counseled against diving. She insisted. All we know is that she never resurfaced."

"Where is Guillotte?" Blaine asked.

"I told him to be here," Merritt said. "You know how he is."

"Did you talk to Gerrin?" Doc asked.

"Yes."

"What did he say? About Triage, I mean?"

"They don't think Triage had anything to do with the women's deaths. We're to go ahead as planned. So really, it's finished. As soon as we get a weather window, those women fly out."

"And the rest is history," Blaine said.

"Amen," Merritt said.

50

THE MOUTH OF THE ENTRANCE SHAFT WAS A ROUND HOLE IN THE
ice four feet in diameter. As Blaine had told her, it was hidden behind
a maintenance shed a quarter mile from the station.

Under the plywood cover, a six-by-six wooden post lay across the
top of the hole, its ends resting in slots cut into the ice. Bolted to the
six-by-six was a cable ladder with round metal rungs that dropped
into darkness. Cavers and climbers had used similar ladders in the old
days, before rappelling and vertical gear changed everything. Like
those, the rungs on this ladder were only a foot wide. And slick.

She glanced at the parka thermometer: seventy degrees below
zero. There were no southern lights just now, only stars pitting the
black sky. The cold was already seeping through her clothing, sneak-
ing past thin spots of insulation. Tiny exposed places on her face
burned. Fire and ice, she thought. At some point, they feel the same.

She started down. It had been some time since she'd used a ladder
like this. The metal rungs were icy, and she'd never had to descend
one wearing seven layers of clothing. Worst of all were the huge
bunny boots. The rungs were so narrow that she could place only the
toes on them, which meant that she had to keep her calf muscles

tensed to prevent her feet from slipping off. By the time she reached the bottom, both legs were jigging up and down in the spasms climbers called "sewing machine legs."

She stepped from the ladder onto the bottom of a rectangular corridor that, as she played her light beam around, reminded her of an abandoned mine shaft. The walls were sheets of thick plywood, now bulging in from the crushing pressure of ice and snow. The ceiling was more plywood, supported every four feet by massive vertical timbers and horizontal crossbeams. Even so, some of the crossbeams had cracked, and seams of ice showed through splits in the plywood sheets.

Because no one had ever lived at the South Pole before 1957, no one had known what the weather would be like. The first crew constructed most of the original station underground, leaving five feet of ice on top. The walls and ceilings had been shored up, mine-style, with timbers. When the place had originally been built, everything must have been plumb and square. Now there was not a plumb line or square angle to be seen, giving the place a tilting, twisting funhouse look. It smelled of old wood and diesel oil and decay.

Cave-in debris blocked half the passage to her left, so she went right, into an open corridor. After a hundred feet that led into a room that must have been the galley—red picnic tables with benches, sagging cabinets, sinks. On the tables sat bowls of cereal as they had been left half a century earlier, no mold growing here, empty beer cans and mugs, some with coffee frozen solid, overflowing ashtrays.

Either they got out of this place in one hell of a hurry, she thought, or they didn't bother to clean up after their last day. Probably the latter. She was about to continue through a door on the galley's opposite side when a cracking noise stopped her. She remained absolutely still, not even breathing, listening. No more noises, but she knew that the entire complex was unstable. The beams and timbers were huge, two feet on a side, but a major shift in all that ice above could snap them like twigs. Not a place to linger.

Thirty feet past the galley she came to a T intersection. Turned right, moved on carefully, the floor here littered with rusting cables, lumber, scrap metal. Came to what had been an entrance on her right, the frame all askew now, door hanging from one set of hinges. Painted in black:

Capt. J. R. Lieder, USN

C.O.

South Pole, Antarctica, USA

Like Columbus claiming everything he could see, and all he could not, for the queen, she thought. South Pole, Antarctica, USA. Different times. She wrenched the door back and shone her light into the room. Two gray metal file cabinets, an overturned chair, and a massive old metal desk like the one in Graeter's office in the station.

Fida lay on top of the desk, naked, curled into a fetal position. His eyes were open, dulled by the gray haze of death. One arm lay underneath him. The other was stretched straight out, fingers spread wide, as if trying to snatch something out of the air. Areas of his skin glistened: body moisture that had frozen and was reflecting her light. Sweat? From a struggle? So thin, she saw, skin over knobs and ridges of bone. His ECW gear, underclothing, and boots lay in a pile on the floor beside the desk.

She ran her light over the room's ceiling. None of the crossbeams had split, but all had unsettling downward curves. Didn't matter. She needed to get closer. She walked in, stood beside the body, started to look for wounds or signs of trauma. Saw nothing obvious at first, but then, peeking from beneath Fida's head, a small, reddish-black circle. Blood? She bent to look.

A sharp noise from the dark passageway behind her, then a sound like giant hands clapping, ice cracking, timbers shattering. One second of dead silence, and the ceiling collapsed. Her last thought was that it sounded like the avalanche on Denali just before it hit.

51

GERRIN PULLED INTO HIS GARAGE, WAITED FOR THE AUTOMATIC door to close, and sat. He turned on the dome light and angled the rearview mirror toward himself so that he could look into his own eyes. It had been a difficult couple of days. First the call from Barnard, later meeting with him. Then the call from Merritt. The videoconference with Kendall and Belleveau. Finally, the sat call back to Merritt. She wasn't a problem. Merritt was a zealot, driven by resentment that had festered for years. He understood her: damned barren by pure chance, unable to fathom why others should not suffer the same fate, especially if her conscience could be salved by thinking some good thing might result.

So the Pole's women would fly like sparks to every corner of the world, and Triage would burn like wildfire through the globe's breeding stock. Or, more properly, like smallpox. There would be the same exponential growth. And there would be pain, but at least it would visit all equally. He took comfort from the fact that Triage had no bias, made no choices, assumed nothing. Only a microbe, it would work just as effectively on the Upper East Side and Rodeo Drive as it would in Lagos and Dhaka and New Delhi.

But did "work" mean sterilize or kill? If he had made the wrong call, millions—*tens of millions,* a thing barely conceivable—of women might die. He was a man of iron control, but now his mind flooded with red visions. Exsanguinated. Bled to death. Two women died that way, an awful thing to see and worse, no doubt, to suffer. He saw rivers of blood, streets awash in blood, lakes of blood, hosts of women drowning in blood, blood like rain, drenching the earth.

And yet, and yet . . . What were the options? From the beginning, his scientific, rational, calculating brain had reduced it all to sets of probabilities, clean and simple, rows and columns of data, percentages, projections. Certain global catastrophe later or heroic action now. Heroic in the strictly medical sense: treatment sure to harm but employed as a last resort when no action at all meant sure death. Physicians did it routinely, millions of times every day all over the world. Amputating gangrenous limbs. Excising cancer-riddled eyes, noses, colons, lungs. Killing people slowly with toxic chemicals to keep tumors from killing them quickly.

In the end, he did not really believe that Triage would kill millions of women. Could not believe it. They had planned too carefully, prepared too thoroughly, tested too rigorously. Triage was not designed to kill. Now, a place like Pole, *that* had been designed by nature to kill if any place on earth had. Surely something down in that otherworldly hell had caused those women's deaths.

So he had lied. He had lied to Barnard, over and over. He had lied to Kendall and Belleveau when he'd said he agreed with Kendall's plan. And he had lied when he'd told Merritt that the three Triage leaders had chosen to go forward as planned, when in fact they had agreed to pursue Kendall's suggested course. He felt remorse over lying to his fellow Triage leaders, but what choice had there been?

In the mudroom, he took off his shoes and left them neatly aligned in one corner, unlocked the inner door, and stepped sock-footed onto the hall's thick green carpeting. A small thing, but one he had come to expect with pleasure. In the kitchen, he brewed tea and took a cup, thick with sugar, toward his leather recliner in the living room. He said, "Lights." Said it again, more loudly. Nothing. Five thousand dollars for a voice-activated system, and this. It had worked that morning. He would have to check the security system later. He used the wall switch.

Before he seated himself, someone knocked on the front door, and he answered. Two men. One he had never seen before, *very* big, with short, straw-colored hair and a remarkable face. "Good evening, Dr. Gerrin," he said. Another man stepped from behind the first. It was Donald Barnard.

"Hello," Barnard said.

"We need to talk to you." Bowman stepped through the doorway and walked straight toward Gerrin, who moved backward step for step, as if retreating from an advancing wall. "You know Dr. Barnard from BARDA," Bowman said. "I work with another agency."

"It has been a very long day, I am afraid. This is not a good time." He glanced at his watch. "But if you call my office tomorrow, you can—"

"Have a seat on the couch." Bowman had walked, and Gerrin had backed, through the entrance hall and into the living room.

"It won't take long," Barnard said, following. He was surprised at how much traffic noise he was hearing. An older house, built even before the nearby Beltway.

Gerrin seemed not to notice. He looked from one to the other and placed his cellphone on the coffee table in front of him.

"Amazing devices," he said. "Especially the voice activation. Someone is breaking into your house in the middle of the night? One word brings the police with sirens screaming. Very comforting."

"When it works," Bowman said.

Gerrin picked up the phone, put it down again. "No reception bars. How strange."

"Everything disappoints, sooner or later," Bowman said. Earlier, he had explained to Barnard, "Some signal jamming, highly localized. Easy on, easy off."

"So," Gerrin said, "how may I help you gentlemen?" His irritation had passed, and he seemed composed. Barnard thought, If a man like Bowman had just pushed into *my* home . . .

"The South Pole," Barnard said.

"Which we discussed in my office."

"I have some more questions."

"Really? I thought we addressed your concerns well enough."

"We know that you lied to Dr. Barnard," Bowman said. "We need to know why. And we need truthful answers. Lives may be at stake here."

Gerrin locked eyes with Bowman, and Barnard had to admire that. "Or what? You'll spirit me away to some distant land for extreme rendition? Waterboarding and such?"

"We wouldn't need to spirit you far. Waterboarding is medieval and messy. This is the twenty-first century, Doctor. We've come a long way." Bowman took a smartphone from his pocket, started a video, and handed it to Gerrin. After twenty seconds, the slender man turned pale. When he gave the phone back, his hand shook.

"Emily Durant," Bowman said. "Why did you ask for Hallie Leland to replace her?"

"The government personnel system computer asked for her, actually. She had the specialized skills needed to finish an important project." Gerrin looked from one man to the other. "You must have known that already. Why did you come to my home? Really, I mean. What is this about?"

"Dr. Durant's death may not have been accidental," Bowman said.

"How would you know? No one has seen the medical examiner's report."

"We have. Tell us what you know about her death. The truth."

Gerrin sighed, set his cup on the table, leaned forward, elbows on knees. His composure had returned, which Barnard found very strange. "All right. I will appreciate your discretion here with what I am about to say. I was told—we are talking back-channel now—that drugs might have been involved."

"Why did you lie to me about that?" Barnard asked. "You said you didn't know."

"Please consider my position. A stranger comes to your office asking for details about the death of a senior scientist in a facility for which you are responsible. There is no official report on this death yet, but you have unconfirmed information that could do huge damage to the dead person's reputation, as well as to your organization. Not to mention your own career."

Barnard started to ask another question, but someone knocked on the front door. Gerrin looked at them, eyebrows raised.

"Go ahead," Bowman said.

Gerrin left them and returned with a young man Barnard recognized at once. "Gentlemen, this is my assistant, Muhammed Kandohur Said. He kindly offered to look at a computer here that has been misbehaving. Muhammed is an exceptional young man. Graduated magna cum laude from MIT two years ago. He is from Karail, in my native country. Have you heard of it?"

"No," Barnard said.

"Not surprising, really. Few Americans have. Muhammed, this is Dr. Barnard and, ah, his associate."

The young man, polite and diffident, shook hands with each in turn. To Gerrin he said, "My friend Hasim is dropping me off. We weren't sure you would be home yet. Shall I tell him to go now? He will pick me up later." To Bowman and Barnard, sheepishly: "I still do not have a license to drive."

"Yes, go and do that," Gerrin said. "Then we will look at the computer. My friends here were just leaving."

"What did you think?" Bowman asked, when they had driven a few blocks.

"I thought about how much effort it took to keep from wrapping my hands around his neck and squeezing some truth out of the bastard," Barnard said. He shook his head. "Haven't wanted to do that for a long time, Wil."

52

WHEN SHE HEARD THE CRACKING SOUND, HALLIE DOVE UNDER THE desk and crouched in the kneehole, an instinct-driven reaction, too fast for conscious thought. She huddled and prayed that the massive desk was as strong as it looked.

This collapse took much less time than the avalanche—not more than three seconds, ending with a huge *whoomp*. She didn't move, wanting to make sure the cave-in had stabilized. She was unhurt and breathing but would exhaust the air in her little cave quickly. When the carbon dioxide load became too great, she would fall unconscious and then suffocate.

She had the headlamp and two handheld lights. Her cellphone, which would be useless. An energy bar. Matches. The Leatherman multitool. Light would not be the problem. Nor food and water. She would live or die by air.

She guessed her hole to be about two feet high, three feet wide and deep. She had waited out mountain storms in snow caves not a whole lot bigger, and worked through cave passages a good deal smaller. Here, she was crouched on her knees, bent over sideways in the hole, perpendicular to the way she wanted to go.

She pulled off her mittens, found her Leatherman tool, and formed it into a pair of pliers with tapered jaws.

You have to breathe easy, she told herself. Don't overexert. This will take time.

With her mittens back on, she jabbed the pliers' point into the wall of frozen material blocking the front of the kneehole. It was not as compacted as concrete-hard avalanche debris. The snow above Old Pole had never slid and melted. It had compressed, yes, but that was different. When she jabbed the pliers in and pulled, fist-sized chunks popped out.

Trying to tunnel up was out of the question. Her only hope was to work her way horizontally toward the room's doorway. The room's ceiling beams were long and could support less weight than those in the narrow hall. Maybe the collapse had been limited to this one office.

She kept her breathing as shallow as possible, but soon she started to feel oxygen hunger, a constant, low burning in her chest coupled with an urge in her brain to suck in a huge, deep breath. Bothersome, but something she could control. She did know that at some point the rising carbon dioxide level in her blood would trip an autonomic response. Then she would gasp involuntarily. For a few seconds she would feel relief, but then the urge to breathe would again become irresistible. The cycle would repeat itself over and over until, by exhausting the oxygen in her space, it would kill her.

She kept digging, lying on her belly, shoving icy debris back behind her as it accumulated in front of her face. Halfway out of the kneehole, she stopped and hollowed out a space in front of the desk's lower drawer. She was gambling, and it was taking extra time and air, but it might be worth it. When she had a space big enough to open the drawer halfway, she pulled it out. Inside were four sturdy metal dividers, more common back in the days when files still meant only paper. They were rigid steel the size and shape of a file drawer's interior. Little arms on their sides ran along horizontal tracks in the drawers. There was some proper way to get them out, which Hallie didn't recall or maybe never knew. She grabbed one with both hands, wrenched it around, and it popped free. It would become her shovel. She could move ten times as much ice and snow with each stroke as she had been chipping out with the pliers.

She didn't need a large tunnel, just the size of a manhole cover, big enough to wriggle through and to push debris back behind her. There was always the possibility that the tunnel might collapse, but she could do nothing about that. After a minute, digging with her "shovel," she had advanced another foot. The distance from the desk to the room's doorway was about eight feet, if she remembered correctly. So, roughly eight more minutes of digging. Call it ten. She was unhurt, had the tool and the energy and the will. Whether she had the air remained to be seen.

After five minutes, she was panting and her head hurt, signs that the oxygen level in her tunnel was dangerously low. When her vision started to gray, she would be close to passing out. Her arms and back and neck muscles were burning, but she had to keep chopping and clearing, extending the tunnel, inching forward, doing it over again and again.

She had to work hard enough to progress, but not so fast that she burned through all the oxygen too soon. From rock climbing she had developed the ability to shut out fear and distraction by focusing on the tiniest grains and flakes and color variations right in front of her eyes. She did that here, concentrating on the ice in her headlamp's white circle.

Finally she chopped what looked and at first felt like solid snow, felt something change, chopped harder, broke through. Created an opening, made it larger, breathed fresh air. It had been close. Her blood carbon dioxide level was dangerously high. For a while she lay there panting. Then she pulled herself out of the tunnel, into the hallway. The force of the cave-in had splintered the office's plywood walls on either side of the door frame. Snow and ice had flowed out and now formed a sloping pile that blocked half of the passage.

Something groaned overhead. A cracking noise. The floor twitched.

She looked up, heard another crack, turned and started running. Old Pole was less complex than the Underground, and here there were more landmarks that she'd committed to memory on the way in. Several minutes later, she was standing at the foot of the access shaft. Her light shone all the way to its top.

There was no ladder.

Someone had pulled it up. *Why* would anyone do that? Only two possible reasons: They didn't want anybody going down into Old Pole. Or they didn't want her to leave it. Right now it didn't matter. What mattered was finding a way out. Maybe there were other access shafts. She would have to search the whole complex, corridor by corridor, room by room. There was no telling where else Polies might have gained entrance or where original shafts might exist. At any moment, the whole thing could come down on her. While that was always true in caves, as well, she knew that snow and ice would be less stable than solid rock. Even if she located another shaft, the chances of finding a ladder dangling handily for her convenience were slim. But there was nothing else to do.

She retraced her earlier route, moving through the galley, stopping at the T intersection. She stepped out into the intersecting passage, searching for some rationale about which way to go. There really wasn't one. So she would be like a rat in maze, blundering around blind, relying on the most inefficient search method of all: trial and error.

She had turned right before—a trial in that direction. Not very far, true, but a trial. She turned left, followed that corridor until it dead-ended at a cave-in. She turned around and retraced her steps though that corridor, exploring four other side passages. Two ended in cave-ins, two others with plywood walls. She went back to the point where she had started. Having explored everything the left corridor offered, she would do a more complete search of the right.

Half an hour later, she was back where she had started. Her primary light was dimming. She was thirsty and shivering and feeling weak. When had she last eaten? Couldn't remember. Felt dizzy, took two steps, faltered. Stood carefully, one hand on the ice wall to steady herself while her head cleared. Started to move again, stopped. She stood perfectly still, then stepped out into the center of the corridor. Turned a full circle.

She yanked off her clumsy overmitts and removed the thick wool Dachstein mitts underneath, leaving only a pair of pile gloves. They would keep her hands from going numb for maybe sixty seconds. That should be enough for her to unzip one of the Big Red's pockets and find what she wanted. It took ten seconds to get the stiff zipper working, another five to pull it open. Ten more to search around in the cavernous pocket, feeling and discarding the energy bar, the multi-tool, cellphone, spare headlamp batteries. Finally feeling the unmistakable shape of the thing she sought, she removed a small metal cylinder. Unscrewing its top, she withdrew a wooden match, struck it against the cylinder's abrasive bottom, and waited for the flame to stabilize. Then she very carefully raised it high over her head, as if offering the tiny fire to some ancient deity.

53

"SHE DID NOT STRIKE ME AS THE TYPE WHO IS LATE," GUILLOTTE said.

"No. We'll give her another fifteen minutes, then go looking," Merritt said.

It only took ten. "We were beginning to worry about you," Merritt said when Hallie banged through the door. Then, looking at her more closely: "What happened to your face? How did it get all scratched like that?"

"I'm calling the dive."

"What? Why?" Merritt said. Guillotte moved to one side, between Hallie and the door.

"I found Fida down in Old Pole. Dead. Then I almost got buried by a cave-in. A few feet one way or the other and I'd still be there."

"How did you get out?" Guillotte asked.

"In caving, you follow moving air to find an exit. It worked in Old Pole, too. When Rockie's Cat went down, it exposed one of the passageways. I found it by following moving air and climbed out. The hammers I'd used were still there."

Guillotte was staring at Hallie with something like admiration, shaking his head. "*Incroyable.* You are a tough woman to kill."

She wasn't sure she'd heard him right. "What?"

"You're diving," Merritt said. "Get your gear on."

"I just told you I don't want to dive."

"It doesn't matter what you want."

Hallie suddenly understood. "So this is about the extremophile? And money. I didn't think you were one of those, Agnes."

"We need to kill her." Guillotte might have been ordering escargot. Hallie turned to stare. He said, "I thought yanking out one of those timbers would be the end of you."

She was already scanning for a weapon. The workbench was a veritable armory: hammers, screwdrivers, wrenches, a couple of blowtorches.

"Do not even think about that." Guillotte moved to within arm's reach of Hallie. "It would only make this much longer and more painful than it has to be." To Merritt he said, "Let us get to it." He stepped closer and clamped one hand around the back of Hallie's neck. He had to reach up to do it, but his grip felt like a band of iron. His breath smelled heavily of alcohol. But not just alcohol.

Licorice.

Absinthe.

"It was *you,*" she said. "You fucking psychopath. You tortured Emily to death." She felt her hands ball into fists. His grip on her neck tightened.

"What is she talking about?" Merritt asked. When Hallie had told her about Emily's murder, she had left out graphic descriptions of the torture.

"Let me have a few minutes with her. The cooperation will increase quickly, I can promise you," Guillotte said.

Merritt waved him quiet again. "What are you talking about?" she asked Hallie.

This time, Hallie gave her the details. When she had finished, Merritt was pale and looked like she might vomit. She stared at Guillotte. "That was never part of your assignment. Let her go."

Hallie felt Guillotte's grip tighten even more.

"What did you do with that video?" Merritt asked.

"I sent a copy of the file to some people in Washington."

"She's lying," Guillotte said. "You know we disabled comms. Nothing goes out or gets in."

"I told Zack Graeter," Hallie said.

"You're lying," Merritt said.

"No, she is not," Guillotte said. "Graeter has a copy."

"Then why isn't he here?" Merritt asked.

"I have no doubt he will be quickly." Guillotte shook his head and Hallie felt his grip loosen very slightly. Then he said, "Wait. Why did you come down here if you knew?"

"I didn't know it was you until just now."

"Ahh, shit," Guillotte said. He took his hand from Hallie's neck and stepped back. "Just once, just *one fucking time,* I would like for the luck to come my way."

"You realize what this means?" Merritt said to Guillotte. Her voice was shaking.

"Of course I do. Triage is compromised. To put it simply, we are all fucked. You need to stay calm, Agnes," Guillotte said. "At times like this, the most important thing is to stay very calm."

But Merritt was not calm. Terror and fury were overtaking her. *"What were you thinking?"*

"People like him don't think," Hallie said. "They act on instinct. Or something worse. You knew about this, Agnes?"

Merritt turned away from Guillotte to face her. "Not the torture. That wasn't supposed to happen."

"I don't understand. He's obviously insane. But you? How could you be involved in something like this?"

Merritt didn't answer right away. Instead, she stared at Guillotte. Hallie watched Merritt's face change into a mask of horror, disgust— and guilt. The pain Hallie saw there reminded her of pictures of Dante's sinners in hell.

This was her chance. "What is Triage really about?" she asked Merritt.

The older woman looked down, then back at Guillotte and shook her head. She turned to Hallie, and when she spoke, there was abject misery in her voice. "A group of people committed to saving the planet from pollution. Human pollution."

"You're talking about overpopulation," Hallie said. She saw the women bleeding to death, Bacon suffocating. "My God. Are you going to start some kind of pandemic?"

"No. That's the beauty of Triage. No one has to die."

"Then how can you stop overpopulation?"

"Neutralize the breeders."

"Kill women? For God's sake, Agnes . . ."

"Nobody dies. We don't *kill* anybody. We sterilize them."

"That would take years, even if you could get governments to do it."

"Governments won't ever do anything. That's why we created Triage."

"Then how—?"

"The women here will fly back to five continents. Each will carry Triage. The spread will be exponential."

"Like smallpox. What is Triage, exactly?"

"Merritt." Guillotte's voice had an edge now. "We need to—"

Merritt waved him to silence. "Quiet. We're not all like you. It's a picornavirus carrying a payload: streptococcus engineered to seek and destroy ovarian cells." Merritt's full attention was on Hallie now. Perhaps she thought that confessing, or at least sharing, would ease her pain from learning what Guillotte had done. "It only affects those with a certain genetic marker called the Krauss gene. About half the women on earth have it."

"So it's eugenics all over again. Modern-day Nazis. But how could you infect the women here? I don't imagine they all consented to—"

"Doc's been very busy these last ten days with exit physicals."

She remembered: the blood drawing and throat swab.

"Now put on your dive gear," Guillotte snapped.

"What?"

"I said, Put on your dive gear. Now."

"No."

Guillotte walked over, fixed black-marble eyes on hers. "You saw what happened to Emily. It would be easy to do similar things to you. Or worse. Gear up. Now." To Merritt he said, "We will dispose of her first. Then I will deal with Graeter."

"But if you kill me, you won't be able to fake a diving accident," Hallie said.

"Oh, you will be quite alive. The needle did not kill Emily, as you recall. It just helped her . . . emote. The difference here is that if you don't obey, when I finish, you will be begging us to let you put on your diving gear. And to die, as well."

They must have sabotaged some part of her equipment. She had no way of knowing what. So she could gear up now, without coercion, or resist and suffer the consequences. End result the same. If she cooperated, at least she would be in better shape to deal with whatever surprise they had prepared for her.

"Okay," she said.

Guillotte held her gaze for another few moments. She felt a twinge in her gut. Eyes of the Beast, she thought. Whoever said the devil on earth would look like an ordinary man was right.

They helped her don gear. She thought they would put her into the dry suit that had failed but then understood that they were too smart to do that. She might have told others about the leaks. If she were to be found dead in the flooded suit, it would look suspicious. And even if they didn't find her body—likely, given the cryopeg's depth—if she and the failed suit were both missing, it would also give rise to questions. So they gave her one of the station suits. They even switched on her headlamp after securing her helmet over the hood. They would want to make sure that if her body was ever found, everything would be in order. Except the one thing, whatever it was, that they had done to the equipment.

At last she pulled her mask down, seated it properly, and started shuffling forward, Guillotte supporting the tanks from behind. Merritt walked ahead to stand beside the hole. Hallie caught her eye, making one last attempt to connect, but Merritt looked away.

Almost to the shaft, Hallie pretended to catch the tip of one fin on something. She stumbled, pitched forward, grabbed the rack of scuba tanks, and yanked it over with all her strength. As tanks hit the floor, she disappeared beneath the surface of the water in the shaft.

She had feared being positively buoyant, unable to sink fast enough to get away from them. But just the opposite: she plunged like an anchor. She hit the inflator button on her dry suit's chest.

Nothing happened.

So they had disabled the suit's inflating system. She kept dropping, and the deeper she went, the faster she sank.

54

IF SHE COULDN'T ADD AIR, SHE WOULD HAVE TO SUBTRACT WEIGHT.
She ripped her belt's quick-release buckle open and dumped twenty-
five pounds of lead. Almost immediately her descent slowed. She
looked for the white anchor line, but her light beam showed nothing.
Her uncontrolled descent had not been dead vertical, then. She would
have to make a free ascent and hope that she spotted the line or the
shaft mouth on the way up.

Her computer's luminous green readout showed a depth of thirty-
two feet. She had been sucking hard on her mouthpiece but had been
too focused on the uncontrolled descent. Only now did she realize
that the regulator was not delivering air. It seemed quite possible that
water this cold could freeze up even the best technical regulators. She
pushed the purge button. Nothing happened. Finning hard to slow
her descent, she removed the regulator and knocked it against the
heel of one hand. It still didn't work. She picked up her backup regulator, hanging on a bungee-cord necklace. She pushed it into her
mouth, bit down, inhaled.

Nothing.

Forty-eight feet.

She understood. It wasn't only the dry suit's inflator mechanism. After she'd tested both regulators on the surface, they had simply turned off her air and argon supplies while she'd been shuffling toward the shaft. It would have been easy for Guillotte to do that, without her feeling a thing, as he walked behind her.

It was one of the oldest and most common causes of fatalities, overeager divers killed by their rush to get in the water. They hurried through all the predive donning and forgot the most important thing of all: opening valves to send air to regulators and the buoyancy-control system. How many dead divers had she read about who were found with their air turned off? Too many to count. Since divers used the same gas they breathed to inflate their buoyancy compensators and dry suits, they hit the water and, unable to arrest their descents, plunged too deep to reach the surface on the one lungful of air they had taken with them into the water. It was possible to reach back and turn on the air oneself, but an uncontrolled descent's suffocating panic and bursting eardrums destroyed many a diver's presence of mind. She tried that now, but with so many layers and the thick dry suit, she couldn't even come close to the valve knobs.

Finning furiously, she arrested her descent and began slowly rising, looking desperately for the line or shaft, seeing nothing. At thirty feet her chest was on fire. Her hands and face tingled, and her peripheral vision started to close down. She was near the point where spasms would start convulsing her diaphragm, a result of the autonomic system's involuntary attempt to breathe. She might resist that for a few seconds, but then the carbon dioxide buildup would trip a switch in her brain. Her mouth would open wide, and a silent, final gasp would fill her lungs with water.

Her peripheral vision narrowed. As though looking through the wrong end of a telescope, she saw what seemed to be blobs of liquid, molten silver trapped against the ice ceiling. It was exhaled air from Emily's and her own dives. She knew that it had only about 5 percent less oxygen than fresh air.

She aimed for the largest silver bubble she could see, one about the size of a watermelon, in a cavity in the ice ceiling. She spat her regulator out and pressed her lips into the silvery mass. The hole in the ceiling was almost a foot deep, allowing her to push her face into the air pocket. She opened her mouth and breathed.

She held the air deep in her lungs for several seconds to let her system extract the maximum amount of oxygen. She put her face back in the water, exhaled bubbles away from the pocket to keep the air in it fresh, then took in more air. She did this until she felt her body's air hunger fade, and then she kept doing it longer to stabilize her blood oxygen level.

She filled her lungs and pushed down, away from the ceiling, rotating 360 degrees, trying to light up the white guideline with her headlamp beam. She saw nothing but cloudy water. She exhaled, breathed again from the air pocket, and this time added the illumination from handheld lights to her headlamp beam. The extra lumens did it. She spotted the line twenty feet to her left.

She exhaled deeply to exhaust as much residual air as possible, then filled her lungs as fully as she could. She swam into the shaft mouth and started ascending. She had not been down long enough to worry about decompression sickness, and the water's pressure, which had worked against her descending, now helped, especially without the weight belt. Pockets of gas in her dry suit expanded, speeding her rise, as did the air in her lungs, forcing more oxygen into her system.

She looked up at the bright circle of the shaft's mouth and hoped that it would be enough.

55

SHE ROSE TO THE SURFACE, EXHALING A THIN STREAM OF BUBBLES
on the way up to keep her lungs from exploding as the pressure less-
ened, and floated there without making a sound. At first, she let only
her lips and mask show above water. She had no way of knowing
what she would find in the dive shed. Guillotte and Merritt might
well be waiting there—just to make sure she didn't return. If they
were, this time they would knock her unconscious or kill her before
putting more weights around her waist and shoving her back into the
hole.

She waited and listened for several minutes, hearing nothing. As
quietly as possible, she worked free of her diving harness and let go
of the double tanks. Still fully charged, they were negatively buoyant
and sank out of sight. The edge of the dive shed's ice floor, with its
plywood covering around the shaft mouth, was two feet above the
water's surface.

She performed a slow, careful 360-degree rotation, listening for
any sound Guillotte or Merritt might make. Nothing. No scraping
boot, indrawing breath, rustling clothing. She had begun to shiver,

the first stage of hypothermia. She needed to get out of the water. But looking up at the edge of the circular shaft gave her pause. In the salt water she was positively buoyant. Her body weight was about 135 pounds. The dry suit, underlayers, fins, and mitts added another 25. Every inch of her and gear that came out of the water would reclaim its full weight. Looking up at the lip, she knew she would have to get at least far enough above it to perform a mantle, the climbing move she had shown Graeter to help him escape the crevasse. To do that, she would have to lift three feet of her body out of the water: head, arms, and shoulders above the edge, which meant that her torso in the shaft would be above water, too. So at least 50 percent of her body and the dry suit—say 70 or 80 pounds.

The question would be whether she could submerge with a full breath, fin and swim straight up, and pop out high enough to hook her arms and elbows over the lip of the shaft. It was a very good thing that they had floored the shed with plywood. She would have no chance at all trying to claw her way out of the hole over slick ice.

It would be the height of black irony, she thought, to have saved herself from dying as Merritt and Guillotte had intended only to freeze to death two feet from the surface. There was still the possibility that one or both of the others might be up there waiting for her. If they were, she would fight, of course, and probably could overcome Merritt, though the encumbering dry suit would be a huge disadvantage. She would have no chance against Guillotte.

She needed to push herself deeper into the shaft, as deep as possible until her buoyancy overcame her strength, but her mitted hands could find no purchase on the smooth ice walls. She unbuckled both of her dive computers from her left arm and held one in each palm, straps around her knuckles. Each computer was worth $2,000, and using them as imitation claws would destroy them, but this was not the time to be worrying about money. The computers had rectangular metal cases with sharp corners and edges. Her hope was that when she slapped them against the ice wall, they would dig in and grab enough to let her push herself down a couple of feet, then repeat the action until she had gone as deep as her buoyancy allowed.

If that worked, she would propel herself upward with fins and arms. Their energy, plus that of the buoyancy, would have to shoot her far enough out of the shaft. If not, somebody would find her floating right there in the hole, frozen solid.

56

"I'VE NEVER BEEN ON A WARRANT SERVICE BEFORE," BARNARD said. He was sitting in the front seat of a white Ford Expedition with mirrored glass all around. Bowman was driving. A salt-and-pepper team of deputy U.S. marshals, Dolan and Taylor, sat in back. Dolan was the salt, Taylor the pepper. It was, Barnard had to admit, exciting in a way he had not felt for a very long time.

"Just so we're clear, you wouldn't be part of this one were it not for Dr. Bowman. No disrespect, you understand," Taylor said. He was a big man, not as big as Bowman but thick in every aspect, from neck to calves.

"None taken. I'm grateful to be included."

As they neared their destination, Dolan said, "We don't expect any problem, but we always follow protocol. All you two have to remember is stay behind me and Taylor. Okay?"

Bowman and Barnard both acknowledged. Barnard said, "I don't think that judge appreciated our visit."

Bowman shrugged. "Comes with her job. She was the on-call."

"Pretty young for a judge," Dolan said.

"And pretty good-looking. I didn't realize they came in that model," Taylor said.

"Yeah," Dolan said. "Even at two in the morning. Go figure."

"They never look that good on the bench," Taylor said.

57

IT TOOK THREE TRIES, BUT HALLIE FINALLY HAULED HERSELF OUT
of the shaft. She lay on her belly for half a minute, unable to do anything more than pull off her mask and gasp. If somebody wanted to
bash her head in, they could just have at it. As soon as she was able,
she sat up, removed her fins, and looked around. The valves had broken off three single tanks, which escaping, high-pressure air had
transformed into giant, caroming bludgeons. The interior of the dive
shed looked like a tornado had blown through it. One tank had
smashed halfway through the Quonset's wall and stuck, a giant silver
sausage hanging from a ragged mouth.

Guillotte was not there. Merritt was, lying on her back, right
where she had been standing when one of the tanks killed her. She
looked like someone had hit her in the face with sledgehammers.

Hallie searched for a weapon and grabbed a big ball-peen ham-
mer. Her clothes were gone—Guillotte must have taken them. So he
was still healthy enough to do that. Calling the station was not an
option. This was the Dark Sector. No telephones or radios here.

She had to get back to the station. Thought about what she was
wearing: long underwear, two Viking insulated dive suits, the thick

neoprene dry suit, hood, wool gloves, and dive mitts. Not your regulation ECW, but it would have to do. She jumped up and down and windmilled her arms to build body heat and push warm blood out to her extremities.

Outside the shed, the snowmo she had driven down remained. But even before she went to look for the key, she knew Guillotte would have taken it, and in fact he had. She would walk the half mile to the station.

Hallie used neither headlamp nor flashlights, for fear of alerting Guillotte, who had to be moving around somewhere. The cold began to nibble here and there after just a few minutes. She knew it would penetrate a dry suit and diving underwear much more quickly than it would work through all those ECW layers. No time for sauntering. She started trotting. And almost immediately, she stopped. She had gone anaerobic that quickly. She would have to walk, like it or not.

But there was another cause for concern: she could feel the thick neoprene suit stiffening in cold it was never designed to encounter. The dry suit was designed to function in water down to twenty degrees. It was not designed to function at seventy-two degrees below zero—probably closer to one hundred below, with the wind. Trotting in the suit was impossible, and just walking was becoming hard work. So much resistance was generating body heat, a good thing, but she kept tiring and going anaerobic, which forced to her keep stopping. Each time she started off again, the suit was stiffer, less yielding. She was still a quarter mile from the station when it became completely rigid. It was like being encased in a suit of armor with no joints.

Seconds passed. Standing still, she felt her body heat dissipate quickly. She knew that the White Death was coming for her. It did not touch her whole body at the same time. Working its way through weaknesses in her thermal layers, it felt like a succession of icy hands being laid on her flesh, one after another, gradually spreading. It would not be long before her whole body was in that grip.

She looked at the glowing station. People were in there eating, working, walking the corridors, perhaps making love, those few who still had the energy. Light leaking from those windows stopped far short of where she stood in the blackness. Inside the lit rooms, no one could see anything outside. Including her.

58

GUILLOTTE HAD BEEN BOTH QUICKER AND LUCKIER THAN MERRITT.
As soon as he saw Leland grab the tank rack, he sprinted for the door.
Flung it open, dove through, hit the snow, and rolled behind the
parked snowmos. It took a full minute for the tanks to empty, and it
sounded like industrial demolition the whole time.

When all was quiet, he got to his feet and went back inside. Merritt was moaning, so he knew she was still alive, but from the look of
her she would not be for long, and that was fine with him. Gerrin had
made her, instead of him, head of the Triage team at Pole, and it had
rankled ever since. He had never liked her bossy, supercilious manner,
nor even the way she looked. Fat, red, and wrinkled, she'd made him
think of a spoiling apple. Dead, she would be one less detail for him
to worry about.

She was even worse to look at now, though, so Guillotte went
outside, sat on the snowmo, and tried to think things through. It was
a few minutes past six P.M. The station sat links became active once
every twelve hours, at roughly six A.M. and six P.M. He had to assume
that the comm engineers would have diagnosed and fixed the mal-
functions he'd been causing. Could not afford to think otherwise.

Graeter would not know that he, Guillotte, had killed Durant. Nor would he know everything about Triage, because Leland herself would not have known all of that before she came to the dive shed. She'd seemed genuinely surprised by Merritt's sanctimonious little speech. But Leland might have told Graeter about Doc and Blaine, and they were not the kind who survived prison. They would say anything to keep their rear ends inviolate.

Even if they did not give Guillotte up, he knew that Graeter could be watching the video right then. If Leland had not known it was him until she smelled the absinthe on his breath, it meant she had not recognized him in the video. The camera angle or light or both might have been bad. But Graeter was much more familiar with all Polies than Leland, and he might well see that Guillotte was Durant's killer. If that happened—and Guillotte had no choice but to assume that it would—the station manager would mobilize the security team and go looking for him. And he would talk to McMurdo the instant comms were up again.

Guillotte understood that the penalty for committing premeditated murder of U.S. government employees in a U.S. government facility could be death. New Zealand was nominally the country with jurisdiction over criminal acts in Antarctica, but the Americans would insist on prosecuting murders in their own facility in the States. Life in prison was the best he could hope for, a needle in the arm more likely. He would rather die by his own hand than suffer either fate. But he did not think it would come to that.

He pulled the cuff of his mitten back to look at his watch. Nineteen minutes past six. Should be enough time. But only if he moved fast.

59

SCREAMING FOR HELP WOULD BE A WASTE OF ENERGY. THE SUIT
had locked up just as Hallie's left foot landed after striding forward.
Her right arm had swung to the front, as well, her left to the rear.
There she stood like a statue of one frozen in the act of walking, not
frozen herself inside the suit but so immobilized that she might as
well have been.

She tried to move her arms, working in all directions, imitating the
curl motion of weight lifters, then trying to push back the other way.
She could move a half inch within the suit but wasn't strong enough
to crack the thick, multilayered neoprene. Next she flexed her legs,
tried bending over at the waist, twisting. Nothing worked.

She thought how ridiculous it would be to freeze to death here,
trapped in a suit that was supposed to be a life-support system. Even
worse was the thought of Guillotte running free. There was no telling
what he might do.

For a moment rage took over, and her muscles tensed and struggled against the suit. It was like trying to run in a block of ice and
accomplished nothing but a slight wobble side to side. She tried again,
and again, but the suit was not going to break or bend.

She stood, catching her breath, thinking. *There is always a way.* She just had to puzzle it out. She couldn't go forward or backward, up or down. Couldn't bend the suit or break out of it. Yelling for help wouldn't do any good. She considered urinating, thinking that warm liquid might soften the suit's lower half. But she knew that there wasn't enough liquid in any human bladder to do that. She would end up standing in a few inches of frozen piss.

She remembered reading a story, perhaps apocryphal, about a climber, buried in an avalanche, who produced a turd, waited for it to freeze solid, and used it to dig himself out. But even if she managed that, she wouldn't be able to reach it inside the suit.

She was beginning to shiver. Her teeth were chattering. A cold, empty space was opening in her chest.

This would not be a quick death. She had read accounts, none apocryphal, by stranded mountaineers who froze into comas, thinking right up to the point of unconsciousness that death was certain, then waking to discover that they had been rescued. It would be slow and increasingly painful for a long time; then would come numbness, everything growing weak and dim, and a long, gentle falling away from the last light.

Her rational brain grasped that. Then, like birds startled from a tree, thoughts and images began to fly from her mind. The lovely, burnt-honey smell of horses. Taps at her father's funeral. Her mother's hands, small, but rough and strong. And people she loved, her mother and father, two brothers, best friend Mary Stilwell down in Florida, Don Barnard.

And Bowman. For all the others she felt sadness but not regret; she had lived with them as fully as she could, knowing that loving and being loved were life's greatest gifts. But with Bowman, regret did come. So much would be left undone between them: the moment when she might have said, "I love you," another when they might have exchanged vows, and then all the other possibilities—including even children. She was thirty-one. Still young for a scientist, and certainly not old for a mother.

One thing left undone was especially troubling. Bowman came

from a ranch in Colorado and had grown up horseback. She came from a horse farm in Virginia and had as well. And yet they had never ridden together, had never shared the experience of melding with half a ton of pure beautiful power. Both had recognized how special it would be. They had talked about it so often that it had become a kind of personal idiom with its own definite article: "When are we going to do The Ride?" But they had never made it happen. *She* had never made it happen.

She remembered Merritt's talk about how it became harder and harder to stay away from danger. She knew it was true. She had worked in BSL-4 labs with the most lethal pathogens known to man and had loved every minute of it. Eventually even that had become routine, and she'd asked Barnard to put her in the field, where even greater risks reopened the adrenaline spigot.

She yelled then, not specific words but a raw and guttural howl. Breath and energy finally ran out, and she fell silent. She looked up, but no lights stirred green and purple around the black bowl of sky, no meteors cut white streaks, and no stars twinkled, as if even they had frozen to death.

She took a deep breath, closed her eyes, and waited for the same fate.

60

GRAETER PICKED UP A DART, ALIGNED THE BARREL BETWEEN THE thumb and first two fingers of his right hand, cocked his arm back. Shook his head once and put the dart on his desk. Where the hell was Leland?

A moment later, his door banged open and a Dragger barged in. At least he thought it was a Dragger, given the grease-smeared overalls and black bunny boots. But it was a Beaker in Dragger's clothes. And not just any Beaker. It was Hallie Leland.

"What are you doing in that outfit?" he asked. "In fact, what are you doing here? I was trying to find you."

She told him how a gust of wind had rushed across the ice, wobbling her in the frozen suit. How she had shifted her weight to that side, tilting the suit a fraction of an inch more, then shifted the other way, back and forth like pumping on a swing to go higher, until finally she'd felt herself tilting and falling and hitting the ice, cracking the suit.

She told him about Fida: "I think Guillotte killed him and left him down there to make it look like a suicide." Then she recounted what had happened in the dive shed. He stood.

"I'll find Guillotte. And I hope the son of a bitch tries to fight."

"Why?"

"Because," he said, gathering up his badge folder and gun, "then I can shoot him a dozen times."

61

DOLAN KNOCKED ON GERRIN'S FRONT DOOR. NO ONE ANSWERED.
Taylor had gone around to cover the rear of the house. Dolan pounded
with the heel of his fist. Inside it must have sounded like thunder.
Anyone would have heard.

"Well, easy way or hard way," Dolan said. He had brought a
crowbar for just such an eventuality. Motioned for Bowman and Barnard to stand back as he got ready to drive the bar's straight end between the door and the jamb.

"Hang on," Bowman said.

He stepped to the door and took a stainless steel device from one
pocket. Dolan started to say something but stayed quiet and watched.
Bowman laid the thing over the door's lock set and touched a sensor
on its side. For a few seconds nothing happened. Then the sound of
metal moving against metal and a distinctive click. Bowman repock-
eted the device. Dolan stared at him.

"It works with high-end locks and old ones," Bowman explained.
"They have enough steel in the tumblers. Not as messy."

"How in hell did you—?" Dolan started.

"Don't ask," Barnard said.

Dolan glanced at him, nodded. "Copy that." He keyed his radio, raised Taylor. "We're in. Hold your position."

He drew his service weapon, eased the door open, and stepped inside.

"U.S. Marshals," he shouted. "We have a warrant to search these premises. Anyone here present yourselves or be subject to arrest for obstructing federal officers."

No response.

Dolan went to the back door and let Taylor in. Barnard and Bowman waited while the marshals cleared the first floor. They followed them upstairs and waited in the long hall while the marshals looked into every room until only one, at the far end, was left. The door was closed. Dolan motioned for them to approach.

There were no more rooms. The house did not have a basement. Taylor eased the knob around, pushed the door open gently. The two marshals went in first, separating immediately, weapons up.

The red dots of their laser sights centered on the forehead of the small, dark-skinned man sleeping with a pair of noise-canceling headphones on.

Dolan turned on the ceiling lights.

Taylor, beside the bed, prodded the sleeping man's shoulder. "Dr. Gerrin. Wake up. We have a warrant," he said.

The man's eyes opened slowly, went wide at the sight of two big men aiming guns at him. He sat bolt upright. Started to speak, realized he still had the headphones on, yanked them off.

"Dr. David Gerrin, we have a duly authorized warrant to search these premises," Taylor began.

The man's mouth opened and closed repeatedly, but no words came.

"You can stop," Barnard said.

"What?" Dolan and Taylor looked back at him.

"It's not Gerrin."

62

THE DIVE SHED WAS STILL LIT, AS HALLIE HAD LEFT IT. MERRITT LAY where she had fallen, her face a stove-in, frozen red mess.

"Like she got hit by a fifty-pound bullet," Graeter said.

"Must have missed Guillotte," Hallie said.

"If he's not here, the son of a bitch must be back in the station."

They hurried outside, ready to jump on Graeter's idling snowmo. Both stopped at the same time.

"What is that?" Hallie asked.

"A Cat D9," he said. "Nothing else sounds like it."

But it was not a Cat D9 they saw materializing out of the gloom several hundred yards away. It looked, in fact, like the face of an advancing black wave, just visible against the ice. "What the hell is that?" Graeter said. "And who's running the Cat?"

"Guillotte. Has to be. He's killed the lights."

"Why would—" Graeter started to ask. Instead he exclaimed, "That's a fuel bladder he's pushing. He's going to blow up the station."

"We need to get him off that machine," Hallie said.

"He's locked himself into the cab for sure. And that glass is designed to protect operators in rollovers and landslides. Forget bullets. We'll have to evacuate the station before he reaches it."

"No phone, no radio comms—remember? The Dark Sector. We can get there, but that still won't leave enough time to get everybody out."

"Son of a *bitch*."

"I have another idea," she said.

"What?"

She took the first aid kit from the snowmo's emergency box and used it like a brick to smash the headlight and taillights.

"We're going stealth," she said. "You drive."

63

"GET OUT OF BED. KEEP YOUR HANDS WHERE WE CAN SEE THEM."
Dolan's voice was neither harsh nor courteous, just barely civil. He
and Taylor weren't pointing their weapons at the man, but neither
had they holstered them.

"Yes, yes. Of course." The one who was not David Gerrin was
wearing blue flannel pajamas with white stripes. His terrified expression, as he climbed out of bed, suggested that he was accustomed to
dealing with very different kinds of police.

"I'm sorry, I don't remember your name," Barnard said.

"It is Muhammed Kandohur Said."

"Who is he?" Dolan asked Barnard.

"I am Dr. Gerrin's executive assistant," Said answered for himself,
regaining a fraction of composure.

"Where is Dr. Gerrin?" Barnard asked. "And why are you here?"

"I am house-sitting for him," Said answered. "As for his location,
I am not sure I should . . ."

Dolan reached behind his back and brought forward a pair of
handcuffs. "You can answer questions here or go with us."

Said's face lost what little poise it had regained. Where he had come from, Barnard thought, the phrase "go with us" probably implied a one-way trip to some medieval hellhole.

"He has left on vacation." Said's eyes were fixed on the handcuffs, which Dolan held out between them, the lower cuff swinging back and forth like a pendulum.

"Where?" Barnard asked.

"I do not know that," Said blurted. He tore his eyes from the handcuffs to look at Barnard. "I honestly do not. Please believe me. Dr. Gerrin did not say, and it was not my place to ask."

"He left you no way to get in touch with him?"

"No. I did ask about that, but he said he wished to relax on his vacation. Leave work behind, as he put it." Barnard looked at Bowman, and they both exchanged glances with the marshals.

"We'll still search," Dolan said. "The warrant is for the premises. Owner doesn't have to be present for us to execute it."

Barnard turned back to Said. "Did Gerrin say how long he would be gone?"

"No."

"Did he say anything?"

"Yes."

"What?"

"He said, 'You should expect some visitors.' I thought he was talking about friends."

64

GUILLOTTE LOVED OPERATING HEAVY MACHINERY. IN THE FRENCH
Army, he had wanted to be a tank driver, but they'd used him for
close-in killing instead. That was really his true calling. Regardless,
he also found sexual pleasure in sitting atop all that roaring, throb-
bing power. And it was so easy, even with his right thigh aflame with
pain where one of the tanks had struck a glancing blow. Right now,
he had little to do but sit in the Cat's comfortable, high-backed operator's seat and input minor course corrections with the left joystick.
The machine's gigantic blade protruded a foot on either side of the
bladder's sled, so keeping it centered and moving forward was no
problem.

The hard part would come later: triggering the emergency signal,
then managing not to freeze to death waiting for the Twin Otter. The
pilot would have his own challenges, landing on an ungraded iceway
lit only by a few flares. If that plane crashed, though, its pilot would
be the lucky one. He would die too quickly to feel anything. Guillotte, on the other hand, would freeze to death, unless he found some
way to kill himself with less pain and more speed.

He hummed "La Marseillaise," gazing up at the southern lights, thinking of nothing in particular. He had never felt regret or remorse, guilt or pity, so he did not care that the station and everyone in it were about to be incinerated, nor that Triage was wrecked. He had not much cared whether the plan worked or not, really. He knew that Merritt, Blaine, and Doc were true believers in the Triage cause. He, Guillotte, believed, too—in the money he was being paid. For him it was a job of work, nothing more.

He gave the throttle lever a hard push forward, but it was already jammed against the travel stop. There was nothing to do but sit and wait for the behemoth to crawl to its final destination. Really, there was no rush. The station certainly wasn't going anywhere. He would push the fuel bladder underneath it, between two sets of stilts. Then he would open one of its valves and let gasoline run far enough that when he lit the long, liquid fuse he would not blow himself up along with everything else. He was looking forward eagerly to this part. Few people are ever privileged to see such an explosion. Here in the black polar night, it would be even more spectacular. Like standing close to the sun.

He nudged the left joystick gently, correcting the dozer's course a few degrees right, and settled back to enjoy the remainder of the ride.

65

GUILLOTTE COULD NOT HEAR THE SNOWMOBILE AND SAW IT ONLY as a vague shape angling in and then creeping along beside the bladder's front end a hundred feet ahead. He saw very clearly three red flares ignite in rapid succession and describe small arcs through the air before landing on the bladder's broad, flat top.

His first thought was to jump over the blade onto the bladder while the dozer kept moving, but the possibility of his bad leg causing him to slip and fall beneath the machine dissuaded him. Instead, he stopped the Cat, clambered down, and limped forward, planning to hop onto the bladder and throw the flares away. It was never easy to hurry in bunny boots, and his injured thigh slowed him even more.

The bladder's top was shoulder-high, and its sides were rounded and as slick as black ice. Guillotte jumped and jumped, trying to claw his way up. With two good, strong legs, he might have made it. But his legs were skinny and weak, and one was hurt. He kept sliding back down, and before long, his legs had no more jumps in them.

He knew that the bladder, manufactured by a company called Aero Tec, wasn't really made of rubber. Its core was multilayered Kevlar, the material that gave body armor its stopping power. That, in turn, was coated with layers of industrial-grade polyurethane. Viewing a demonstration, Guillotte had seen technical advisers attack a water-filled bladder just like this one with axes and knives. They'd succeeded only in tiring themselves out.

He did not know, but strongly suspected, that the bladder was not designed to withstand magnesium flares burning at about three thousand degrees Fahrenheit.

There was no point in trying to run. Injured and encumbered by the boots, he would not be able to get far enough away to survive the explosion of two thousand gallons of gasoline. He looked at the station, still distant, unreachable by him or the blast. He looked up at the black dome filled with dead stars. The southern lights had vanished. He tried to recall when he had last seen the sun, but couldn't remember.

Then it was as if he had fallen into it.

As soon as Hallie lofted the last flare, Graeter drove them back toward the station at full throttle. The ice was not smooth, like Bonneville's salt flats, but corrugated with sastrugi. Traveling fifty miles per hour, Hallie had to use all her strength to stay aboard, but she figured Graeter had looked at the death options—fire or ice—and decided to take his chances with the latter.

The explosion's roar was loud enough to be heard even over the engine's scream. Neither of them turned around, so they didn't see it begin as a tight, white ball that bloomed into roiling fire, black and red and orange and yellow, billowing outward in great whorls and blossoms, as though trying to burn up the darkness.

She did feel the heat on her back, like standing close to a huge bonfire. She glanced around then, understood that they were safe, tapped Graeter's shoulder. He slowed, turned, stopped. It took some time for two thousand gallons of gasoline to explode, so there was still plenty to see. A fist of heat hit her chest and face, and the flames kept churning and rising, and she thought how strange it was to see ice on fire.

66

DOC WAS IN THE GALLEY WHEN THE BLADDER EXPLODED AND YEL-low fire filled every window. The light was so bright that even with his glasses on he had to squeeze his eyes against the sudden pain. The blast wave rolled over the station a second later, and the whole struc-ture wavered. The thick stilts, designed to protect against snow burial, allowed the energy surge to pass like wind flowing around a wing.

Doc didn't know exactly what was happening, but given every-thing else that had transpired recently, he sensed threat deep in his gut. He turned away from the window and headed for his office.

67

HALLIE HALTED AT THE ENTRANCE TO THE LABORATORIES ON LEVEL
1 with Graeter, Lowry, and Grenier behind her. All four were wearing
hooded white Tyvek suits, gloves, booties. Surgical masks were pulled
down below their chins, ready for use.

"I don't expect Blaine to fight," Graeter said. "But I haven't done
this before, either, so . . ."

"I used to be a cop. Wanna know how we did it?" Grenier said.

"Goddamned right," Graeter said.

"We go in, me and Lowry on one side, you and Doc Leland on the
other. If the door opens in, the one closest to it works the knob and
shoves. If it opens out, the one on the far side reaches across and
swings it open and back. They have to step around it, but no avoiding
that. Everybody's flat against the wall this whole time. That's in case
anybody in there's thinking about shooting his way out."

"Here?" Graeter said. "Blaine? You really think so?"

"You wouldn't believe what I seen comin' through some doors,
Mr. Graeter. Better safe than sorry."

"Anything else?"

"Yeah. Soon as he's in sight, take him down. Don't hesitate a second, and don't worry about hurtin' him. Me and you will put him on his face, Mr. Graeter. Just grab an arm and kick his leg out from under him. I'll be doing the same thing on the other side. Ben, you put a knee on his neck until we get the poly plastic cuffs on him. Sound okay?"

"Just like *Law and Order*," the big scientist said.

"No," Grenier said. "That's bullshit. This is for real." He looked at the others. "Ready?"

"One last thing," Graeter said. "Hallie, don't worry about Blaine. You secure the lab and everything in it—computers, instruments, God knows what else. Good?"

"Good."

"Let's roll," Graeter said. They put their surgical masks in place. He went first, followed by Grenier, Lowry, and Hallie. They passed into the main laboratory corridor, walked almost its full length, and stopped at the outer door to Blaine's lab. Graeter tried the door. It was locked. He used his master key, stepped to one side, opened the door.

Every laboratory had a small outer office with two desks, file cabinets, computers, and bookshelves. Lowry and Grenier squeezed against the wall to the left of the inner door, which opened outward, left to right. Hallie and Graeter did the same on the other side. Graeter tried the knob and it turned. He looked at Grenier with raised eyebrows. The other man nodded, reached across, turned the knob, and yanked the door open.

Graeter lunged forward. Hallie was right behind him. The hell with hanging back. She saw it an instant before he did.

"*Stop!*"

She grabbed his shoulders, hauled him out, and slammed the door shut.

Lowry and Grenier had caught their own glimpses. Neither a career in science nor one in law enforcement had prepared either for what they had seen, judging from the looks on their faces.

"Jesus Christ," Grenier said. "What the hell happened to him?"

Blaine lay on the floor, faceup, to the left of the room-length lab bench, six feet from the doorway. He was dressed, so only his head and hands were visible. The flesh they could see was shriveled and desiccated. His face, collapsed in on itself, resembled a giant raisin. The rest of him looked as though his bones had dissolved inside his body. His limbs and torso had shrunk, so that he appeared to be wearing clothes much too big for him. Tendrils of orange matter emerged from his ears, nostrils, mouth, and eye sockets. The stench was indescribable.

Instead of answering, Hallie rifled through the office until she found a roll of duct tape. She used it to seal the spaces between the door and jamb all the way around.

"Let's get out of here," she said.

She used tape to seal the outer door as well. Back in the corridor, the men stood staring at her, waiting for an explanation.

"Here's what I think," Hallie said. "I found the extremophile dead in my lab. I would bet that he did something that brought him into direct contact with it. The thing metabolizes carbon dioxide. It might consume carbon in any form. Our bodies are about twenty percent carbon. It could have colonized his and metabolized its carbon content. If we cut him open now, we might find him full of that orange biomatter."

"I seen a lot on the street," Grenier said. "But never nothin' like that."

"Bad things happen when you mess with a god," Hallie said.

PART THREE

Homecomings

There's no place like home.

—DOROTHY, *THE WIZARD OF OZ*

68

"YOU REDECORATED," HALLIE SAID.

There was a chair in front of Graeter's desk, and the walls looked different, cleaner. He glanced at his watch—his one watch. "There's some time before flyout," he said. "I need to make sure I understand what happened before you go. So many different pieces. Some I still don't get. This report is going to be a real royal bitch."

Saturday had passed without a weather window for flying. Today, Sunday, the temperature had risen to minus fifty-six and was supposed to stay in that range for eight hours. Between his administrative work and her sleeping, this was the first time they'd been able to spend time together. Graeter handed Hallie a mug of black coffee, poured from a brewer he had placed on a table that had appeared behind his desk. She sipped, grimaced.

"Navy coffee," Graeter chuckled. "Cures all ills."

"Probably melts spoons, too. How did it go with Doc?" she asked.

"The idea of life surrounded by psychopaths in a supermax where bright lights burn twenty-four/seven terrified him. He spilled a lot of beans, but here's the gist: he, Merritt, Blaine, and Guillotte were working for an international group called Triage. From what I can gather, these are not card-carrying members of the lunatic fringe. They're legitimate scientists from around the world. We'll probably never get all of them. But three guys were at the top. One was David Gerrin. Mean anything to you?"

"No."

"It did to me. He's director of the Office of Antarctic Programs at NSF, no less. You said Merritt told you what they were planning to do."

"They wanted to 'save the planet'—her term—using an engineered pathogen to sterilize millions of women without their knowledge or consent," Hallie said. "The last group of female Polies flying out were going to be their disease vectors. Doc infected them here over the last week or so. Before winterover, they would fly out to countries all over the world. It would spread exponentially, like any cold virus. But the streptococcus bacteria had been engineered to seek and modify ovarian cells."

"They could do that?"

"Sure. The genetic engineering would have been challenging, but definitely possible. Twenty years ago they were joining genes from flounders and tomatoes to keep them from freezing, after all. The science has come a long way since then."

"And Emily Durant was killed because of what she learned about Triage from Blaine?" Graeter asked.

"Yes. On the video log she said that she had asked both Merritt and Doc if they knew anything about Triage. Blaine was already aware of what she knew. One would probably have been enough. Three sealed her fate."

"Tell me again what got *you* here?"

"They couldn't just haul in any old scientist. That might have looked suspicious, especially on such short notice. They needed a female from North America. The fact that I matched Em's qualifications and could get here fast sealed the deal."

"Fida was killed because they were afraid Emily had told him about Triage, too," he said.

"Right."

"That still leaves Lanahan and Montalban and Bacon."

"Merritt said no one was supposed to die. I can believe that. But there are always unintended consequences. Did Doc give up the other two?"

"Ian Kendall is a Brit. Retired now, but worked with Crick, the DNA guy. Jean-Claude Belleveau is a doctor in New Delhi."

"That's incredible," she said. "I mean, I believe you. But men like those doing something like this? I just can't understand it."

"You know as well as I do that things are going to hell here. And I don't mean Pole."

"Earth."

"Right. There are an awful lot of people out there sick to death of governments fucking up or doing nothing."

"Can't argue with that."

"So some capable people taking it on themselves—doesn't surprise me that much. I would bet good money there are more out there."

"It's scary when you think how close they came."

He picked up his mug, put it down again, looked at her. "Listen, I need to say this: if you hadn't kept digging about Durant's death, those infected women would probably have been on the plane out of here today."

"You'd have figured things out and stopped them."

"Maybe. I'd like to think so, anyway. But honestly, I'm not sure."

She didn't argue. Time would pass, and he would see the truth. Better to let him find it himself. But his mention of the women reminded her of something.

"I understand that the standard rapid strep test worked on this strain, so we know which women are carrying the infection. But I got busy packing and lost track after that. What's the situation now?"

"The women have to stay at Pole until they're not contagious. One month, minimum. That does mean they'll be here for winterover. Not an easy thing, but no way to avoid it."

"So are all those women going to end up sterile?"

"No. The bad news was that everybody got sick," he said. "But the good news is that to test for the Krauss gene, you only need a cheek swab. Seven out of thirty-six carried the gene. And as you already know, you were not one."

"Just luck of the draw," Hallie said. "But a close call."

"Speaking of those, did you find out how they sabotaged your dry suit?"

"They didn't. The suit's knees were reinforced with carbon-fiber patches. I think that extremophile was metabolizing them." She reflected for a moment. "Damned good thing Emily didn't have that style suit, come to think of it."

"Why didn't it start metabolizing you? Like Blaine?"

"Nothing known can survive in pure argon gas."

"So that thing won't be saving the earth."

"Afraid not." She sipped coffee. "What happened to the picture on your wall?"

"She was living in my head rent-free. I moved her out."

"How's that feel?"

"Like cool water in a desert."

"What about them?" The young sailors' framed photos were no longer on his desk.

He smiled. With sadness, but a smile. "I laid them to rest."

"They'd be happy," she said. "For you."

"You think?"

"Absolutely." Talking about the dead young sailors had reminded Hallie of Emily. Her eyes grew hot. She looked away, then back again. "I'm going to set the record straight for Emily. She will be honored. The courage it took to dive that hellhole four times. I couldn't have done it." Hallie just shook her head. "And so much else."

"Figured you would. Set the record straight, I mean."

Neither spoke for a time. Then she said, "Think you'll stay at Pole?"

"Have to, through the winter. After that . . ." He shrugged. "We'll see." He looked at his watch again, then directly at her. "I don't say this to many people. You're special. I'm glad to have met you."

"And I you," she said. "God. Look at me tearing up." She wiped her eyes. "Did you hear that?"

"Can't miss a One-thirty on final. You'd better hustle. They won't do much more than a touch-and-go when it's this cold."

He came around from behind his desk and stuck out his hand. She put hers on his shoulders, kissed him on the cheek, and gave him a hug. "Take good care of yourself, Zack." She patted his arm and turned for the door.

"I'll buy you and your friend a good dinner when I get back."

"I'd like that. He would, too."

On her way out, she got a close look at the new picture on the wall by the door. It was a submarine surfacing, its black bow shooting skyward through a white collar of foam.

69

IAN KENDALL'S WIFE HAD DIED TWELVE YEARS EARLIER. WITHOUT children or close relatives, he'd kept the home in Chiswick, a leafy, pub-strewn London suburb. The house was two stories of beige brick with red-stone accents at its angles and peaks, tall windows, and matching yews in the front yard.

Built in the reconstruction frenzy after World War II, it was sound except for a crack that had opened five or six years ago in the brick-work of the back wall. The crack started at the foundation and rose almost to the eaves. It had opened a little more with each passing year, not a structural threat—yet, anyway—but clearly visible.

Kendall had brought in a man to affix a trellis to the wall and plant English ivy, which grew eight feet a year. By now, the crack was completely hidden behind a façade of snaking vines and slick, shiny leaves.

Shortly after his wife's death, Kendall had hired a large, meticu-lous Jamaican woman named Gardenia to keep house. On Wednes-days she rode the tube out from the city. She cleaned, did laundry, changed linens, and "neatened" the place. He always let her know when he was going away so that she could find other work if she chose.

Thus she was surprised, this particular day, when Kendall didn't answer her knocking. A friendly and courteous man despite having done something important in science, unlike so many of the arrogant and disdainful she cleaned for, he never kept her waiting on the small porch. She knocked again, louder, and a third time, and still no one came.

He had shown her a spare hidden key, after forgetting his own in the house or losing it once too often while out. It was so unlike him to be away without calling that she retrieved the key from beneath a flower pot and let herself in.

"Dr. Kendall, are you here, sir?" she called, two steps inside the door. "Dr. *Kendall*?"

She put the key on a kitchen counter and thought about what to do next. Elderly people who lived alone tended to die alone. Often, after becoming very unpleasant, they were discovered by landlords or housekeepers. She took a deep breath and let it out slowly, steeling herself. Dr. Kendall had treated her well for more than a decade. He deserved better than being found by some stranger.

He was not downstairs. She climbed to the second floor and searched it all, leaving his bedroom for last. The door was closed. She knocked, waited. Knocked again. Swallowed, afraid of what she would surely find, and eased the door open.

The bed was neatly made, everything in place. The room smelled musty, in need of a good airing, but not like death.

Back downstairs, she had to admit that this time he'd simply forgotten to let her know he would be away. Not so surprising, really. He was almost eighty, after all. She would mention it to him when he returned, and he would reimburse her for her tube fare. He might even offer to pay her for the whole day. She would not come back here, though, until he called. It was a long way from Brixton Station to Chiswick.

70

SHORTLY AFTER GARDENIA VISITED IAN KENDALL'S HOUSE, THE *Times of India* newspaper reported a crime in South Delhi's Jor Bagh district. A Delhi police spokesman stated that a victim had been found in an alley, dead of multiple stab wounds, not far from the free medical clinic where he practiced. His wallet and cellphone had been stolen. His watch, wedding band, clothing, and a solid silver crucifix had not. Police said they believed the assailant could have been interrupted in the act.

The brief report appeared below the fold on page 3. Delhi was the crime capital of India and had been for nine years. Homicides were nothing special, and this particular victim, whose name was being withheld pending notification of next of kin, was not even Indian.

71

DAVID GERRIN WAS WALKING BACK TO HIS HOVEL IN KARAIL WITH
two plastic jugs of water. The new home was a shack of plywood and
cardboard and rusting metal. He and a dozen families shared an open
pit toilet beside which lay a bag of lime no one used. The nearest
water he considered less than life-threatening lay almost half a mile
away, and he waited until the sun was long down before starting such
a trek, even in February.

Difficult, all of it, but better some time here than life—or death—in
an American prison. He could endure it all for months—a year,
even—in exchange for the anonymity this vast and teeming slum en-
gendered. Eventually he would work his way back into the world,
slowly, patiently, one stratum at a time, all the while shedding layers
of his old self like a molting snake.

He believed that Karail was the last place authorities would suspect him of going. In addition, the Dhaka police were perfectly useless. His call for the dying woman had demonstrated that, as he had
known it would. She would never have made a breeder, so he had
thought it worth a try at least. Horribly corrupt and rarely visible
even in the city proper, the Dhaka cops had written Karail off com-

pletely years ago. It was a world all its own, seething and primal, but if you knew its ways, as he still did, you could survive. Not easily or pleasantly, but it was possible.

He kept to himself, dressed badly enough to blend in, went unshaven and dirty, though it would not be long before he had to wash in muddy Gulshan Lake, which formed Karail's border. Now he was halfway home from the well, a trip that had taken him farther than he liked to go from the slum's steaming center, when he came upon a boy standing over a woman on the sidewalk. He was trying to pull a cloth bag out of her hand. The boy could not have been more than twelve. His shirt and shorts were ragged, his feet bare. His calves were almost as big around as his thighs.

The woman was too old to be a breeder, so Gerrin set his water jugs down, walked up to the two of them, and pushed the boy away from her.

"Stop this," he said in Bengali to the boy. To the woman: "Go away." She rose and scuttled off.

He turned to face the boy and caught the familiar stench of garbage and filth, smells he himself was absorbing. This boy was one of those deep-slum denizens who ventured out to hunt the edgelands at night, where things like an old woman with a bag of spoiled lemons might be found. As Gerrin himself had done so long ago.

The light here was dim, only a couple of unbroken streetlamps in two full blocks. Even so, the boy's eyes shone, huge and white and bright with hunger, but with something else as well, very intent, scrutinizing, registering. Gerrin thought he saw something familiar in the boy's face, those eyes. Intelligence recognized itself.

"Tell me why you were robbing that woman," Gerrin said, thinking he knew already how the answer would form.

"I am so sorry, sir." The boy's voice was as thin as the rest of him, but he spoke clearly, keeping his eyes on Gerrin's. "I will tell you. Please do not beat me. My sisters are starving to death, and so am I." The boy put his head down and his hands behind him, in a pose of submission. "Please, sir."

He did not think this man would beat him, though. He had been beaten often enough that he could tell, in seconds, what would happen next. This man was not one of those. He had a heart. The boy had learned many valuable things about the human heart.

Gerrin saw one of the boy's hands come from behind his back. It held a rusty knife. Gerrin stepped away and said, "I am no threat to you. And I have nothing worth stealing."

"There is *always* something worth stealing." The boy moved toward Gerrin and raised the knife for a stab to the left side of his chest.

A hiss, and he froze in mid-strike, his hand at the top of its arc. A small red spot appeared over his heart. Gerrin watched blood run down the boy's torso. The boy gazed at it, his mouth open. The knife fell from his hand, his hand dropped from the air, and he collapsed like a pile of disconnected parts onto the sidewalk.

Two men stepped out of the shadows. One held a pistol with a short silencer, muzzle pointed down. Both were Bangladeshis, dark-skinned, with close-cut black hair and clothes so absurd—pressed gray slacks, shined black shoes, short-sleeved shirts with tropical flowers and birds—that for a moment Gerrin thought they might be lost tourists. But no tourist would be reholstering such a pistol beneath the loose shirttail.

"Dr. Gerrin, you will come with us." The voice was neither polite nor abusive, just barely civil, as though he were talking to a waiter.

"Who are you?"

"It is only a short distance. You can shower and put on clean clothes. It must be difficult for a man like yourself, going about so."

They moved like a big scoop, one on either side, bringing him along.

"You are not from the city police," Gerrin said.

The two exchanged glances and laughed. "No, that we are not. Thanks be to God."

"What is your name?" Gerrin tried to sound authoritative. In his condition, it was not possible.

He understood that this had to do with Triage, and that somehow they had tracked him down, despite his certainty that no one could.

Escaping from two such as these was not an option. The best he could hope for now was a trial before the International Criminal Court in the Hague.

The worst . . . For a moment his knees felt weak, and he knew it was not from hunger. Then he reminded himself that there was no death penalty with the ICC. He might spend twenty or twenty-five years in a relatively comfortable prison. He would be old when they released him, but there would be some years of life remaining. He would make the most of them. Perhaps he would even write a book while in prison. Surely some publisher would pay for the true story of the notorious Triage plot.

The first flash of terror passed, and he was surprised to find himself feeling something almost like relief. Carrying the secret of Triage for so long had corroded something within him horribly, and he knew it. Living in Karail, even briefly, had been worse than horrible and had brought back so many unspeakable memories that at times he'd thought his mind might crumble. No, a clean, well-lighted cell would not be the worst place on earth. He had just walked away from that.

They turned right at the end of the block. It was so dark that Gerrin did not see the black Mercedes until a third man opened its door and the dome light went on. The driver touched a remote control, and the trunk popped open. Gerrin's two escorts picked him up—one could have done it easily enough—put him in, and closed the lid. As much as he hated being treated like this, it was easy to understand why they would not want him in such a car. He hoped that was the reason, in any case. The trunk was hot, but even here a Mercedes was lined with a velvety plush. Other than him, it smelled not bad for a trunk—the spare tire's fresh rubber, that clean fabric, a sweet gasoline tang.

He thought about where they were taking him. A clandestine office of some kind, hallways echoing, most rooms dark. The messengers— for that was all they really were, fancy car aside—would deliver him to a security official in an off-the-rack dark suit, a white shirt too big in the neck, and a horrendous tie. He might be invited to sit, or perhaps not, given his condition. He would be told the reason for his detention and informed of whatever rights he had left, which, this being Bangladesh, were assuredly minimal.

They had mentioned a shower and fresh clothes. Prison garb, perhaps. He would be remanded to a holding facility while extradition proceedings played themselves out. There were only two possibilities that he could imagine: the ICC or the United States. Gerrin had not prayed in many years—in fact, for as long as he could remember—but he did now, briefly. Anything was worth trying to avoid the latter destination.

After a shorter time than he had expected, the car stopped. Sounds of doors opening, the soft rasp of leather soles on pavement. The trunk opened.

"You can get out now."

Gerrin looked around. It was even darker here than the place where they had started. He saw no government offices, no safe house, no buildings of any kind, in fact. Behind the two men, there was a strip of littered, empty land, then a ragged chain-link fence, and beyond that, only empty darkness.

"I am fine. This is not so uncomfortable." He understood how ridiculous that sounded, but he could not make his muscles remove him from the trunk.

The two men lifted him out as easily as they had put him in. He extended his legs, tested them, his ex-runner's knees aching. "What are we doing?"

"You are not a young man any longer. We cannot have you suffer a heart attack or some such thing before we deliver you." The two men exchanged glances, smiled.

"We walk a little."

Deliver me? "I feel perfectly well."

They scooped him along again, one on either side, to the chain-link fence. The ground was littered with trash, bottles, blowing paper. He could see that someone had cut a gash in the fence and peeled back the two sides. Nothing but darkness beyond. Like the mouth of a cave. Or hell.

The man who spoke reached toward his holster, and Gerrin could not stop himself from making a sound, half whimper and half groan. From his pocket, the man withdrew a slim metal case, rectangular and shining. He opened it, offered an unfiltered cigarette to his partner, and took one himself. The other man lit both, and they stood there smoking with great relish.

"Do I n-n-ot get one, too?" Gerrin asked. He was losing control of his mouth.

"You don't smoke."

"A last cigarette. I should get a last cigarette. It's how they do it." Babbling, he disgusted himself, but he could not stop the words.

The two laughed and shook their heads. When they were finished smoking, they flicked the butts away. The companion urinated with gusto. They put Gerrin back into the trunk.

They traveled for what he estimated to be about an hour. Then he felt several stops and starts, heard snatches of conversation that he could not understand. Lifted from the trunk, he stamped his feet to restore circulation, stretched his hands and shoulders.

When he opened his eyes, having finished his stretch, the two men and the driver were gone. Standing before him was a huge man with short, straw-colored hair, his cheeks rough with stubble, a red-checked *shemagh* wrapped around his neck. He wore dusty jeans, a khaki shirt, and a monstrous automatic pistol in a shoulder holster. Gerrin recognized him. The giant who had come with Barnard.

Behind the man stood two others dressed similarly. They had holstered pistols and carried assault rifles, neither M-16s nor AK-47s but a kind he had never seen. It would have been impossible to take the men for anything but Americans. Tall, thick with muscle, well-fed, and, most of all, the gun-muzzle eyes.

"Dr. Gerrin," the big man said, and Gerrin shuddered. You hoped to hear a voice like that only once. He had the eyes of a natural predator—one who would know very well how prey went to ground, and where.

"Why do you not just kill me here and save us all the t-t-trouble?" Gerrin's fear was talking again, words just bubbling out. It wanted to know what would happen to him, and he could not make it stop.

"What?"

"Just do it. Get it over with. Those others were supposed to, but they lost their nerve. So go ahead."

"That's not how we operate," the other man said, and he glanced over his shoulder. Gerrin noticed for the first time a hangar with an odd black helicopter crouching inside.

"What *will* you do with me, then?"

"The right thing."

72

HALLIE WALKED OUT OF THE JET BRIDGE AT DULLES AND ALMOST
ran straight into Bowman. She no longer asked about things like how
he could be in a secure area without a ticket. She dropped her carry-
on and hugged him long and hard while the crowd flowed around
them.

"Let's go someplace." He carried her bag and most of her—
exhausted after four days and nights of traveling, again, on top of the
Pole time—away from the busy gate area. In a deserted one nearby,
they stood facing each other.

"Did you get my email?" she asked.

"No," he said, and she looked surprised.

"Did you get mine?" he asked.

"No," she said, and he looked just as surprised. "I thought you
were mad, Wil."

"I wasn't. I thought *you* were," he said.

"I wasn't either," she said.

It took a moment for their brains to sort everything out.

"As you were leaving, you told me there was something else," she said.

"So did you," he said.

"What did *you* mean?" she asked.

He told her what he had written in his email.

Once over her amazement at such a misapprehension, she told him what she had written in hers.

A small boy tugged on his mother's hand. He was bouncing along the Dulles concourse in the kind of sneakers whose heels blinked with colored lights at every step. They were passing a gate area that was empty save for a tall blond woman and a giant of a man. The two were holding on to each other as if afraid of being pulled apart by something. Like a big storm, the boy thought. Giant wind. Shaped like a funnel. He could see it, but he couldn't remember the name.

"Mama, what's the thing called that picked Dorothy and her house up?"

"A tornado," she said. "Why?"

"Those people," he said. "What's wrong with them?"

She glanced quickly. "Don't point. Nothing's wrong. They're just so happy to see each other."

"Why is she crying if they're so happy?"

"Sometimes happiness hurts," his mother said, which he thought was the most ridiculous thing he had ever heard. Still, he found it hard to stop watching them. They were—what was the right word?— *different.*

Just then the blond woman happened to look straight at the boy. The man followed her eyes. Caught by both, he froze.

"I *told* you *not* to *stare.*" His mother frowned and squeezed his hand.

The woman held his gaze. Then she looked at the man and pointed at the twinkling sneakers and they both smiled. She waved to the boy. He waved back. Then she and the man hugged some more.

"See? She's not mad," he informed his mother, who dropped his hand and told him to keep up.

Tornado. A storm that *tore.* Ripped things apart. Plucked up houses and barns and cows. And people. But looking back at them one last time, he thought that even a tornado might not tear apart those two.

AUTHOR'S NOTE

The construction of this novel's dark atmosphere required certain modifications to real life at Pole. Food, amenities, and Polies themselves all suffered somewhat in the translation. Let me acknowledge at the outset that those who toil at the bottom of the world are for the most part competent, companionable, and sane.

That said, it is a hellish environment that can exact extreme tolls from both body and mind. Murders and mayhem are not common, but neither have they been absent. One source of inspiration for this novel was the mysterious 2000 death of scientist Dr. Rodney Marks. For reasons unclear, to this day U.S. agencies have stonewalled New Zealand police attempts to investigate. NZP senior sergeant Grant Wormald said several years ago, "I am not entirely satisfied that all relevant information and reports have been disclosed to the New Zealand police or the coroner." In January 2007, a document pried loose with the Freedom of Information Act stated that "diplomatic heat was brought to bear on the NZ inquiry." The case remains open to this day, with an interesting coda for those inclined to conspiracy theories: one of the few Polies in a position to know what really happened disappeared, also mysteriously, at night from a ship in polar waters not long after Marks died.

There is no disputing the fact that the South Pole station is awash in good liquor (and, according to more than a few, other mood enhancers) that fuel Thing Nights and more. One Polie noted, "There is an unbelievable amount of alcohol down here. Pallets of booze were flown in." And while all is usually calm on the southern front, things do happen. In 2008, two intoxicated Polies brawled over a woman. One suffered a broken jaw and both were summarily flown out—sans jobs. It's safe to say that lesser disputes which don't break bones (and get people fired on the spot) are more common and less publicized.

And while some of this novel's elements required poetic license—in reality, cellphones cannot be used at Pole—the novel's central theme, overpopulation, required none. Though a solution to the crisis would ameliorate the planet's biggest threats—climate change, global warming, environmental degradation, water shortages, famines—overpopulation goes largely unaddressed in the public square. Because population control involves white-hot issues like contraception, abortion, and sterilization—voluntary or otherwise—it has become virtually a taboo topic for politicians, scientists, and major media. For those who wish to know more, one rational take on the topic is *2052: A Global Forecast for the Next Forty Years,* by Dr. Jorgen Randers, a professor at the BI Norwegian Business School.

Frozen Solid is, of course, a work of fiction, but the science is very much grounded in reality. It examines what would happen if highly capable vigilante scientists decided to solve overpopulation on their own, with means available today. Though it hasn't happened, a pathogen (meaning a conjoined bacterium and virus) like Triage is certainly possible. Hallie Leland cites one example of research in this area and it is very real, conducted by Dr. Vincent Fischetti and Dr. Raymond Schuch at Rockefeller University. They confirmed that the survival of the deadly anthrax bacterium, *Bacillus anthracis,* "is directed and shaped by the DNA of bacteria-infecting viruses." The bacterium provides a home for the virus, which in turn prolongs anthrax's life and directs its actions—classic symbiosis. Would it be impossible for scientists to reverse-engineer that kind of relationship, for good or evil? To me, the answer seems obvious. In fact, though my research didn't uncover an extant microbial "depopulator," I would not be a bit surprised if one were flourishing in government or private-sector labs—maybe in both.

ACKNOWLEDGMENTS

My literary agent, Ethan Ellenberg, saw promise in the concept that became *Frozen Solid* and provided reassurance during the inevitable dark times when my own faith was weakening.

I am more grateful than I can say for the support and belief in my work from Ballantine Bantam Dell's publisher, Libby McGuire, associate publisher Kim Hovey, and editor in chief Jennifer Hershey.

Mark Tavani, my editor at Ballantine, again and again went far beyond the call of duty to help me shape this novel. I said it in my other novel's Acknowledgments and I will say it here: Mark puts the lie to the oft-heard criticism that editors today don't edit. He sure as hell does, and brilliantly.

Special words of thanks to senior publicist Cindy Murray and assistant director of marketing Quinne Rogers. Steve Messina, an indefatigable production editor, shepherded the book during its long journey from thought to print. Finally, it's true that the devil is in the details, and I'm grateful to Ratna Kamath for managing those demons so effectively.

As always, my wife, Liz, was my first reader and critiquer. Through more "story meetings" than I can count, she was more helpful than I can say. Other readers and critiquers included Walllis Wheeler, Tasha Wallis, Damon Tabor, and Jack Tabor.

About the Author

JAMES M. TABOR is the bestselling author of *The Deep Zone,
Blind Descent,* and *Forever on the Mountain* and a winner of
the O. Henry Award for short fiction. A former Washington,
D.C., police officer and a lifelong adventure enthusiast, Tabor
has written for *Time, The Wall Street Journal, The Washington
Post,* and *Outside* magazine, where he was a contributing editor. He wrote and hosted the PBS series *The Great Outdoors*
and was co-creator and executive producer of the History
Channel's *Journey to the Center of the World.* He lives in Vermont, where he is at work on his next novel.

www.JamesMTabor.com